Sky Pirates

by

Gregory A. Kompes

Fabulist Flash Publishing
Las Vegas, NV

Copyright 2016 by Gregory A. Kompes

All rights reserved worldwide.

ISBN: 978-1523475247

Editor: Leslie E. Hoffman

Cover Design: Gregory A. Kompes

The material in Sky Pirates represents the artistic vision of the author published herein and is their sole property. No part of this text may be reproduced, stored in a retrieval system, or transmitted by any means—electronic, mechanical, photocopying, recording, or otherwise—without written permission of the author. The author may be contacted through Fabulist Flash Publishing.

Fabulist Flash Publishing
PO Box 570368
Las Vegas, Nevada, 89157

For more books by Gregory A. Kompes,
please visit www.Kompes.com.

Dedicated to:

Darlien C. Breeze, Bonnie Apple, Nancy Sansone, Ellen J. Dugan.

> WHAT can I give thee back, O liberal
>   And princely giver, who hast brought the gold
>   And purple of thine heart, unstained, untold,
> And laid them on the outside of the wall
> For such as I to take or leave withal,
>   In unexpected largesse? Am I cold,
>   Ungrateful, that for these most manifold
> High gifts, I render nothing back at all?
> Not so; not cold,—but very poor instead.
>   Ask God who knows. For frequent tears have run
> The colours from my life, and left so dead
>   And pale a stuff, it were not fitly done
> To give the same as pillow to thy head.
>   Go farther! let it serve to trample on.
>
> ~Elizabeth Barrett Browning

Sky Pirates

by

Gregory A. Kompes

One

Clash of metal. The unmistakable sound catapulted Lord Parker Greene from his comfortable cabin chair aboard the HMS Barkley. From the muted shouts, metal scrapes, and rhythmic, steel clatters against steel, Lord Greene instinctively clasped the handle of his sword in the scabbard. Most men might have rushed through the door into the fray; Greene chose to hold back a moment; he listened and soundlessly locked his door.

Greene returned to his table, took the time required to neatly refold the letter he'd been reading from his niece, Mildred, and tucked the papers into his breast pocket. Greene dipped his pen, noted the time on his beloved pocket watch, and quickly wrote in the open journal with his deft script: 1851 July 7…8:57 AM…Pirates. He blew on the page before closing the small book and tucking it into his pocket.

Six quick bells rang in his room, the signal for "All Hands on Deck for Battle."

Lord Greene moved with precise action. He took his great coat from its hook and slid his arms into the sleeves. He opened the top bureau drawer and assessed the contents. Greene hoped to return to this room, but there was no telling now if this might be his only opportunity. Parker Greene choose the silver compass with its secret compartments—a family heirloom—the small leather bag of gold coins, his pocket pistol, the leather folio of small tools, and, finally, the well-worn locket. As he selected, Greene tucked each item into their own place in one of the many interior pockets of his great coat.

The shouts and sounds from the dozens of men answering the captain's call outside his cabin faded. Greene gently placed his scabbard over his head, unlocked and opened the door, and peered into the empty hall. He gave a last survey of the room, wishing he could also take his walking stick and favorite hat. But, he'd have to leave those behind.

"Sir, we are boarded!"

Greene swung to see a short, handsome, blond young man of twenty or twenty-one running toward him. The man held a sword too big for his stature.

"They've out maneuvered us, My Lord."

The fear in the boy's eyes sent an arrow into Parker Greene's heart. "We'll get through this together, lad." There was no way to know if these words were true, but he knew it was his job, his duty to give faith and fortitude to the man.

The young airman—a stoker based on his coal stained face, arms, and hands, plus the goggles bouncing around his neck—tried to offer a smile, but it came across more like a wince.

"Back to your station. You and the lads there, keep stoking as fast and furious as you can. It may be our only hope. And, find two strong men to guard the cargo."

"But...Captain Meadowbrook has called for all hands on deck."

"Do as I've told you, and we shall possibly survive this ordeal."

The boy didn't move.

"Go!" Greene shouted at the airman. He watched as the short stoker turned and ran back the way he'd come.

The silence of the next moment felt like being in the eye of the storm. "I'm getting too old for this." He pushed the thought aside and replaced it with: "I serve at Her Majesty's request."

Greene crept down the hall toward the staircase that would lead him to deck. He took each step, one-at-a-time, listening. Lord Greene put an eye to the keyhole, taking in the limited view it offered. With sword poised, he pushed open the door and drove his weapon cleanly through the chest of the pirate standing there. Blood spurted from the perfect chest wound, a direct skewering of the heart; his enemy dropped to the deck with a quiet, blood-filled gurgle. The death sound melded with the chaos of the scant schooner crew attempting to fend off a sea of pirates.

There was no time to enjoy his victory, as another pirate, this one, like the last, clad in remnants of various uniform pieces from Her Majesty's vast fleet, drove forward at him. Greene met that onslaught and each subsequent parry with his own volley of jabs and lunges. His great skill, unmatched by this villain, allowed Parker Greene to quickly gain advantage while sparks rained from their glistening steel weapons as they clanged and scraped. When the pirate drew back to regain his footing in the growing puddle of blood and slop beneath their feet, Lord Parker Greene, private emissary of Her Majesty, Queen Victoria, cleanly sliced off his head, leaving the writhing corpse spewing blood and sinew all over Greene's new boots.

"Damn!"

Little more than a beat passed; he recovered the dead man's sword, and, two-handed, joined in the fighting between Her Majesty's Royal Mail Airmen, defending their ship, and a band of joyful pirates, doing all they could to overtake them.

Parker Greene slipped and slid several feet along the deck, but quickly righted himself. Amidst the sickly sweet smell of blood and gore were many small gears, cogs, pins, and pieces of wire. Before the emissary could think further about them, two large pirates, each a head taller than him, came at Greene, one with sword, another with something akin to an old-fashioned battleax. The attackers grunted and threatened. Lord Greene, with nimble might, met the sword bearer's assault with a two-fisted, double-sword action. The left hand holding back the thrust, the right hand sword plunged into the oncoming assailant's chest.

The second man, dressed in a combination of air and sea uniforms, both from the last war, utilized the moment, while both of Greene's hands and weapons were otherwise occupied, to swing his mighty, ancient impaler in Parker Greene's general direction. Lucky for the Lord, another of Her Majesty's finest slowed that ancient weapon in mid swing with a piece of the Barkley's shattered mast. The delay, only a second, allowed Greene to withdraw his bloody sword and plunge it once again into the chest of the oncoming enemy.

"Good show for a botanist," the assisting airman offered.

"Couldn't have done it without you, sir." The two nodded and then went once again against their own, newly arrived opponents.

For each man Lord Parker Greene cut down, three more seemed to approach stepping on and over the corpses that now carpeted the groaning deck. Their column reminded him of ants, each man mindlessly following the one before him. Greene worked his way along the outer edge of these approaching insects until he came close to the ship's rail. There, sidled up to Her Majesty's short mail schooner, the Barkley—a small air-, water-, land-ship built for speed, not fighting—was an airship more massive than he'd ever before witnessed. Its sides glistened in the afternoon sunlight, its deck large enough to hold six of Her Majesty's 90-foot, mail schooners. Huge masts, wrapped in steel that flecked sunlight into his eyes, were topped by gargantuan propellers. From his current perspective, the pirate's ship was so massive that Greene couldn't see either its bow or stern.

How can the thing stay aloft?

In his mind, each propeller-topped mast took a space; he easily arranged and rearranged all the pieces until he understood how all the dozens and dozens of gears must fit together leading below decks to the great steam boilers. By turning the pistons and driving the propellers at the top of each mast—with his fascination in the unknown-to-him technology getting the better of him, Parker Greene didn't see the man approach from behind. For a flash, the pain was exquisite. Then, blackness.

Two

Mildred Greene slid the large twirl into her smock pocket and pushed on the garden gate. The heavy wrought iron with rusted filigree tops high above her head didn't budge. "Oh, bother," she said to no one in particular, being alone. She fingered the twirl in her pocket, removed it, studied the over-sized key, placed it back into the hole, and turned it. She heard the click and knew that she'd once again locked the 10-foot high gate. Mildred gave it another turn and again placed the twirl in her pocket and once again pushed on the gate. Still, it didn't move. She felt her cheek, annoyed at the heat of the flush that rose there. She pushed again, harder. The metal blockade gently groaned, but refused entry.

None of the gardeners or stable hands were within view. Mildred gazed toward the great house, hopeful a servant or houseman might be near the manor, but the whole of the vast property seemed empty and deserted. The young woman turned and surveyed the long, high ivy-covered garden wall. She certainly couldn't climb over that. So, back to her task; Mildred braced her shoulder square against the bars, took a solid breath, and shoved with her full weight. Being only sixteen and slight, without breasts to speak of or curves in any other place to use as ballast or leverage, her action had no effect whatsoever.

She stepped back, took the lace handkerchief from her pocket, and wiped her brow. "This simply won't do," Mildred said aloud and turned on her heel, her muslin skirts slowly catching up. After following the path, she arrived at the workshop near the big barn. It took a long moment for her eyes to adjust to the darkness inside. Before she could see him, Cole spoke:

"What is it, Millie, I'm busy."

She made her older brother wait for her response. He was so rude to her at times, yet so loving at others. This, obviously, was of the former, not the latter. Mildred, who hated being called "Millie," even though both her brother and tutor used that horrible name when speaking to her, chose not to be offensive back to him. She, after all, needed his help, or at least his brawn, to gain entry into the garden. She chose her words and tone carefully. "Cole, can you please step away from your important task? I find that I'm helpless at the moment."

"What is it you require, dear sister?" He crossed the dusty floor and hovered over Mildred. "For, you must want something important if you're being so kind." Cole poked an oil stained finger into his sister's side, which made her laugh.

"Stop, your fingers are filthy. Whatever are you working on?" Her curiosity got the better of her and, for the briefest of moments, she was more interested in her brother's work than her own.

"Oh, Millie, come, let me show you." Cole took his sister's hand and pulled her toward the large workbench covered with gears of all sizes. "I've taken apart the workings of the old clock."

"Whatever for? Uncle Parker will be angry." Mildred knew that their uncle would also chastise Cole for his lack of jacket, open shirt collar, and rolled up sleeves. Uncle Parker would have said: "You're dressed like a commoner." But Mildred left well enough alone. It was not her task to be her brother's keeper.

"Uncle will be gone for weeks, maybe a month."

"But, Cole, why have you taken it apart?" Mildred surveyed the many pieces and parts in disarray on the table. "How did you get it all down here?"

"A little at a time. I took it apart up in the tower and then, when I couldn't figure out the cause of the problem, little by little I've carried it down here."

"If you do get it fixed, how will you get it back up there?"

"I'll deal with that when the time comes." Cole moved around the bench and picked up a large gear and a smaller one. "Do you see this?" he asked.

"Of course, I'm not blind."

"No, this," he positioned the two gears in front of Mildred's face where a space formed between their interlocking teeth. "It's broken. There's a piece missing."

Mildred didn't respond. Instead, she looked closer at each piece, both those Cole held and those still on the table. She didn't touch them; that would have dirtied her hands. In her mind, each piece of clockwork took a space; she arranged and rearranged all the pieces until she understood how all the dozens and dozens of gears fit together. It was only after those few moments that she finally spoke again. "Cole, silly boy, it's not broken." She pointed to another cog, "That's where all three of these intersect." Still, she didn't touch the oily, dirty clockworks. Again, she reviewed all the pieces in her mind, saw them fit together and begin to turn in harmony. "I wish you had shown all this to me before you took it apart. If you want my help with this project, you'll need to reassemble the entire clock back up in the tower."

"Who said I want or need your help?"

Her brother's feelings were obviously hurt. It was in his tone and written on his sensitive face. "Why did you even come in here?" Cole's eyes were harsh when he made eye contact with his sister.

"Oh, I can't get the gate open. I've got the key," she held it up, "it turns in the lock, but, the hinges are rusted shut, I think."

Cole pushed past his sister and stalked toward the garden gate. A sound stopped him. He lifted his head and scanned the sky.

Mildred stopped behind him and turned her face skyward, too. There, several miles away, the unmistakable sound of wind against propeller as one of Her Majesty's mail schooner airships glided across the sky. Mildred hoped that the sight of the flying machine indicated that there would be a letter from her beloved uncle Parker.

She dreamed of being a pilot. Truly, she dreamed of being a great many different things: pilot, inventor, lord of the manor, plant hunter like her uncle and father…something, anything that allowed her to make decisions about her own future rather than having those choices thrust upon her. As she contemplated her lack of future, Cole continued without words to the task at hand.

He placed his two strong, suntanned hands as near to the top of the gate as he could reach and pushed. It gave a bit, but not enough to offer access. "Push at the bottom, Millie."

Mildred easily fit below her tall brother.

"One. Two. Three," said Cole. They both pushed on three and the gate, after a final, loud screech, gave way. Cole opened and closed the gate several times. "These hinges need to be oiled," he said more to the gate than his sister.

"Thank you," Mildred whispered to her brother who had already turned and was sulking back to his workshop.

Mildred picked up the basket she'd placed on the ground and entered the high-walled garden. Every direction offered views of overgrown plants and weeds of all colors, shapes, and hues of green. She attempted to navigate the main path toward the fountain whose stone filial she could just make out, but briers, prickers, and other grasping plants and weeds accosted her every step. Yet, the place was not scary to her as she peered over the tall weeds and grasses and watched an army of honey bees flitting among the fragrant flowers blooming above the thick growth.

Mildred contemplated the small basket on her arm. The collection of hand tools there would be of little use at the moment. She thought of dropping the basket at her feet, but feared she'd not find it again amidst the verdant tangle, and so took it with her as she exited the garden. Again, she placed it on the ground near the gate and made her way back up the path, past her brother's workshop, past the path leading back to Wickwillow Manor, beyond the gravel road, and into the big barn.

The greyed wood of the barn's strong walls housed long rows of stalls and pens. The dirt floor packed hard as stone. Smells of hay mingled with those of animals and manure filled her nostrils while neighs and bays mixed with the scuffle of hoofs entered her ears.

"Good morning, Miss Mildred. What can I help you with?" asked the old stable master.

"Oh, dear, Isaac. Always my savior." Mildred touched his arm ever so lightly. With a guardian so often away, traveling the world in search of new plants, Mildred grew close to the house servants and grounds staff, who had, after all, raised the two Parker children. "I've decided to follow Uncle Parker's advice and take up a vocation. I've gained entrance into Mother's garden, but my little tools are simply not up to the great task of—"

"Lady Parker's garden? No one has been in there since..." Isaac stopped himself from finishing the statement. There was no reason to remind the young woman of her mother's passing sixteen years ago to the day, may she rest in peace. "Happy Birthday, Miss."

"Thank you, Isaac." Mildred had no desire to speak of her birthday. Instead of the joyous occasion her natal day, her arrival on the planet, should be, everyone knew, everyone remembered that it was on this day that the Great Lady Parker, her mother, departed from this earth. She often felt whenever anyone saw her, that their only thought was that in her birth she had killed her mother. Furthermore, she knew that the vast majority would prefer her mother's continued good health over Mildred's non-joyous arrival.

Of course, her horrid entry into the world was only surpassed by the disappearance of her father a year later; a fact also blamed on the demise of Lady Parker. For, everyone knew that without his beloved wife, her father, Lord Cecil Greene, simply couldn't go on. He disappeared during a plant hunting expedition with his brother, Mildred's dear uncle, come guardian, Parker Greene. Her father was the most decorated plant hunter in the world; a man frequently summoned and dispatched across the entire globe with all the resources of the British Empire at his personal disposal in search of new and interesting plants for Her Majesty. No one knew what had happened to him. It was believed that he wandered off into the jungle and was killed by a wild beast.

She pushed the horrid thoughts from her mind and pressed on with her mission. "It was Uncle's suggestion." She thought about that conversation with her uncle, how he was both kind and stern at the same time. She breathed through her mixed emotions and continued: "He said, before he left for Indonesia, that as the woman of the house, and as a good English woman at that, that it was my duty to maintain the garden. Do you have some tools I may use?"

"Miss?" Isaac was confused.

"A hoe. A shovel." Even though sad and frustrated, Mildred maintained her patience as she always did with Isaac.

"Perry!" the old stable master shouted. A young boy popped his head up over one of the many horses lined up in the great stable.

Mildred and Cole often discussed the fact that their uncle continued to maintain a barn filled with live animals, while everyone else in the country was acquiring mechanical horses to ride about, pull their carriages, and even work their fields.

"Help Miss Greene," Isaac said to the young boy. He turned back to Mildred. "Whatever you need, you ask Perry. He will help you with all the heavy lifting and anything else you require."

Mildred doubted that Perry, Isaac's grandson, a boy of twelve or thirteen, would be much help at all. She didn't protest, instead saying: "Thank you, Isaac."

After a few moments of negotiation, hunting, and searching, Perry did his best to steer a wheelbarrow, filled with all manner of tools and buckets, down the path back toward the garden. While Mildred didn't believe Perry would be of much help when it came to the heavy lifting, she hoped, all the same, that she would enjoy the young man's company over the many hours and days her new vocation would consume.

Three

*L*ord Parker Greene awoke with a start to the sounds of swords clashing. He instinctively tried to reach for his sword astonished to discover himself shackled. Greene studied the getup: hands, bound in iron cuffs encircled with heavy, rusty chain. He followed the chain to a loop through cuffs at his ankles which then threaded through an iron coupling in the wooden floor. As his vision cleared, he was flabbergasted to discover he was in his own, private chamber aboard the HMS Barkley.

He stood, tried to stretch, but couldn't move his arms beyond his chest. Greene tested his tether's distance and found he could move rather freely for about three feet in all directions from his berth. While his range didn't allow him access, he was pleased to discover that his walking stick remained resting upright in its corner. His hat was still on its peg.

Greene's head ached. He reached for it, but was reminded of his imprisonment by the rattling iron. "At least, I'm alive."

After some maneuvering, he felt the pockets he could touch with his limited range of motion; it seemed that everything he'd selected to take with him, the watch, compass, and even the small pistol were still on his person. The only thing not there was his sword, although, after further assessment, he realized his scabbard remained over his shoulder. "How curious." Greene smiled to himself at his captor's choices.

All the while, as he studied his surroundings, the battle that caused him to awake continued unabated, not close by, but near enough to hear the individual clink and clash of sword against sword. Was it possible that the fight between the pirates and the Barkley's crew continued?

Greene moved as close as he could to the portal. If he pulled the chains to their furthest point and tilted his head in just the right way, he could see that his airship was now aboard the deck of the great pirate ship. Despite the horrible headache he felt, Parker strained his neck a bit more and, for a brief moment, caught a glimpse of another of Her Majesty's mail schooners floating next to the pirate's ship, just as the Barkley had been before he'd been knocked unconscious. From his current precarious vantage point, he saw an army of pirates—not their bodies, only their heads—moving from the deck of their ship onto the schooner's deck. Hundreds and hundreds of them moving in that ant-like column, just as they'd boarded the Barkley.

"Ah, you're finally awake."

He turned and stumbled to find a dwarf dressed in a page's uniform akin to those worn hundreds of years ago during the reign of Henry VIII.

"We weren't sure if you'd come back around after that nasty bump we gave your noggin." The dwarf smiled at Greene before closing the cabin door and approached a bit closer. "Now, don't try anything silly, Lord Greene. You want to stay on my good side." The little man turned a bit. "Which is this side." His eyes sparkled when he laughed and exposed a cheek with a small, ragged scar. "I may not look like much to you," he continued in a singsong way, "but with this,"—he showed off a ring on the pinky of his right hand—"with this, I'm a giant."

Like so many, Parker Greene was drawn to dwarfs, as if they were curious creatures, rather than humans. He couldn't help but smile at the petite man's good nature, all the while inspecting the ring as best he could from his current distance to discover a flat surface with a spike, like a sun dial in the center.

"It may not seem like it at the moment, but truly, we mean you no harm." As he spoke, the dwarf opened up the flap of a leather satchel, the strap of which looped over his shoulder.

"It didn't seem like that when you were slaughtering my fellow airmen. Did anyone survive?"

"Well, when men resist, we cut them down." The dwarf had raised himself with some effort on to Greene's berth. The small creature smelled of mint and lavender soap. Not like a woman, exactly, but he was the freshest airman Greene had ever encountered. Now, standing eye-to-eye, the small man said: "Some young crew survived, most didn't. Others have been captured and…dealt with. Please turn around so I can take a look and change the dressing on your head." He held up the bag he wore around his neck that caused the red cloth flower on his breast to rumple.

Lost in thoughts of the small crew he'd grown to like, Greene tried to raise his hand to inspect his head, but the chains kept him from it.

"You'll get used to the limitations those present."

Lord Greene's heritage and breeding surfaced. "How shall I address you?" he asked and turned away from the diminutive man to allow him access to his head. If he was going to be pawed over by this little creature, he certainly was going to get some desired information.

"Silas. I'm Phineas Silas." He went to work removing bandages and replacing them from a fresh stock he pulled from his bag. There was a slight tug on Parker's hair, but the pain felt no worse than before Silas had begun working. "There, all finished."

He had to admit to himself that the dwarf's hands were quick and nimble; his work barely increased the throbbing pain in Parker Greene's head.

With both hands on Greene's shoulders, Silas guided the man around so they were once again facing each other. "Here, chew on this." He held up what appeared to be a sliver of bark toward Greene before attempting to push it into the prisoner's mouth.

Parker studied the sliver of bark the dwarf offered, but didn't take it, pursing his lips tight together.

"This will help with the pain." Silas raised it closer to Greene's mouth. "And, it will also take the edge off of your hunger. When we're boarding a mail ship, everything else pretty much stops, so there won't be a hot meal for any of us for some time, now."

"What is it?" he asked and quickly tightened his lips again.

"Well, I'm not a doctor or an herbalist, but I've chewed much of this in my life, and it will help you feel better."

"Yes, but what is it?"

"It's hickory that's been soaked in a poppy solution. It's not like you need to worry about your growth being stunted." Silas showed two rows of doll-sized, stunningly white teeth.

"Opium?" Lord Greene was aghast. He'd broken up two opium rings to clear the Channel for the trade. Of course, that was a much different story. Suffice it to say, the stuff was addictive and ruined lives. He shoved that from his mind.

"The choice is yours, sir."

Greene weighed the pain he was suffering versus the possible consequences. "What's going to happen to me? What are your plans for me? Why have you taken the whole ship? What are you after?"

Once again, Silas presented his twinkly smile. "I'm just a page. I don't make choices or decisions. I carry out orders. You'll have to wait. The captain will decide your fate."

"Who is your captain? What ship are we on?" How could he not have thought to ask those questions earlier? He had so many questions: like, how were they able to keep afloat, without much movement, while stopping one of Her Majesty's fast mail schooners?

Silas' tone turned incredulous: "Why, you're on the Balsa Robin, captained by Lord Fletcher Flynn!"

Now, it was Lord Parker Greene's turn to be indignant. "Fletcher's in charge? He was never knighted." Greene kept up with all the Orders, Honors, Decorations, and Medals awarded by Her Majesty. He and Fletcher Flynn had been schoolmates, rivals. They'd played the same sports, each as captain for their houses. Both had graduated at the top of their year. Greene went on to university. He couldn't recall where Flynn went off to. Greene tried to remember when last he'd seen or heard from or of Flynn. It was so long ago that no recollection, beyond the last cricket contest, came to mind.

The men stood silent, eye-to-eye, staring at one another.

A large explosion shook the ship. Silas grabbed on to Greene for support. The dwarf, after the rocking subsided, crammed the piece of bark into Greene's mouth before he bounded from the berth and out the cabin door leaving Greene to wonder what might have happened.

He began to work his tongue to position the bark so he could spit it out. In that process, he got a good taste, enjoyed the flavor, and appreciated more the sudden, almost immediate relief from his pain. As he chewed, he considered more questions. Did Her Majesty's airmen fire off a cannon in retaliation? Had a stray bullet or spark set off a powder keg aboard the Balsa Robin…?

The Balsa Robin. Greene had heard stories about the ship; like everyone else, he believed them only to be legends and myth. But, here he was, a prisoner on the fabled ship. It existed. He could now attest to its great size and formidable might—that portion of the legend was true, and he feared what other truths he would now discover. While he didn't know the particulars, Parker Greene now knew that it was possible to build and fly such a massive contraption. He reached, well, attempted to reach into his inner pocket to pull out his small diary, but the endeavor was abated by rattling shackles and chains. He made the best mental notes he could all the while wondering if the opium laced bark he found himself chewing would create fantastical stories and hallucinations.

four

"Good evening, Miss Mildred, Master Cole," said Lorain Canton as Mildred and her brother sat down at one end of the expansive dining table.

Despite the summer heat, all the windows were closed to any possible breeze; a large candelabra, with more than a dozen light and heat bearing candles, lit their supper of venison, boiled potatoes, and spicy greens. Miss Canton, assuming the role of "mother" as usual, asked: "How have the two of you passed your day?"

Neither sibling spoke.

Miss Canton continued the conversation: "I walked along the river path all the way into town and purchased a new hat at Miss Beachwood's. She's created some wonderful hats, Millie. You should stop by and pick out something for yourself."

Mildred nodded toward the tutor, knowing full and well that she wouldn't be buying a new hat any time soon. Silly trappings did not interest her. What she truly desired were mechanical tools to help her clear the weeds and debris in the garden. Sadly, those she wanted only existed in her mind; no one had yet built any such thing on a small enough scale to be useful in a garden.

"It has been reported to me that you gained entrance into your mother's garden today," Miss Canton said with direction and intent.

"I did," said Mildred. She pushed the piece of potato around her plate. She was hungry and loved Cook's potatoes, but yet, it was simply too warm this evening to eat.

"And, what is the drive behind your entrée?"

At her silly use of the French word, Cole pointed at his plate with his utensils causing Mildred to stifle her laughter.

"Uncle suggested I take up a vocation and that gardening was an acceptable form of activity for me. Today, I gained entrance into Mother's garden." She scrutinized her brother for his reaction to the statement, but Cole's reaction was hidden as he instead heaped a second helping of meat and potatoes onto his plate while still chomping on a mouthful of food like a cow working its cud. The image caused a smile to grow on Mildred's lips.

"Well, Lord Greene is a very great man, and if he feels it's time for you to have such a large project…" her words trailed off as the serving girl arrived and took her half-eaten dinner away. "And, what about you, Cole? You look a mess, so you must have been up to something manly today?"

Cole simply grunted, using the cover of his full mouth to allow him not to answer.

Mildred wanted to share what she knew of her brother's endeavors that day, but chose instead to remain silent. They may not agree on much, but they had a pact never to feed one another to Miss Canton; it would be too much like feeding a Christian to the Roman lions. She recalled her beloved Lord Byron's verse:

While stands the Coliseum,
Rome shall stand;
When falls the Coliseum,
Rome shall fall;
And when Rome falls
- the World.

The new serving girl arrived with pudding and served it all around. The small cake with sugar on top appeared dry. Mildred ate a berry from her plate. It tasted fresh and wonderful and she wished there was more than the one atop her cake. Yet, she knew if she asked for more berries Miss Canton would go off on another tirade about how impolite it was to ask. What good does it do to have servants if we can't ask them for things?

"Oh, I just can't wait any longer," squealed Miss Canton. She produced a stiff wrapped package from her lap. "Happy Birthday, Miss Millie."

Mildred's eyes lit up as her tutor passed her the gift. She gently untied the ribbon and turned over the package to let the paper open. Inside the heavy trappings were three dainty handkerchiefs. Her delight turned to sadness. "Thank you, Miss Canton," she said in a tone dryer than the cake.

"It's your birthday, Millie?" Cole asked as he licked icing sugar off his dirty fingers.

"Yes," Mildred said with a pout.

"You should have reminded me."

"That certainly isn't my job. If you cared at all about me, you would have remembered."

The three were silent.

"May I be excused? I have a letter to write." Mildred avoided eye contact with the others.

"Of course," said Miss Canton.

Mildred stood, dropped her napkin on the table, and strode out of the room. She remembered her gift and turned to retrieve it to find her brother's long arm reaching across the table to take her pudding without apology. Mildred retrieved her gift, nodded to Miss Canton, and retreated from the room.

Her heels clicked on the stone floors as she briskly walked toward the staircase. Mounting the stairs, she absently unbuttoned her collar and several additional buttons. Taking one of the new handkerchiefs, she wiped the moisture from her neck and cheeks before arriving at the second floor. She turned to the left and walked past the small tables and hanging portraits of someone else's ancestors. As the story had been told many times, her father had purchased Wickwillow Manor and its estates a number of years before she or Cole were born, before he'd even married mother, and the place had come furnished, including the dark, ancient pictures and dusty marble statues that lined the long, second-floor hall.

Thoughts of her father filled her mind and she stopped, absently staring out the hall window that offered a view of the vast stretch of meadow. She could see a light, a lantern perhaps, coming from the hunting cabin at the edge of the wood. Mildred wondered who might be there. Was it some young couple on a romantic tryst? Perhaps a hunter, skinning a rabbit? Maybe a school girl, like her, run away from her horrible tutor, hold up for the night.

"Miss? Can I bring you anything?"

Mildred turned to the house girl in her crisp uniform and white cap. The girl was barely older than her, but they'd never talked. Not about anything more than bed linens and coal scuttles. She considered asking for more berries. Maybe the girl could sneak them up to her. But, Mildred also knew that Miss Canton would discover that she'd asked and... "No. No thank you."

The girl left her mistress and Mildred opened her door and was greeted by a pleasant whoosh of air. Unlike the rest of the house, she kept her windows open against the heat in hopes of enjoying a breeze from the surrounding countryside, at least when her Uncle Parker was away. The girl wanted to leave her door open to encourage the evening coolness into her bedroom, but knew that such a thing was unacceptable. Every passing servant would poke a nose in to see if she required anything and upon departing the room would just close the door anyway. That was the rule of the house, all doors and windows were to be kept closed at all times.

She shut the door behind herself before removing her vest and skirt. She knew it was unacceptable to be in such a state of undress, but it was simply too blasted hot to sit in so many layers of fabric. Yet, it also seemed too early to retire to her dressing gown. She took up her robe and placed it nearby just in case someone knocked upon her door.

The view from her bedroom windows included the sweeping pasture that spread out for hectares from the back of the house to the line of willows at the river's edge that gave the village of Wickwillow its name. She watched a mother and foal run together across the fields of tall grasses and wildflowers as the few clouds in the sky turned purple and orange in the last minutes of the setting sun. Moments such as these made her wish she was more accomplished at drawing or painting. It would be nice to capture such a lovely scene.

Mildred opened a small, empty book and wrote the date: 7 July 1851. Below that she added: Wickwillow Manor. A bit further down the page: "Entered mother's garden today for the first time."

She got up and retrieved the twirl from her smock pocket. She placed the key at the right side of the page and traced it, doing her best to add in the intricate scrollwork that adorned its top.

She continued to write: "At Uncle's urging, I now have a vocation of gardening. Everyone seemed silent about dear Mother and her demise on this day sixteen years ago. At least I. and L.C. remembered this special day. L.C. even gave me a gift."

Mildred fingered one of the handkerchiefs, noting the delicate lace and pretty embroidery that adorned the sides, its looping lines creating her monogram "MG." She wanted to like her tutor, but didn't. Lorain Canton put on airs and acted as if she were the lady of their house. Everyone knew Miss Canton had her sights set on her uncle; the last thing Mildred wanted was that woman as a permanent member of their family. She considered how evil all the fairy tale stepmothers were and shuddered.

Cole burst through her door. "Sister, Sister!" he sang out.

At the sound of the door, Mildred reached for her robe, but seeing it was only her brother, there was no need required of modesty. He'd pulled his own shirt out from his trousers and most of the buttons down the front were undone, exposing his chest.

"You, sir, are a cad," she said with a little smile. Mildred enjoyed saying such a vulgar word as cad. Truly shocking. Cole didn't bat an eye, and she realized just how much she loved her handsome brother. She wished she could be freer like him, like most men. But, alas, she was a woman and others had a great control over, not only her future, but her manners in the moment.

"True. Too, true," Cole said, flopping himself into a chair and throwing one leg over its arm.

They sat for a moment in silence.

"Mill, I'm very sorry. I didn't really forget your birthday." Cole reached in his pocket and took out a handful of springs, wheels, and cogs. "It's supposed to be a rabbit. It's supposed to walk. I couldn't get it to work." He set the toy on Mildred's desk.

"It's wonderful, Cole." Her mind went to work immediately, trying to puzzle out a solution that would help the metal creature walk. She said to her brother: "Let's just say you owe me another favor."

"How many does that make now, dear Millie?"

Mildred thought for a moment. "Two thousand, six hundred and fifty three…no, fifty two since you helped me gain access to the garden." She smiled at her brother who had reached over and picked up her new little diary. He read the brief entry and tossed the book back onto her desk.

"Someday, Mildred, I'll create very special gifts for you that will totally eliminate the list of favors I owe you. Once I better understand gears, I'll be able to build all sorts of wonderful items. I'm going to change the world one day with my inventions."

She was touched that he used her proper name. With a softened tone, she said: "I know, dear Cole. I know."

Cole had been saying such things for as long as Mildred had memories. Sadly, he wasn't very well inclined toward mechanics or invention. He didn't seem well suited to anything. He certainly didn't have their father's green thumb. Any plant Cole even got near died. He wasn't dashing like their

Uncle Parker. Cole continually fell from the horses he tried to ride and held no mastery of swords or bows and arrows. He was better at taking things apart than putting them back together. He had no retention of book knowledge and failed his university entrance exams. And, at eighteen, he had yet to charm anyone of the female persuasion. But, Mildred gave Cole great credit. He never gave up, even when morbid or depressed about his lack of accomplishments, he continued to try and try again, all the while maintaining his silly, joyful attitude.

"Well, I'm going back out to the workshop." Cole stood and kissed his sister's head. "I love you, Millie."

She forgave the nickname, this once. "I love you, too, dear brother."

When Cole departed, the young girl quickly took apart the little rabbit, reconfigured a cog and a spring. She put the thing together again, wound the little crank, and set the rabbit down. It walked in a circle. Another adjustment and it now gently hopped across her desk.

Mildred drew out a fresh piece of paper and, while the rabbit marched back and forth across the surface, began another long letter to her uncle. It was her daily duty to write to him with all the details of her and Cole's day. As she dipped her pen into the ink, small droplets stained the paper. Mildred envisioned a mechanical pen, one that was already filled with ink, and that wouldn't dirty her fingers. It was a satisfying vision that came to her, so she pushed her uncle's letter aside, looked around to be sure no one had entered the room without her knowledge, and, feeling satisfied she was fully alone, reached into the secret hiding place in the desk, removed an old, worn, leather book, opened it to the next available page, and drew her vision of a mechanical pen, with notes about how it could be filled with ink.

five

After fifteen minutes to dust off and wash up, an underling ushered Parker Greene into Fletcher Flynn's cabin. The immense room held all manner of appointments, a bed, a map table, a desk, and so on; this room instead was a large sitting room, replete with over-stuffed, red velvet chairs and long sofas covered in smoky-gray tufted satin. In one corner, a grand piano forte, with its claw feet chained to the floor, was played by a dwarf, not Silas, but another undersized human with a shock of red hair. Greene wondered to himself how odd that a dwarf with stubby, fat fingers would be such a master of the instrument. Along the outer wall, under the windows, billiard balls rolled slightly on the black felt covering of their large table.

"Greene, you ol' sharp!" called Fletcher Flynn who practically leapt from his chair, tossing a book aside as he strode across the room with hand extended.

He grew enthusiastic, once again seeing Flynn, the boy he'd been in love with so long ago; catching himself, he shoved those emotions back deep inside and held his solid ground, not taking the proffered hand. "Sir, I am not now, nor have I ever been a swindler at cards or any other game."

Flynn, unperturbed by the rebuff, said, "Always the gentleman. I'm sorry if I've offended you. It's just so good to see you. It's been ages." Fletcher Flynn used his outstretched hand as a tool to show off the room. "What do you think? Rather unique for an airship?"

Greene remained silent.

"A drink? How about a little whiskey between mates?"

"I've never been your mate." Parker's mouth watered—was that at the thought of a belt of whiskey or the thought of finally becoming Flynn's mate?—he did his best to hide his desires. In that very moment, he gave up on thoughts of trying to escape that evening. There were too many guards. The ship was too big for him to have clear knowledge of its decks and passageways. Parker acquiesced: "Why not have a few drinks with an old school chum?"

"That's the spirit!" Fletcher snapped his fingers; another dwarf, dressed in the uniform of a page, appeared with drinks on a tray. Flynn took one for himself and then the wee creature moved closer to Greene who took the second crystal glass from the silver salver. "Come, sit!" Flynn took up a chair to the far left of the room and indicated the second to Greene.

Lord Greene crossed the room, silently counting. He'd been adding up footsteps in his head as a way to gauge the size of the halls, rooms, and main deck. He took a seat just as the piano player changed to a new tune, something heavy and romantic that Parker had never heard before.

"Such a prize. To have captured one of the greatest mechanical minds, one of the true intellectuals of Her Majesty. To Victoria!" Flynn raised his glass.

Greene followed suit. "Victoria!"

Both men downed the contents of their glasses. Before Fletcher had set his on the table between them, a dwarf arrived. He filled Fletcher's glass and placed the decanter between the men. The dwarf, never making eye contact, bowed slightly and backed away from the men. It was Flynn who refilled his guest's glass. Greene did not protest.

"So, Parker, why where you discovered on one of Her Majesty's mail schooners? Certainly, you aren't working for the Royal Mail as a guard or letter carrier? The last I heard of you, you'd been chasing plants, or some such, right?"

Greene had rehearsed his response hundreds of times during his service to Her Majesty. The words now came tripping easily, almost gaily from his tongue. "Just catching a ride. The schooners are the fastest airships around—"

"Tut, tut. The Balsa Robin is the fastest airship that exists."

"Well, then, next to the Balsa Robin, the mail schooners are the fastest. I'm heading, in a round-a-bout way, to my next location. I'm still a plant hunter for Her Majesty."

"And, what location would that be?"

Greene thought for a split second. "South America."

"You're rather far away from that part of the world." Fletcher Flynn swallowed down the contents of his glass and poured several more fingers of the brown liquid into the cut crystal. He offered more to Greene, who shook his head. "As you wish."

"When I left England, the first available ship was headed to the dark continent. I took berth and hopscotched down the center of Africa, ending up trapped in the Congo for some time. The Barkley was the first ship to pass through headed toward the Caribbean, where I could once again jump around a bit through Her Majesty's little colonies, until I could gain access to a ship to take me further south." Greene didn't know if Flynn believed his story. It didn't really matter.

"Why not just set out with a ship of your own?"

"In the past, it's been easier this way. Hasn't worked out to be so this time." Greene pointed to his glass and his host filled it. He maintained a dejected attitude for some time. "And, you, a pirate."

Flynn smiled broadly. "If you choose such a title, I guess I'm obliged to wear it."

"Well, what else can I call it when you are attacking and stealing Her Majesty's airships? Killing her airmen? Stealing the royal mail?"

"Well, yes, from that vantage point, I suspect you might call us pirates. We prefer a different title. We are settling the scores for the atrocities performed in Her Majesty's name: The killing, raping, and plundering of the peoples of the world. While so much of the world is suffering and starving, Victoria and her people living in England enjoy the wealth of the world. The British Isles remain bucolic, while the rest of the world falls deeper and deeper into squalor. So many others suffer, while lords like you enjoy the wealth of other nations." In his growing rage, Flynn threw his glass against a nearby wall; it shattered into millions of pieces. Without missing a single beat, or flinching at the action, the piano player continued to play unperturbed and the serving dwarf arrived with a fresh glass and decanter of whiskey on a silver tray.

"A Robin Hood, then?"

Both men held eye contact in silence for a long moment. Greene worried for an instant that he'd gone too far and the captain of the Balsa Robin would have him murdered. But, with each passing instant, the skin around Fletcher Flynn's eyes crinkled more and more until the man let out a bout of uncontrolled laughter.

"Shall we go in to dinner?" Flynn asked as he stood.

Greene obligingly followed Captain Flynn across the room. A dwarf opened and held the door for the two men, who entered a formal dining room. The table was set for six, but, other than the pint-sized servants,

Greene and Flynn were the only ones in the room.

"Will there be others?"

Flynn took in the room. "No." He moved to the head of the table. "Here, come sit to my right."

Greene did as told. He stood at the table, waiting for Fletcher to be seated first. He contemplated the possibilities. He still had the small pocket pistol. He could easily kill Captain Flynn in these few moments while they were alone. Even if the army of dwarfs were to kill him for the deed, he'd have killed the captain of the Balsa Robin. Of course, if he were to die, he'd never discover how this ship actually worked. He'd not really stop the pirates from stealing the ships, because surely, some sub-lieutenant or midshipman would quickly take power and control the mission in their own form. And, frankly, Lord Parker Greene, while serving at Her Majesty's request, was himself curious as to why they'd been stealing the ships and mail. To what ends? And, of course, just because Flynn captained this ship didn't mean he was also the one in charge wherever the home or base was set. No, there were too many questions yet to answer.

"Parker? Won't you sit?" Flynn asked.

Lord Greene took his seat.

"So glad you've decided not to kill me at this moment. You'd miss a very fine dinner." The captain rang a small bell and an army of little men, all dressed like sixteenth century pages, carried in platter after platter of all manner of meat, vegetables, and fruits. "Really, help yourself to anything you find appetizing. While I do love formality and ceremony, I toss it all aside at dinner. I have them make a feast and let whoever I've asked to join me just graze at will."

The spread across the table amazed Parker Greene. Exotic meats from far-flung lands and strange vegetables—some he'd seen during his travels and others that were new to him. Not only were many of the dishes strange, but their preparations were remarkable and surprising with heads and plumage announcing to the diner what the creature had once been.

After both men finally tasted the heaps of food they'd chosen for themselves, Lord Greene asked: "So, Flynn, what are your plans for me?" Parker embraced the spirit of the evening and sloshed more wine into both his glass and that of his host.

"Well, that depends on you, my friend."

Greene winced slightly, noticeably at the word "friend."

"We've cast off or killed most of those who were on your ship."

"It wasn't my ship," Greene said tossing a bone, picked clean, back onto his plate. He hadn't thought of the Barkley's captain until now. "What happened to Captain Meadowbrook?" He watched Flynn suck on a forefinger, juice dripping down the sides of his mouth. The sucking sounds and visual aroused Parker.

Removing a finger from his mouth, Flynn said: "I'm not really sure. We've attacked two ships since we got yours." Captain Flynn rang the bell and a page appeared. He whispered to the slight, blond chap who quickly left the room. Within a minute, a Nubian dwarf returned with the burden of a great ledger. The thing was nearly as big as the man. He made a clicking sound and two other little men appeared at his sides, the three of them held the book open for Flynn to peruse.

"Meadowbrook, one commander, and several officers were cast off in a long boat. Most of the flight crew and riggers died fighting us." Flynn paused while he studied the large ledger. "Strangely, your entire under-crew, the stokers and engine men, all survived and have been brought into our own under-crew. So often, those lads go the way of the riggers, which is no use to us."

"It wasn't my ship. But, I'm happy to hear the captain survived and so much of the crew." Parker smiled thinking that the handsome blond boy was probably shoveling coal or wood into the boilers. *Why am I so interested in a boy so below me?*

"We were really hoping to gain a few riggers from you; they so often die in the fighting."

"I'm curious about how this ship operates. It's massive size. Those huge propellers."

"We'll be arriving home tomorrow. Depending on your choices over the next few days, I'd be happy to personally give you a tour and access to everything. That is, if you choose correctly. If not, well, we'll be making other arrangements."

Six

The gate creaked opened giving entry to Mildred and the stable boy, Perry. The two stood for a long moment taking in the overgrown garden. When something rustled in the tall grass near the wall, Mildred caught her breath. It wasn't from her own fear, but Perry's; he tensed and stepped closer to Mildred. The young boy's hand grazed Mildred's, but he never took hers into his own; that would be wrong.

"Well, this isn't going to weed itself," said Mildred, more to herself than her young companion.

"No, Miss," said Perry, who didn't move.

Mildred took a step onto the dew covered grass. Her apprehension eased and a calming presence came over her. She closed her eyes and envisioned the garden as she knew it could be. She saw in her mind a handsome woman with ample hips gliding through the large, high-walled garden, clipping flowers and herbs, and placing them in a basket on her arm, all the while the woman hummed a familiar tune. With a bit more focus on her vision, she realized that the woman she was seeing was, of course, the mother she'd never known. Mildred never questioned how she knew this.

"Perry, I can see our future and have decided that we will begin right here. Please start with the grass along the wall. Cut it low. I'll begin here at this first paving stone." Mildred thought for a moment, and added: "If you come across any plant that isn't grass or a weed you know, please stop your progress and come get me."

"Yes, miss," said Perry. He wiped his brow on his sleeve, raised himself on tiptoe to look over the weeds and plants so much taller than him, and reached into the wheelbarrow and took out a small scythe.

Cole picked up a small sprocket. Despite its size, the piece was quite heavy. He walked out of the workshop, down the path toward the house, and then he ducked his head and entered the small door at the corner. He stayed to the right, walked through a second door and ascended the narrow, dusty staircase. When he arrived at the top, a breeze revived him and Cole placed the piece of the clock's inner workings on the wooden floor. After taking a moment to catch his breath, the young man ran down the stairs, taking them two and three at a time. This was how his morning progressed, shouldering the large and small gears, cogs, and sprockets back up to their tower room, as his sister had requested.

While he worked he hummed the tune his mother used to coo to him at bedtime. Cole questioned in his mind why he was so unsuccessful despite his best actions. He worked hard at everything, why just see the sweat he was now amassing in his current task. Cole opened another button at his shirt collar in defiance.

He wanted to invent something new, something different from anyone else. He liked getting his hands dirty as he took apart the machines around the house and farm, yet he rarely had any success on his own at putting said equipment back together. Yet, somehow, his sister always seemed to see the problem. She'd study a thing, close her eyes for a moment, and then, most annoying of all, have the perfect solution. She never took credit for that, but allowed Cole to accept the accolades.

A swallow lit from the rafters in the clock room. Cole wiped his brow with his shirt sleeve and then surveyed the many parts scattered across the floor.

"Well, boy," he said to himself with a tone quite similar to his father, "you'll have to get her up here to help you with this."

Cole's stomach growled, announcing his desire for lunch. As he exited to the out-of-doors, he watched his sister, covered in dirt, make her way with Perry up the path. The two of them were comical as they tried to maneuver the overladen wheelbarrow toward the barn. Without any more thought, Cole rushed to their aid, took over the handles, and deftly maneuvered their heavy burden toward the compost heap.

"Take off another favor," he said to his sister.

Seven

When Greene returned to his cabin the previous night after his dinner with Flynn, he hadn't been cuffed and chained again. . It felt good to undress, to wash himself, and to sleep in a nightshirt instead of his heavy uniform.

Now, Parker Greene wandered the ship freely; he nodded to the deck hands, as if it were his own ship, and they nodded back. Ever an early riser, he'd awoke, dressed, and wandered onto the deck of the Balsa Robin unmolested and perched on the ship's rail long before the sun peeked over the horizon. He enjoyed the feel of his walking stick in his hand. Parker unconsciously ran a finger along the rounded, carved filial that topped the thing.

While staying out of their way, he watched as all manner of men in all manner of dress, ran to and fro, moved barrels and crates, climbed rigging, furled and unfurled various sails, mopped, polished, and generally cleaned in a frenzy he'd never before witnessed on a ship; at least not one in flight. Greene found many of the shoeless men handsome with their thin waists and broad shoulders. Shirts open at their necks revealed deep-tanned, often haired chests that caused him to catch his breath with desire. At those thoughts, he couldn't help but think of the young, handsome blond man from the Barkley who was now stoking boilers below his feet, strangely glad that the lad was still alive.

While he felt a sense of freedom, Lord Greene couldn't help but notice that the eyes of all the men he could see were also keeping a watch of him. He took the moment to survey the deck: three mail schooners locked into positions. He wanted to inspect the couplings and discover how they managed to hold them upright in their mooring slots. Simply amazing.

As the sun rose a bit more, the call came from the crow's nest high above his head: "Land ho'!" Such a lovely, singsong voice gave out the cry again: "Land ho'!"

Lord Greene turned and spied a large, lush green island, with three other smaller islands keeping watch over her.

The activity all around him increased. Men swung and leapt into action. The great ship slowed and hovered, before beginning an easy descent toward the smallest of the four islands.

As they drew closer, a line of buildings came into view. They were some of the largest buildings Parker Greene had seen anywhere, ever. He finally realized what was happening. As they progressed closer and closer to the building in the middle of the long line of more than a dozen of nearly the same size, its great panel doors were opening, one-by-one, like a huge accordion. As each panel moved it made two sounds: a click and clack in tight rhythm. Click-clack. Click-clack.

Inside the building was dark. And then, the sound of what seemed a million bees buzzed deafeningly. With that hum came a brilliant yellow glow from within not just the terminal with the open doors, but from the windows of all the other adjacent and adjoining structures. As they lit up, Parker could see how they were each attached to one or two others. It was like a hive connected to a hive connected to a hive.

He found himself with a strong desire to participate as the energy of anticipation of returning home built around him. He surveyed the deck for something to do: maybe toss an anchor or take up a rope or…but there was nothing for him to do. It now felt as if the deck had been abandoned. There weren't men scurrying anywhere now. No barefoot riggers worked the line or sails. No calls were offered from the crow's nest above.

Eight

"Children!" Miss Canton called from one of the many manor doors. She clanked an old bell like the schoolmarm she'd once been. "Children!"

Cole and Mildred jostled together along the path as they race-walked to the house.

"Slow down," she reprimanded.

"Stop poking me, you cad," squealed Mildred to her brother as they entered the dining room.

"Mildred! Don't use that vulgar word." Loraine looked around to be certain none of the servants had heard.

As the children took their places at the table, the serving girls arrived with trays of cooked meats and roasted vegetables. Cole heaped food on his plate, while Lorain and Mildred each took their own turns at serving themselves dainty portions.

"What have you children accomplished this morning?" As usual, Cole had already filled his mouth with food, so Lorain turned her full attention toward Mildred.

"Perry and I have begun clearing away the weeds and cutting the overgrown grasses in Mother's garden." Mildred sounded proud of her endeavors. "I wish mother had kept track of her garden in a book. It would be nice to know in advance where the paths lead and what plants we should look out for."

"No one has been in there for a very long time, Sister," Cole began through a mouthful of potatoes. "I'm sure whatever plants were there have long ago been replaced by weeds.

"Not so. I discovered a whole row of rose bushes this morning. They're overgrown and gnarled, but roses none the less. I wish father were here with us because he would be able to tell me how to care for them…" her words trailed off with her thoughts. Unlike the others, who had given up Cecil Greene for dead, she still believed, nigh knew that her father was still alive and that one day, in one form or another, the man would return home to take up his rightful place in proper English society.

"Millie, my dear, why don't you look over the shelves in the library? I'm sure you'll find many books on plants and flowers that will be of help to you." The tutor smiled sweetly at her charge. "I only ask that you read them inside the house and not take them outside where you might forget about them, and they'd be ruined by the weather."

As if on cue, thunder rattled the window panes.

"Oh, bother. It's going to rain all afternoon now, I suspect," said Mildred who had already been looking forward to her next discovery among the weeds.

The three ate without speaking as rain began to drum on the windowpanes.

"May I be excused?" Mildred asked as she placed her napkin on the table. "Since the weather is so foreboding, I think I will spend some time in Father's library."

"Of course, Millie," said Miss Canton.

Mildred walked through the great entrance hall with its grand staircase, gaudy crystal chandelier, and life-size portraits of an aged couple. She'd taken to calling them Helga and Roulf after characters she disliked from a penny dreadful story. Mildred opened the door to her father's study, entered the large, dark room, and left the door open behind her. She took a match from the table and lit two of the lamps before beginning her search of his vast library.

"Can I help you find something, Miss?"

Mildred turned at the voice of the old houseman. "Hello, Marcus. I'm looking for books on roses.

The man walked deftly to the center of one of the floor to ceiling bookcases that surrounded the room and lined the walls, and pointed. "You'll find books on English flowers and plants here."

Mildred moved to where he'd indicated. The two stood close to each other for a long moment. "Thank you, Marcus. That will be all."

"Would you like some tea, Miss?"

Despite the rain, the room remained warm and close. "No, thank you."

"Very good, Miss." The houseman left the room, closing the door to the library as he departed.

Mildred didn't care for Marcus. He'd been her father's valet for as long as she could remember. Obviously, her Uncle Parker trusted the man enough to allow him to stay on and run the house. But, there was something about Marcus that Mildred didn't care for. It was as if he was always watching her; he was always polite, even if stiffly so, appearing whenever Mildred left a door open. Yet, she simply didn't like the man.

After selecting several books from the shelf, Mildred sat at her father's great, ornately carved desk, and began turning page after page of the books, hoping to find the rose she'd discovered in the garden. As she thumbed through the leaves, her mind began its work, cataloging each flower and fact into her mental filing system. It wouldn't be long before she knew everything about every English rose and flower that existed, and, furthermore, she'd have instant recall of all the content for the rest of her life. That was how Mildred learned. She read something and had it forever.

Nine

In awe, Lord Greene watched as the great Balsa Robin was guided by lines dropped from her sides that had been taken up by men on the ground. Yet, the ropes weren't pulled by them; instead, they were hooked through a lattice of metal connectors which, as they moved and shuffled, perfectly glided the airship into a resting berth. The slow motion adventure culminated with a very slight thud; Parker maintained his footing without issue the entire time.

Now, inside the massive hangar, the hive of activity within the building was matched on the ship. Gang planks were lowered. Men, and surprisingly women, boarded the ship from the ground and began the great task of unloading the ill-gotten cargo. The bees of this hive, spoke a collection of different languages and dialects—some Parker Greene had heard before and others he hadn't. The crew's skins were all possible shades from the whitest Irish linen to the blackest African night.

Once again, Parker felt he should be doing something, participating. Despite his title, he wasn't a man to shirk responsibility or duty. Even here, a prisoner as it were, he still felt a strong desire to work for his keep. Yet, no one, not even one of the many dwarfs he'd met and who had acted as his handlers, had come to him to give charge or order. And, so he watched the proceedings.

Ropes were released from the hull and many men, normal sized and smaller, captured them and began leading the Balsa into her berth. The great bird was slow, even tempered, and gentle as it entered the cavernous hall. A series of gentle thuds worked their way from bow to stern. The ship was being locked into place. A haze of smoke filled the space and threatened to engulf the entire barn, but just as Parker Greene reached for a handkerchief to cover his mouth, hundreds of panels opened in the ceiling, allowing release of the fumes.

Then, the moment of silent clarity broke. Shouts from all directions came. Lines of small men and women came toward the ship at four different entrances below the main deck and in even rows. Their empty hands were filled, and they walked back the way they had come, through a myriad of doorways and passages.

Sections of deck opened wide and colossal cranes swung over the deck and, after some attention to detail, one by one, the pirated mail schooners were lifted whole from their births aboard the Robin, swung gingerly and slowly off the boat, and then lowered to a massive track and rail where they were then tugged out of the main building and out of view.

As he watched the Barkley follow this fate, he had a twinge of regret. His personal effects remained in his cabin, and he hoped he'd be able to retrieve them. At the thought of the possible loss, he touched his breast pocket where his niece's last letter remained folded. He could feel the weight of the small pistol in the other inner pocket. And, he now had use of his walking stick once again. He'd survive no matter what happened. Yet, Greene wondered what the fate of the Barkley and the other ships would be. Would they, after the moveable contents had been removed, be broken down for their wood and fixtures? Would they now become part of the pirate's fleet? Would...

"Lord Greene?"

"Yes." Parker Greene turned toward the soft voice to discover another dwarf, this time a woman. He'd only seen female dwarfs at county fairs and on stages, never so close. He was amazed that she was mostly like a miniature person, except the proportion of her head to her body was out of sorts.

She took his hand. "I'm to show you to your temporary quarters."

A shudder ran along his spine. "My things have..." he pointed toward the direction where the Barkley had been. The whole ship was gone, taken. He looked around, attempting to find the ship, but he couldn't discover it.

"Not to worry, sir. Your personal possessions will be removed from the ship and placed in your quarters."

"Everything?"

"Well, not the furniture, sir. But, everything that is yours." She tugged lightly at his hand. Her small fingers were soft and gentle, a woman's touch. And she, like the others, sported a grotesquely sized ring.

Lord Greene allowed himself to be led by this fair creature off the Balsa Robin and on to land as all around him, hundreds of men and women, continued with their tasks of off-loading the great ship.

Ten

"Dear Uncle," Mildred wrote on a fresh piece of paper. It had been several weeks since she'd received a letter from him. Despite not knowing what he was doing or where he was, she continued to write a new letter to him each afternoon or evening, and Marcus posted it each morning to the business address that her uncle had told her was underwriting his current exploration.

She knew it was an intricate thing, this getting letters from the small village of Wickwillow to wherever her uncle was at any given moment. His trips, while financed by industries, were sponsored by the Queen, so his mail traveled via the Royal Post. Somehow, they knew where her uncle was and could get letters to him. Of course, most of the time, he was out slashing his way through this or that jungle and wouldn't receive her letters until he returned to camp, or sometimes boarded a ship to sail or soar to a new location, or even to return home. But, he encouraged her to keep writing. He said that he read many of her notes over and over during the lonely evenings and lengthy voyages.

Many times, his own missives arrived in large batches. She'd open them all and then sort them by their dates and devour each one, one after another, learning of his escapades with giant snakes, killer spiders, all sorts of native tribes, and the vast collection of new plant specimens he'd discovered, named, and cataloged. Many of the letters included intricate drawings of the plants, animals, and people he'd encountered, too. Mildred loved her Uncle Parker's drawings and narratives and awaited their arrival with great anticipation. And, because she enjoyed his epistles so much, she dutifully wrote her own each day as he'd requested, even though, by comparison, life at Wickwillow Manor was anything but daring or exciting.

"Millie!" Cole burst into her rooms and cast himself onto the settee.

"You're a manner-less brute!" Mildred exclaimed. "Your shirt is undone, your trousers dirty. No wonder you can't ever seem to woo a girl."

Cole ignored his sister's ranting.

"Your room is the only cool place in this blasted house."

"You could certainly open your own windows."

"No, I can't. The aroma from the barn and stalls wafts right up to my room. It's simply dreadful."

"We live in a massive home with dozens and dozens of bedrooms. I simply don't know why you won't switch. The servants would gladly help you move your belongings."

"Well, Sister dear, I refuse to move. The view from my windows is the best in the whole house. I can see the river. I can see the road. I have a clear view of the orchards. And, I can see all the way across the cut pasture to the woods. I wouldn't trade my view for the world. In fact, my view is of the world! But, it would be nice to have a breeze that didn't smell of pigs."

Mildred was amused by Cole's assessment of life. She loved him, but his attitude that Wickwillow was the world caused her sadness. She longed to leave. Not forever, but to have his opportunities, a man's opportunities. She wanted to accompany their uncle on his journeys. To sail to the corners of the world… To soar to…

The heat once again got the better of her, bringing Mildred back to her current reality. As they sat for a moment in silence, she conceived an idea for a mechanical fan. It wouldn't require a window for fresh air, but would be able to force the air out already cooled. She began to reach for her secret notebook, but quickly remembered that her brother was there.

"Is there anything you wish to tell Uncle?" She picked up her pen, poised to add her brother's thoughts to her letter.

"Tell him…tell him…tell him my sister is a pest."

"That's a letter you'll have to write yourself," said Mildred, un-phased by Cole's antics. "Did you get all the clock parts back up into the tower today?"

"Almost. I have two more pieces, but with the rain this afternoon, they had to wait until tomorrow."

"Well, I'll spend some time in the garden in the morning, get Perry started with his chores there, and then I'll come visit you in the tower before lunch." She'd continued to have visions of the clockworks since Cole had shown her the pieces. She'd worked out how the gears moved the hands and also how the massive bells should chime. She surmised that a small cog was the cause of the clock not working, but wouldn't know for sure until they'd reassembled the thing. As she'd thought about the inner workings of the clock, she'd also devised a mechanism that, when attached to the drive shaft she envisioned for the entire manor, would run the clock automatically so that the servants wouldn't be forced to pull the ropes and weights each day to keep it running.

She'd had the idea for the drive shaft when the new hot water boiler had been installed in the cellar under the kitchen. The men doing the job laughed at her when she'd asked them to explain how the thing worked, but they'd given her the details all the same of how the water was under pressure and because of that pressure could be delivered anywhere in the manor. They'd explained about the pressure valves and were very serious as they spoke and tapped the gauge with its dangerous red zone and its automatic release valve. That's when Mildred had the idea for the steam-driven shaft.

Of course, Mildred hadn't told anyone what she envisioned for the house, not yet anyway. She had been figuring that it would take a few more favors banked from her brother to bring the plan about.

"Where have you gone, little Sister? You've dripped ink all over your letter to Uncle."

Mildred looked down at the splatters on the paper. "Oh bother."

"Why do you say that all the time? It's an annoying little phrase."

"Never you mind. I like it. And, it's better than constantly cursing like you do all day long."

The siblings again sat in silence, enjoying the coolness of the evening, a byproduct of the afternoon's thunderstorm and Mildred's open windows.

"I'm hungry," Cole said. He threw his legs over the edge of the settee and righted himself. "Care to join me?"

"No, I want to finish my letter and read a bit before going to sleep. How is it you can eat as you do and never gain any weight?"

"Don't know. Don't care." He stood up, moved to Mildred, and kissed the top of her head. "Goodnight, dear Sister."

"Goodnight, cad," said Mildred with a chuckle. She waited for him to leave the room and close the door behind himself before she reached for the hidden notebook and added her latest ideas for the clock mechanism and drive shaft to the well-inked pages.

Eleven

The dwarf woman deposited Lord Parker Greene in a chamber. She gave a little wave in his direction before she closed the door. Like all the other little people he had seen in the short time he'd been with the pirates, she had a slightly oversized ring on the middle finger of her right hand. He wondered about those rings; if all the small ones wore them, but no one else, they must hold a significance.

Returning to his chamber wasn't much of a walk, but the halls and passageways had been confusing. Parker had lost his bearings, although he could still hear the bee-like humming; the sound permeated everything.

The room wasn't uncomfortable. If fact, despite its size—only slightly larger than the average ship's cabin—it was well appointed. The bed had more cushion and bounce than his bunk on the Barkley; the sitting chair was lovely, covered in bright green damask; a side table had empty cabinet space below and a pitcher of water and basin atop; and, there was a good-sized table with two chairs. He'd asked the woman how long he'd be kept here, but she didn't answer.

On the table, in a glass bowl, was a selection of tropical fruits, most he'd seen before, like the yellow banana and the green star fruits. Others, he'd not seen before. He took an unknown fruit, sniffed it, bit through the skin. It had the flesh of an apple and tasted like it might be a varietal or some odd combination of apple and pear. It tasted good, and he ate all but the seedy core.

As he consumed the banana, Lord Greene contemplated his next move. What could he do? He was on a tropical island, kept and maintained by, from the looks of the vast operation, very intelligent men. These weren't the pirates Queen Victoria thought were stealing her ships and killing her crews. These men had purpose. They had direction. There was meaning behind their desire. Captain Flynn spoke of their actions being a form of retribution for the Empire's deeds.

No, before he could develop a true plan of combat, he had to learn more, know more. He had to hope they wouldn't kill him, so he'd have time to discover what was going on with these men, these pirates.

He tossed aside the banana's peel and took up a star fruit. He wished he had a knife, but alas there was none present; he replaced the star fruit and began to peel a small citrus fruit, not exactly an orange, but something similar. His efforts ended when he heard a knock. He returned the fruit to the glass bowl, stood, and went to the door. Parker turned the handle, but the thing didn't budge. "Yes," he said.

"We have your possessions, Lord Greene. May we enter?"

"Of course." Parker stepped back from the door as it opened.

A group of female dwarfs, dressed in beautifully embroidered and beaded dresses of vibrant hues, entered carrying his things. Without a sound, they moved into the room, placed each item where they felt it went, and, without a word, left the room. The unmistakable sound of a lock being secured punctuated their departure.

He looked around the room; Greene discovered the fruit had been replenished; a knife and clean rag now sat on the table next to the glass bowl. His empty scabbard hung on the back of the door. His hat rested over the top of it. His duffle leaned in a corner and upon inspection seemed to contain all his possessions.

Lord Greene took out a few of his things and discovered a stack of letters addressed to him, unopened. He looked through the stack; each letter was from his niece, Mildred. Without further thoughts of his prison or jailers, Parker tore into the missives, devouring his ward's sweet words and the images they brought of his beloved Wickwillow Manor. For the next several hours, Parker Greene could smell the earth, feel the weeds, and enjoy the machinations of Loraine Canton as she made Mildred and Cole's lives miserable. As he read the lovely words written in well-turned script, he realized for the first time that Mildred had a great command of English, she was a grown woman, or nearly so; it was time to marry Millie off. He'd been slack in his duties regarding these children and, if he survived this endeavor for Her Royal Majesty, he vowed to do better by them.

Twelve

Cole stood silently at the garden gate. He admired how much work Mildred and the stable boy had already accomplished. Nearly twenty feet of the main, central path had been revealed. The center path, made up of large, smooth, flat pavers, was about four feet across. Each side edged with chiseled stone borders more than a foot tall holding back overgrown flowerbeds. To the right, those beds contained old, gnarled rose bushes nearly six feet high. Many of the stems and stalks were as thick around as a man's arm. A smell caught up in his nose and he remembered his mother hugging him tight, her skirts dirty, her hands gloved, and that smell fo earth and roses and something else, something he smelled now but couldn't identify. He willed the rising tears away from his eyes. The two rose bushes nearest the entrance had unopened buds the size of a fist. The things were massive. Around, following the garden wall, Perry was working a scythe, mowing down bushels of grasses taller than him.

From Cole's position, he could only see his sister's feet and ankles. The remainder of her was hidden by the weeds and plants that surrounded her. He debated his options. He wanted her help with the clock. He hated to admit that, but he knew his sister would be able to clearly direct him about what gears and cogs went where. And, if he took her advice, he also knew that the clock would work when he was finished, and furthermore, that she'd allow him all the credit and glory for the accomplishment. Cole resented Mildred, just a bit, for having better skills and abilities than he did, especially when it came to mechanical things. Although, everyone would admit that her skills were better in all things than were his.

Despite wanting her assistance, he also didn't want to bother her. She was obviously taking this new gardening vocation seriously. She seemed to take everything quite seriously. So, for a long while, he simply remained at the gate and watched the bees and butterflies drift over, around, and through the tangle of greenery that once was and soon again would be his mother's garden.

It was impossible to be there and not think of her. He was only three when she died, but Cole had clear memories of her. One of those memories involved this garden. He sat with her on one of the yet to be exposed benches along the wall. They were in the shade, eating a picnic lunch out of a wicker basket so big he could have fit inside. They didn't use utensils to consume their food, but instead ate everything, even the peach jam, with their fingers. And, as they got stickier and stickier, and laughed more and more, dozens of bees arrived, drawn by the sticky sweetness. Cole remembered being startled and afraid when a bee lighted on his mother, but she laughed and said she was the queen of the bees. As she laughed more and more bees arrived and settled on her arms, skirts, and even her head and face. Still she laughed and smiled.

Cole shook the odd memory from his head, thinking, as he had over the years, that it must be a dream, or something he'd made up.

"Brother!" exclaimed Mildred as she rushed toward him, brushing her hair back with a dirty, gloved hand. "Let me show you my garden."

"Your garden?" Mildred smelled just as his mother had sixteen years ago. "This was then, is now, and always will be Mother's garden."

"Oh, I didn't mean to hurt your feelings or Mother's memory." She placed her arm through the crook of Cole's stiff arm. "Really." She laid her head on her brother's strong chest. "I guess I am taking ownership as I work here. I hope you can find a way to be okay with that."

He knew he should say something, but he couldn't bring himself to speak.

They walked together along the so-far-exposed path. The paving stones held a green, mossy patina that was a bit slick. She showed him the roses and their massive buds. She offered conjecture about their color, but then laughed at herself as she admitted she didn't really know what colors would emerge. Cole was patient and allowed his sister to show off all she'd discovered and found.

"Now, dear brother, shall we begin work on your clock?" Mildred stripped off her gardening gloves. "Isn't it delightful that we both claimed projects to work on that would improve the house and grounds before Uncle returns from his trip?"

A bee gently buzzed and lighted on Mildred's arm. She took no notice of it.

"Okay. Okay. Let go of my arm," Cole snapped. He immediately regretted his tone, but at the same time, all he could think of at that moment was getting out of the garden and back into the full sunlight and fresh air outside the high gated walls.

The siblings walked together out of the garden. They didn't touch and were silent as they traversed the path toward the little door at the corner of the house that would lead them up to the clockworks.

Thirteen

Lord Greene was so engrossed in his niece's letters that he didn't hear the recurrent knocks on the door. That same door burst open and a very tall, incredibly handsome man, with dark, long hair, a well-kempt goatee, and clothes so tight Parker could make out each muscle of the intruder's arms, chest, stomach, and thighs startled him. He instinctively wanted the man to turn around, to see what that view might offer. It had been too long since he had made love with someone. Parker instinctively reached for his sword, which, of course, wasn't there.

"Sorry to intrude, but when you didn't answer my repeated knocking, I grew concerned." His voice was strong, but kind. His attitude and style direct.

Parker stared at the man, lost in his deep, deep, brown eyes.

"It appears you don't remember me, so allow me to introduce myself. I'm Able Currant."

"Currant? What sort of name is that?" Parker wracked his brain; that strange name seemed somehow familiar.

"Don't really know. My father always suspected some great, great, great grandfather misspelled something when he was drunk and, well, here we are." Able Currant laughed in a good-natured way causing Parker Greene's knees to go a bit weak.

"Lord Parker Greene," he said formally and held out his hand. "You say we know each other? That we've met before?" Greene knew he'd have remembered meeting this one, with his languid, rippling muscles, chiseled jaw line, Roman nose....

The pirate took Parker's hand. "Oh, we're offering titles, are we? Well, I'm officially Lieutenant Ablest Currant. Everyone here calls me Able. Actually, there are some jokes..."

Their eyes locked.

Electricity passed into Parker Greene, drawing him a step closer as his breath caught. Parker wanted to reach up, touch the man's face, kiss the handsome stranger. But, he refrained, forcing himself to release the man's hand and look away for a moment. Something. He should say something. Change the subject. What had they been talking about? That they'd met before? Preposterous. He'd have remembered. Create a subject. Was there nothing he wanted to know? It dawned on him…

"Why am I being held captive? Captain Flynn said I'd be shown around. I'd get to see the under decks of the Balsa Robin. I'd—" He could feel the heat of blush at his neck, upon his cheeks.

Able reached up with a finger and placed it on Parker's lips. Parker Greene was silenced. The man's finger felt callused and rough. The thought of that finger, pushing into him, opening him, loosening him nearly caused the man to swoon.

"There are many things for us to discuss." Able stepped closer. The heat their bodies generated merged. He lowered his hand. "We ask each arrival a question. Your answer to this question will determine your future. It will decide whether you live—"

Parker swallowed hard. He leaned, ever so slightly, into Able Currant. Through the taught cloth of trousers their maleness touched.

"—or die," finished Able.

"What's the question?" Parker asked breathless. Their tight stomachs and hard chests were now touching.

"I'm not the one to ask it," Able whispered. His breath entered Parker's slightly parted lips.

"Who…is?" He licked his lips, nearly licking Able's lips.

"I'm to take you there now." Able gently brushed his mouth against Parkers and then stepped back.

Parker Greene was pulled forward into the wake created in the air between them; he tugged on his jacket and eyed Lieutenant Able Currant who held the cabin door open, the bulge in his crotch joining the show his other muscles were making of his tight clothes.

"After you," said the man, a twinkle in his perfect brown eyes.

Fourteen

Mildred wiped a cobweb from her face. The thick gloves that she'd removed during their walk she now put on again as she surveyed the small dank room. The light was dim and specks of dust danced in it. Spiders, Mildred knew, where at that moment peering at them from the dark corners and recesses created by the exposed wood framing of the tower.

"I've placed all the big pieces here against the wall, and all the small pieces in this spot on the floor where there's more light." Cole surveyed his work, hands on his lower back, elbow sticking out, without looking directly at his sister.

Mildred first surveyed the frame for the clock. She took a long moment studying it, both with her eyes opened and closed. When her eyes were closed, she could see clearly where each piece belonged. She could, if she chose, see the clockworks in motion, or stopped. She knew hers was an amazing gift. She'd once tried to explain it to her brother, but it was obvious that he didn't understand and that he thought she was a little crazy. Because of that, she never shared with anyone what she saw or how she saw it.

As she pieced the clock back together and then took it apart in her mind, she questioned which piece or pieces were missing and those pieces, two small circular gears, glowed in her mind.

"Okay," she finally said, her eyes open, looking deep into her brother's face. "This is the first one to go in. She touched the biggest gear leaning against the wall. It fits over this long pin. Just be careful as you insert it not to damage any of the other pins or brackets."

With great effort, Cole lifted the gear that was bigger than his chest and moved it toward the pin. With a bit of instruction from Mildred, he managed to slide it on to the large pin. Once it was in place, Mildred gave the thing a gentle spin. The sound was metal upon metal and sent chills up her spine.

"You'll want to oil this as we go." She surveyed all the pieces. "In fact, I think that should be your task this afternoon. Clean and oil all the pieces you've taken off and provide a good cleaning for all the pins and spokes that are here in the clockworks." As she spoke, she pointed to each place that she knew should be oiled.

"Really? We can't simply put it back together and then oil it?"

"Cole, you've gone through all the trouble of taking the thing apart. It will be easier to clean it all like this, don't you agree?"

"I do, but…" he chose not to finish his thought.

Mildred was losing her patience. "You've asked for my assistance in your project. This is my recommendation. If you choose to follow it, I will continue to help you. If you don't want my help, I have plenty to do myself." She wanted to turn and stomp down the stairs for effect, but decided to wait and see what her brother's response would be.

"Fine, fine," he said, his head hanging down low enough for his chin to touch his chest.

They both heard Lorain's call: "Children! Time for lunch!"

"I'm tired of being called a child by that woman," said Cole.

"Me, too, but what are we to do? I am a child. Well, I will be for a few more years."

They looked at each other and offered small smiles of support before making their way back down the narrow staircase and out once again into the fresh air.

Fifteen

Lt. Currant led Lord Greene through a maze of hallways, each one formed of solid wooden flooring, wood-paneled walls, and thatched ceilings. Parker noticed that the wood of the walls and floors changed every ten or so feet. The cuts and grains didn't match. Just as they stopped at a beautifully carved door, it dawned on Parker: all this wood came from disassembled ships—they used everything here, wasted nothing.

Able Currant knocked at the door, waited four beats, opened it, and, with a hand on Greene's elbow, led the man into a small waiting room. The interior matched the grandeur of the carved entry door. The walls were covered in ornate, though mismatched guilt-framed mirrors which bounced the light from the small porthole-sized window at the side of the room back and forth, up and down, and generally, blindingly around the space.

While still visionless, Able rapped at an interior door.

"Enter," was sternly called.

Able pushed at a wall and it rotated open, revealing a very thin man in slim pants and blouse of simple linen. No jacket, no tie. As Parker continued to survey the man, he realized, barefooted. Had the man just rolled out of bed? Despite his simple dress, he looked crisp and ironed, and, when he turned toward Parker Greene, the sight was shocking.

"Oh, pick up your jaw," said the man.

"You...it's you...it's really you?" That was all Parker Greene could get out.

"Yes, it most certainly is me. That will be all, Lieutenant."

Able bent at the waist, clicked a heel, and retreated, leaving Parker Greene to fend for himself.

"Take a seat, if you wish. Or, there's wine and spirits on that table there, if you'd like." The man continued to read a letter as he spoke and absently pointed.

Parker took the moment to align himself. How could this traitor, this scallywag be the one in charge? Greene had only recently seen him at the opera in London. What was that? Three months ago. Like so many of the others he'd encountered since his capture, this man, this awful human, had been at college with him, too. He'd been the scholar, the hero, the head of his house.

Lord Parker Greene felt the pistol push in his jacket. In a swift move, he could easily kill Baki, the obvious leader of these pirates. Of course, if he did such a thing, it meant certain death for himself. He'd never be able to escape these remote islands. He'd figured out he must be in or near the Caribbean, but where, he didn't know. He'd require a boat or airship, but an airship would require a crew. A water escape would require a small crew, too. Instead, he walked to the indicated table and poured himself a glass of wine. Parker drank it off and then refilled his glass before moving back, closer to Baki Frogs, the king of the pirates.

"Sit...sit."

Parker sat. The office was rather sparse: A side table with the glasses and wine. A round table with a faded map of the world held down by four cannonballs at the corners. A desk with a big chair and two smaller chairs facing, of which Parker took one. No rugs on the floors. No art on the walls except a fine rendering of Her Majesty Queen Victoria.

"Really, it will be just one more moment...."

Greene thought back to that final match. His house against theirs. He against Baki. His given name was Landaus Frogs. Parker didn't know if the man had a middle name. He never did discover why everyone at school called him "Baki." But, that's what he went by. He made up for his short stature by being mean to everyone. He was an ogre to the young boys entering his house. Yet, everyone living there, the upperclassmen, seemed to love him. Maybe it was because he came from a wealthy family and could provide sweets and extras for those boys. Maybe it was because he won every cricket match he played. Every single match, except that final one, the one against Parker Greene's house. There it was, the two of them repeatedly stealing the ball from the other, their feet a blur of movement and grass and ball, crowds of boys from both houses shouting encouragement, instruction, as the two young men kicked and fought for that wet ball. Rain. Yes, it had started to rain. In a moment of pause as he wiped mud and hair and wet from his forehead, Baki looked right at Greene, right into his eyes. He whispered, "You'll never win. You don't have what it takes." Baki, in a quick jab, kneed Greene in the crotch. The pain horrible. And, Baki stole that ball and bolted it into the net. After the goal, as he celebrated with his team, he never took his eyes off of Greene.

Finally, Landaus "Baki" Frogs looked up from his letter, smiled at Parker Greene, and sat in his large desk chair. "So, we finally meet again. Me, the guy in charge. You, said to be the most brilliant man in England."

"You flatter me, sir. I suspect there are others more intelligent."

"Well, your brother was said to be the smartest, until he disappeared. How we would have loved to have captured him! That would have been wonderful. A real feather in our cap. But, he got away; Cecil Greene ran off into the jungle."

"You? Baki, you were the cause of his disappearance?"

He offered a bemused smiled toward Parker. "Most people around here call me 'Sir,' or 'Admiral.' He ran into the jungle like a rabbit. I'm sure he's been eaten by a snake by now. You Greene boys don't know how to win games."

Parker Greene pulled his thoughts back from his brother. There was no reason to get lost there at this moment; no need to show any of his anger to Baki. "So, what plans do you have for me, Admiral?"

"That depends on you, Lord Greene. There are so many projects underway that would benefit from your keen mind, from your knowledge of the plant kingdom, not to mention your understanding of the workings of…well…everything. It was amazing to me when we were boys at school together that you could look at something, close your eyes, and then fix it. Your brother had that skill, too. Though, not as keen as you when it came to gears, if I remember correctly."

Parker Greene enjoyed the moment of flattery, but said nothing.

"We have come into possession of a great many plans and designs for machines of all various sorts. We want someone to assess them, determine if they are practical, and if they'll operate properly once built."

"The contest. You've been stealing the airships to get the contest entries." It suddenly made perfect sense.

"Stealing is such a harsh word. But, in short, yes."

"And, then you've been returning the other mail…."

"That's it, Lord Greene. It has not been our goal to disrupt all mail service around the world. We only wish to become dominant when it comes to machines. So, we've procured as many plans as possible. Some of the men and women do occasionally, how shall we say...acquire a fob or farthing. But, that aside, we've built this series of workshops here on our little island home. We're securing whatever resources are necessary to build the things. But, we don't know what is viable or not until it's built. This is cumbersome from a time and resource perspective. We want to quicken things. And, with your mind, we know we can do that."

"And, if I refuse, Admiral?"

"We'll try to persuade you otherwise, for a while, at least."

"Persuade?" Greene immediately thought of the handsome Able Currant. He'd be able to persuade Parker of just about anything.

"Well, we can offer you a very comfortable life if you join us. And, if you choose not to, we can offer a very uncomfortable life...or end your life."

Parker was intrigued about what a comfortable life would mean to these pirate savages. Going along with this would allow him to discover in more depth what the pirates' plans were for taking over all this technology. Yet, if he came across as willing too quickly, they might question his motives.

"I'll give you twenty-four hours to decide. And, during that time, I'll also give you a taste of the two options."

"Is this the question that Lt. Currant spoke of?"

"No. If you decide to join us, then I shall ask you the question."

"What then?"

"Enough for now." Admiral Frogs rang a bell and a group of dwarfs entered the room. Without words or direction, the little men and women took Parker Greene by the hands and arms and led him out of the office.

Sixteen

Mildred, who had changed out of her gardening clothes into something more appropriate for luncheon, walked down the main staircase. She was greeted at the bottom of the stairs by the jangle of the front door bell. There weren't any servants nearby, so she simply opened the door herself.

"Good afternoon, Miss Mildred," said the tall, middle-aged, yet still handsome man standing there.

"Dr. Ellis, how lovely of you to stop by." Mildred reached her right hand to the doctor, who took it. She led him into the hall and closed the door behind them. "What have you there?"

"Letters, for you." He handed the bundle to Mildred and added: "They're all from your uncle, more than a dozen of them."

"Oh, the ships must have finally caught up with him. We saw a mail schooner yesterday, and I'd hoped there'd be a letter from Uncle Parker." She beamed at the prospect of having this collection of letters that would let her know where he had been. "We're about to sit down to luncheon, won't you join us?"

"That would be lovely," said the doctor who had removed his hat and gloves, but was still holding them in his hands.

"Where are my manners, let me take those." She took the doctor's things and placed them next to the bundle of letters on the sideboard before leading him into the dining room. "Look who has come for a visit," Mildred announced to Miss Canton and Cole who were sitting in silence waiting for Mildred.

Cole bounded up from his chair. "Doctor Ellis, how nice to see you." The young man pumped the older man's hand.

"Nice to see you, too, Cole," said the doctor. "Miss Canton," the doctor said coolly with a nod in the tutor's direction, but he didn't shake her hand.

Lorain whispered into a servant's ear. The young serving maid disappeared, and two more girls quickly appeared with a place setting for the new arrival. They looked confused about where to place the glassware, silver, and china.

"Place Dr. Ellis next to me," said Mildred. She liked having a meal companion to talk to. The location was also strategic because it would keep the doctor away from Miss Canton, who didn't really care for her employer's best friend, and it would give Cole and the doctor the ability to make eye contact.

The servants placed the dinnerware while Dr. Ellis held out Mildred's chair before sitting down next to her.

"What news do you bring, Dr. Ellis?" asked Miss Canton as the first course arrived.

"Well, we've finally heard from Mr. Parker. That's what's prompted my visit." He doled out a large portion of soup for himself from the tureen held by the serving maid. "Miss Mildred has a bundle of letters from him. But, let me assure you, after reading my single letter from the man, I can report that he is doing quite well."

"Has he indicated when he will return?" Miss Canton asked.

"No, not in my brief missive. He has told me that they've discovered two new medicinal plants, and he's sent me cuttings, so that I can begin experimenting with them."

Both of the children ate their soup and listened to the doctor explain the supposed properties of the new plant discoveries.

"Well, that's just wonderful," said Miss Canton, her own spoon poised soup-less.

"What other news do you have for us, Doctor?" Mildred asked, turning her head to her meal companion.

"Well, we're finally to have a new vicar for the chapel. A Doctor Wickliffe. He and his family will be arriving in a day or two from Leeds."

"Family?" prompted Miss Canton.

"Yes, his wife and a daughter and son. I'm sorry that I don't know their Christian names, but I do know," here he turned his attention to Cole," I can report that the daughter is Mildred's age." He punctuated his sentence with a knowing wink in Cole's direction.

Cole, who had kept his head down toward his soup bowl, raised only his eyes toward the doctor just in time to see the gesture.

"Well, isn't that nice, Mildred. You and your brother will finally have some playmates close by."

Mildred and Cole looked at each other, rolling their eyes, and trying not to laugh at their tutor still treating them both like small children.

Lorain rang the little bell next to her to indicate that it was time for the next course even though the doctor had only had two small spoons of soup.

Mildred was suddenly lost in thought. It had been ages since there were any nearby girls to talk to. She loved Wickwillow Manor, but they were so far away from the town that it was simply inconvenient to spend much time with her peers. They used to have the opportunity to meet with people their own age at church services, but the shire had been without a vicar for nearly two years. This was caused by their uncle's absence. Somehow, and Mildred never could understand it fully, but somehow, it was Uncle Parker's responsibility to hire and maintain the vicarage. She'd assumed, based on their large house, all the land they held, and the large number of house servants and farm hands, that they certainly could afford the financial burden, yet throughout her life, years would frequently pass without a vicar in the shire.

"Mildred!" hissed Miss Canton.

"Oh, I'm so sorry," said Mildred with all her innocence on display.

"The doctor has asked you a question."

"I'm sorry, Dr. Ellis," said Mildred.

"Not a problem, my dear." He patted her hand as the fish was served. "I was simply asking what has been employing your time."

"Oh, well, I'm continuing to work on my Latin and French. Thank you for sending 'round those French novels. I especially enjoyed Candide, ou l'Optimisme. Although, I must admit I didn't fully understand L'An 2440, rêve s'il en fut jamais."

"Yes, Voltaire is quite fun, rather delicious, really. The Mercier, well, it can be difficult, but I thought you might enjoy it. We can certainly talk about it some afternoon, if you'd like?"

Mildred thought there was a hint of disappointment in his tone and decided to try reading Mercerir's imagination novel again. She changed the subject. "And, at Uncle Parker's prompting, I've begun caring for Mother's garden."

The others at the table remained silent as the doctor's eyes searched Cole's and then Miss Canton's for some explanation. Both of them avoided him and offered their attention instead to the bony fish on their plates.

"How has that been going for you?"

"Well, it's only been a few days, but I feel I've made great progress. Cole has seen, haven't you, Cole."

Through a mouthful of food, Cole mumbled: "I have. She has."

"There are some great, gnarled rose bushes that I've exposed. And, Perry has hacked through the grasses and come across a lovely statue of a goddess of some sort." Mildred mimicked the statues hand gestures, which caused the doctor to smile. "It's been difficult work at times, it took both Cole and me to pry open the gate, but I must admit that I like having something out-of-doors to occupy my mornings. I do love to read and study, and play the piano, and all of the other things Miss Canton thinks important for me, but there's something nice about having my hands in the earth, there's something remarkable about watching an inch worm inch along a paving stone or a bee lighting from a flower…that gets my heart racing."

The kind doctor's eyes grew damp. "You certainly are your mother's daughter."

Miss Canton rang her bell.

The good doctor took the prompt and turned his attention across the table. "And, you, Cole. What is keeping you busy these days?"

"Well," the young man began. He didn't have the safety of food to cram into his mouth at the moment, having long finished his portion of fish. "I've been trying to fix the great clock. It's never worked, so I've decided to undertake the task."

Mildred watched her brother as he spoke and he seemed fuller, prouder as he talked of the clock than she'd ever seen him before. It bothered her slightly that Cole hadn't mentioned to Dr. Ellis that she was helping him, but she understood. This was Cole's project. He hoped to be an inventor. There was no need to muddy the story by including her.

The meat course arrived and for a few moments they were all silent as they enjoyed the exquisite mutton. Mildred knew the doctor must be relieved to actually have a moment to eat his serving.

As she ate, Mildred thought about the shift in fortunes of the afternoon. With the arrival of Dr. Ellis, she had two new friends and a vicar to contemplate. She had the lush anticipation of reading of her uncle's latest exploits. Not to mention a nagging desire to learn more about how she was like her mother. Whenever her mother was mentioned by anyone, they stopped cold their conversation, took a beat, and then changed the subject. Her questions in letters to her uncle continually went unanswered. Mildred longed to know more of her, the woman who died giving her life. As she cut a small potato, she concocted a plan to show Dr. Ellis her garden, with the hopes that being there would prompt him to talk more of her mother.

When the pudding arrived, Dr. Ellis removed his pocket watch from his vest. He took a few quick bites of the sweet concoction, and then said, "I'm so sorry, my dear friends, but I must go."

"So soon? I was hoping to show you my progress in the garden."

"I'm so sorry, Miss, but I have another appointment to attend to." He took a long swallow of wine before wiping his mouth with a napkin. "Miss Canton, I was thinking that it would be helpful if you would have a few of your house girls visit the vicarage and give it a good clean. It must be dusty after so long an absence of residents. Also, as is the custom and expectation, Mr. Parker's house will be providing Vicar Wickliffe and his family with two house girls and a footman."

"Are there any other expectations, Dr. Ellis?"

The doctor removed his pocket watch, peered at the glass, and returned it to his coat pocket. "Simple courtesy, Miss Canton. They will have an empty larder when they arrive, so it would be a kind gesture to perhaps invite them early and often to Lord Greene's table for dinner and offer whatever services and aid a family such as Lord Parker Greene's can to his vicarage."

Seventeen

The dwarfs led Parker Greene on a circuitous route past countless doors of various shapes and styles. At the end of a particularly long hallway, a door was opened by several of the little hands that were conveying him, and unceremoniously shoved him into the out of doors. It took a moment for his eyes to adjust to the bright sunlight; once they did, he looked around to discover he'd been deposited into a cage with about a dozen other men. All of them were scraggly, thin wearing shreds of clothing. For a moment, he worried for his life, but realized that these men were too weak to approach, let alone harm him.

As his eyes adjusted further, the horrendous smell of human life ending assaulted him. These wretches were sitting and lying in their own filth. Flies and bugs accosted them, yet none of those present attempted to swipe the pests away. In their thin frames, their eyes looked huge and they grotesquely followed Parker as he slowly began to move from one to the next. He kept a distance he felt safe, yet, he moved among them, looked deep and hard at each one.

He was relieved not to recognize any of the men, yet he felt a wave of emotions as he contemplated that this might be his fate.

Parker stopped near one of the men. "What is your crime?"

The man said something, but Parker couldn't discern the raspy sound that came from his lips.

"We..."

It was the man behind him who spoke. Parker turned to observe.

"...we refused to answer."

"Answer what?"

With great difficulty the man continued. "The Admiral's question."

"What was the question?" Parker asked.

The man was silent for a very long time. Parker watched as a fly moved across his face, stopped on the eye, and then it walked along the glossy surface. Parker Greene shuddered at the vision before him, at the thought of becoming like these men. He looked among his companions, beseechingly. None spoke, yet none looked away.

One specimen of humanity, off in the furthest corner, seemed to summon him with only the lift of a fingertip. This man, with a bald head and long moustache and scraggly beard, smiled when Parker Greene moved to him. His lips moved, but no sound came. Parker moved closer.

Finally, after what seemed a great effort, a slew of words poured from the man: "You must answer the question. Give the correct answer, you'll live well, Lord Greene. Give the wrong answer, you'll be sent away. Don't know where. Give no answer, you end up here. Once here, you never get to answer again." The man reached for Parker, but before he gained contact, his hand dropped into his lap. The glassy stare went dull. He was dead.

Parker stood, walked to the door he'd been tossed through, knocked. With what sounded like some effort, the door opened.

Parker Greene offered into the interior darkness: "I understand."

Eighteen

The morning was surprisingly cool. Mildred had the serving girl bring her morning tray not into her bedroom, which was customary, but instead into the conservatory. She enjoyed spending time among her uncle's and father's plants and trees, and more so now that she had a stack of nearly a dozen letters from her uncle to read.

Mildred poured a second cup of hot tea and, just for a moment, turned her face toward the glass ceiling, which allowed the sun to warm her cheeks. She looked around at the many green growing things, some of them with leaves bigger than her, and imagined Uncle Parker hacking through them with the machete he described.

All the letters were from Sumatra, an island many thousands of miles away; in a nation he called Indonesia. Her uncle described horrible devastation caused by an earthquake before his arrival there. His team of explorers had seen tigers and rhinoceros.

Opened next to Mildred was a world atlas. The pictures in the large book allowed her to follow her guardian's travels. She traced the islands in the middle of the vast seas with her finger.

Along with his tight, even words, Lord Greene had drawn pictures of some of the beasts, creatures, and plants that he'd encountered. These gave Mildred a sense of the places he described.

In the third letter she opened, two dried purple flowers fluttered into her lap. She picked them up and held them to her nose and imagined she could smell the jungle.

"Mildred!" Lorain Canton shouted from somewhere in the house.

Mildred neatly gathered up the letters and tucked them inside the atlas before she closed its pages.

"Mildred!"

Next, she slathered more soft butter on the last bite of scone before popping it into her mouth.

"Mildred!"

The voice was growing closer.

Mildred imagined it was a native, searching for her in a forest of massive trees, with chirping crickets and birds singing strange and exotic, but delightful songs. Before she could finish off the last mouthful of tea in her cup, Miss Canton appeared in the doorway to the conservatory.

"Here you are. Why didn't you answer me?"

"I'm sorry Miss Canton. I was engrossed in uncle's letters."

Lorain ignored Mildred's reasoning. "I see you're already dressed for work in your mother's garden. That will have to wait. It's time for your piano lesson."

Mildred tried to hide her dismay. It wasn't that she disliked the pianoforte. Just the opposite, in fact. She loved playing the instrument. Sadly, the student had long surpassed the skills of the teacher, and each lesson now no longer took her further with her study of music, but rather held her painfully in place. She longed for a new teacher, someone who could teach her more advanced techniques; someone who could help her with voicing and harmony.

"Come now. I have a surprise for you." Lorain turned on her heels and advanced out of the room.

Mildred stood, enjoyed the warmth of the last swallow of tea, picked up the atlas, and followed her tutor. She stayed many yards behind Lorain as they traversed from the east side of the house toward the west. When they arrived in the middle, where the various hallways adjoined with the grand entrance hall, she discovered a rather short man looking at one of the portraits. With the sound of their arrival, he turned, the man, not the portrait.

The gentleman smiled ever so warmly through great wrinkles that ensconced his eyes. He offered a small bow.

"I've found her, finally!" exclaimed Lorain to the man. "Mr. Wickliffe, this is Miss Greene."

Mildred offered a graceful outstretched hand and a slight curtsey.

"Miss Greene. It is such a joy to meet you. Your uncle has written such kind words to me about you."

Mildred was confused for a moment. She moved to place the atlas on a side table and that little breath of time helped her brain click back into gear. "The new vicar! Oh, Mr. Wickliffe, how lovely it is to meet you. We've been so long without anyone to guide our souls." Mildred meant the comment to come out as a light-hearted joke, but yet, when she actually said the words, they felt true and sincere. It had been a great long time since anyone had taken charge of the souls of the residents of Wickwillow, not just the manor, but the entire village.

"Well, it's good that I've arrived before you've all totally lost your way." He stepped forward and took Mildred's hand into one of his own before placing his second hand atop the combination. "You've a lovely home."

"Thank you, Mr. Wickliffe. I'm so pleased you like it." In his presence, Mildred felt somehow older, more mature, more like a lady.

"Millie, as I've told you, I have a surprise for you." Lorain waited to create dramatic effect, but in truth, she only annoyed Mildred with the use of the disliked nickname, her tone, and the pause. "Mr. Wickliffe is an accomplished pianist and has offered, through conversations with your uncle, to provide you piano lessons."

Mildred, who was still holding on to the vicar, mostly because she'd forgotten that he actually remained holding her hand, beamed at the newcomer. "Oh, Mr. Wickliffe…." She almost said, "I'd just a moment ago been thinking again that it was time for a new teacher," but instead, catching herself in time, which was quite rare, remarked simply: "how wonderful."

"I'm glad you're pleased. Shall we begin?"

"Now? You've just arrived. There must be a great many things for you to do."

Mrs. Wickliffe has requested that I not be underfoot. And, while there are a great number of parishiners to meet, I'd like to get to know you and your brother. Your Uncle has asked that I do that. So, shall we begin?"

And, just like that, Mildred had a new piano teacher. She led him into the parlor and sat at the piano. "How do we begin?" Mildred asked.

"Play something for me. It needn't be your most difficult…how about you play your favorite piece."

Mr. Wickliffe took a spot to Mildred's left, just behind her shoulder. It was a place that Mildred hated for people to stand. Frankly, she hated when anyone stood over her in any way, but there was something about someone standing in that spot behind her left shoulder that was terribly annoying.

Mildred ignored her discomfort this one time and did as asked. She thought for a moment, placed her hands on the keys, took a very deep breath, and launched into a Mozart allegro. Throughout the performance, she could hear Mr. Wickliffe breathing; it was almost as if his breaths were punctuation for the music. She liked that, but when she tried to emulate him, her fingers stumbled a bit over the keys. She went back to her own breathing, tried to ignore him, recovered her fingering, and finished the piece, quite flushed and embarrassed.

"Good basic technique, but we have much to do." Mr. Wickliffe looked about the room and discovered Lorain Canton standing in the corner. "That will be all, Miss Canton. I must work alone with the girl."

"That will never do. We've only just met you Mr. Wickliffe. I cannot leave you alone with my charge."

Mildred could tell from Lorain's tone that she wasn't so worried about Mildred's virtue as she was about having horrible things said about her teaching. "Miss Canton, he's our vicar. I really don't think a man of Christ would cause me any harm." Mildred knew there was nothing to fear of this charming man with the kind eyes.

"If you feel there should be someone here with us, please send in one of the servants to quietly dust or sew, but you, Miss Canton, must leave us."

Mildred liked Mr. Wickliffe more and more with each passing moment.

"As you wish, sir," said Lorain. She was only gone a moment when Matilda, the youngest of the house maids, arrived with a dust cloth in hand.

"Now, Miss Greene—"

"Mr. Wickliffe, you've slayed the beast, and so I can tell we will be great, good friends. You must call me Mildred."

"As you wish, dear Mildred," said the vicar with a warm smile through those crinkly eyes. "May I sit next to you on the bench?"

"By all means," said Mildred as she scooted to the left.

"I think much of your technique is good, but we have a lot of work to do. Are you up for the challenge?"

"Yes!"

"So, we'll begin at the beginning. Scales. Begin with C-Major."

Mildred began. It was joyful to perform for Mr. Wickliffe. If it had been Lorain who had suggested working on scales after all these years, she would have scoffed. Yet, when this kind man, with his pale skin, dark clothes, and the smell of pipe tobacco asked, she could sense the future, and she liked what she felt.

Nineteen

The small hands that pulled Lord Parker Greene to safety righted him. He was doused with what smelled like tropical rose water. Normally, he would have protested being accosted by these women with their scent, but after what he'd just endured, the fragrance of tropical flowers was preferred.

His jailors now rapidly ushered him through a series of twisting, tunnel-like hallways with low ceilings, dark walls, little light, and close air, and out into an open air market.

"Where is this place?"

"This island is called Victoria in homage to Her Royal Majesty," said one of the dwarfs escorting him.

"This island?" The tunnel they'd traversed hadn't seemed long enough or deep enough to take them from one island to another.

"Yes, we've left the entry island, that's where the Balsa Robin birthed. This is the second of the four islands here."

He took a moment to look around, both at the various stalls and booths selling all manner of foods and clothing, and the little people who accompanied him. They seemed to be a different group, dressed in fine clothing, well-made gloves, and hats with exotic plumage. Nothing like the first group who had been dressed in peasant clothes, or like the dwarfs aboard the airship, dressed as medieval pages.

"Are you trying to figure us out?" Her voice and manner grew seductive.

"I'm sorry to stare," Parker said, taking a step toward the vendors lining the wide street they were standing at. As he walked, the sounds of calling salespeople, hawking their wares, mixed with the birds in the trees all around them. The cacophony was amazing and lovely. The human voices were a blend of accents, all calling and talking in the King's English. It was obvious they'd been taught in the verses of the King James Bible, for they spoke in like patterns.

It wasn't only that they spoke in similar ways, but those selling their goods were all dressed in a unique fashion that Parker Greene had never seen before. Even the women were dressed like shipwrecked men. Their clothes appeared clean, yet well-worn and a bit tattered.

Parker finally spoke: "I've traveled most of our world and I've never, never seen anything like this before. So many dwarfs." He gestured to those who now accompanied him. "So many groups of people, each dressed in different, period fashion. Do the clothes signify rank?" Now he pointed to those in the stalls and booths lining their passage.

"You'll come to understand us soon enough. Depending on how you answer."

He chose to ignore the reference to the question. "Where do all these goods come from? Are you manufacturing all of this here?" It seemed impossible.

The group of little people laughed. "No, no. Well, not all of it. No, this is the salvage from the many ships that our sailors acquire."

Parker truly couldn't tell one of the women who accompanied him from the other. They were morphing, with some leaving and others joining their group as they traveled up this fine avenue of sellers toward what now looked like a mansion or statehouse of some sort.

Parker Greene had been to many of Her Majesty's colonies, and most of them had buildings and architectural styles of red brick and white gingerbread woodwork just like those around him now. Had the pirates stolen an island, as they now steal ships and plans? He decided to let go of his own questions for a bit and just be part of the progress of him and his small entourage. He knew, no matter what he asked or spoke of now, it would all appear to him as a riddle of some sort, so he simply let himself be one with the group.

When he enquired about a fruit he'd never seen before at one stall, one of his ladies purchased it for him with a square coin that was new to him. The vendor cut the ripe, dripping fruit into halves and offered Parker the pieces. The woman took half in her small hand and ate it in several bites, skin and all, but she spit out the two or three deep black seeds. Parker followed her example and was treated to the sweetest, most delectable fruit he'd ever encountered.

"What is this called?" he asked, wiping juice from his chin with a handkerchief. Instead of spitting the seeds out on the ground, he deposited these into his handkerchief, as well.

"Sallow Sallow. It's only ever been found on this island. It doesn't grow on any of our other islands."

"Sallow Sallow?" Parker took mental notes of how the fruit looked, smelled, tasted.

Again, it was a different woman who answered him: "A native name that we have kept. Some things and items we rename, but when it comes to foods, we like the exotic sounding names that they arrive with."

The little women gathered and broke apart, each visiting a different vendors' stall and returned quickly with more exotic fruits. These they quickly cut open and fed to Parker from their dripping hands. He could barely keep up with the colors, tastes, and flavors as they laughed and fed him from their raised hands. By the time they were finished with him, his face was covered with sticky liquid and everyone in the market was laughing in a good natured way.

As they continued up the avenue, they sampled several more wonderful foods, including roasted vegetables and meats, dark coffees and teas with sweet, raw sugarcane. Lord Greene couldn't help but think of those men he had met earlier, starving to death where they lay while all this abundance only a short distance away.

The group arrived at a stone plaza in front of the great building. To the left, a narrow river dumped into the sea. To the right, a row of poles stood tall, atop each wooden post, a head rotted.

A woman with a particularly elaborate hat that involved black lace, brightly colored pastel plumes of yellow, pink, and blue, and a pair of workman's goggles pulled on Parker's arm. He lowered his head to be nearer hers, brushing one of her feathers from his face.

"Those are the men who answered incorrectly, Lord Greene," she hissed in his ear.

Beheading, of course, wasn't new to Parker Greene. The British hold their own long tradition of the practice that even included killing defiled kings and their wives and families. Parker had seen such practices among the natives, especially those here in the Caribbean and in South America. Yet, the thought always sent a shiver down the man's spine. And, the sight... he feared he would vomit the lovely fruits he'd recently consumed. But, with deep breathing and changing his view to the building on the opposite side of the stone plaza, he managed to hold himself together.

"The governor?" he asked.

"The Magistrate. You've already met our leader. He makes all decisions. The Magistrate carries out the wishes of our Admiral and generally keeps the peace. Not that that's ever really an issue."

"And, why have I been brought here? Will the Magistrate ask the question?"

"No, Lord Greene. The Admiral always asks the question. We were tasked with allowing you to see the outcome of a wrong answer." At that moment, the group of ladies who had brought him to this place, as a group, curtsied, turned, and left him there.

Twenty

Cole arrived in the fresh morning air. He'd underestimated the amount of oil required to lube the many gears, cogs, and rods of the giant clock. With his oil can in hand, he headed toward the workshop.

"Hello!"

He looked up to see where the greeting had come from. A young man on a midnight black horse was stopped just short of the workshop doorway.

"Good morning," said Cole as he strode over to the stranger. "I'm Cole Parker," he said.

"Horatio Wickliffe. I'm the vicar's son." He jumped down from his horse. He was taller than Cole by several inches with a mane of black hair to rival that of his horse.

The two young men shook hands and Cole's heart began to pound. His hands grew damp. His knees went a little soft. All of this shocked him as he continued to enjoy the pressure of Horatio's hand, the nearness of this slight younger man with his broad smile and pale complexion.

"Oh, sorry," said Cole as Horatio Wickliffe pulled his hand away to discover it was covered with oil. "I'm working on the clock today."

"Not a problem," said the young man who continued to hold his soiled hand out.

"Here, come with me," said Cole who walked into the workshop.

Horatio roped his horse to a peg near the workshop window and then entered the dark, dusty space. When he got inside, Cole handed him a dirty rag, which wasn't much of an aid cleaning the grime off his hand. In fact, because it held a film of sawdust, it made the matter a bit worse. While Horatio did the best he could cleaning up, Cole refilled the oil can, getting more oil on the workbench than into the receptacle.

"So, what's wrong with your clock?" Horatio asked, more as a way of reminding Cole he was there than actually caring about the task.

"I'm not really sure. It hasn't ever worked. Not during my lifetime anyway. But, I decided it was time to figure it out."

The two men were silent as Cole moved back toward the out of doors.

"So you've arrived?" asked Cole.

Horatio looked confused by the statement.

"When did you arrive in Wickwillow?" Cole clarified.

"Yesterday evening. My father is here. I believe he's giving your sister, Mildred is her name? I believe he's giving her a piano lesson."

"Hmm." Cole wished the young man would go away. He was tall and thin and well dressed. Probably well-educated and off to university soon. They could have nothing in common, so there was little point in getting to know him.

Horatio followed Cole out of the workshop. He took a very deep breath that was mimicked by his horse.

"Well, I want to get back to my chore," said Cole. He'd agreed to meet his sister up in the clock tower after lunch, and if he hadn't oiled everything as she'd said to, she would once again refuse to help him with the next step. That's what had happened for the past several days.

"Would you like some company?"

"I don't mean to be rude, but no, I really want to finish this on my own. The space up there is rather tight as it is."

"I understand." The young men looked at each other. "It was nice meeting you," offered Horatio who started to put his hand out to shake, but then retracted it. "We're supposed to be having dinner together this evening, I believe. That will give us a chance to get better acquainted."

Cole huffed and nodded. For a moment, he caught Horatio Wickliffe's eyes. At first Cole thought the man's eyes were blue, but then, both of them turned their head slightly, and it was obvious that Horatio had translucent gray eyes, the likes of which Cole had never seen before. There was color there, but as the man turned his head, as sunlight played on his face, the color changed again and again to all shades of light grey and light blue. Cole was astonished.

"My eyes?" Horatio asked. "You've noticed my eyes." Now he smiled a beatific smile, a cherubic smile. A smile that would make the angels sing.

That would certainly describe the sound Cole was now hearing in his own head. A choir of angels. He knew something important had happened; he knew in that moment that his life had been changed. While he might not yet know what the change was or what it meant, he knew it had happened.

Today was an important day.

"Yes." That was all Cole managed to say before he turned away from Horatio Wickliffe and, without looking back, contemplated the emotion he'd just felt while he made his way back to the entrance to the clock tower. Just as he was about to ascend the dark staircase, he turned back. Horatio was now back up on that tall, black horse, both rider and animal shook their manes at the same moment, and Cole, out of breath for some reason, waved an oily hand in farewell toward the vicar's son.

Twenty-One

Lord Parker Greene stood in the plaza. His companions left him without explanation. The environment felt like those colonies he'd visited before, allowing him to feel comfortable and safe in his surroundings, despite the heads staring down at him from their tall poles. He turned his face toward the sky, letting the sun warm his face and the pleasant breeze off the ocean cool his body. The weather, the location, this little village all felt like perfection.

He'd traveled the world. So much of it was in chaos. Britain was always the exception to that. Somehow, the Queen and her people at home had kept the British Isles calm, comfortable, and safe. It was the rest of the world, the outlying colonies, both of Her Majesty and other European monarchs, that were in dire straits and chaos. Fighting and border wars kept the general populace of the world fearful, both of invaders and of horrible local dictators. Those heads on stakes were a reminder to Parker Greene of what the world had become. Those with power, whether that power was granted or usurped, would put your head at the end of a pole if you didn't do as they told you.

Yet, here, on this little group of islands, all seemed calm and comfortable. He thought of the people he had seen over the past twenty-four hours, since he'd been off the Balsa Robin. None of them carried weapons, at least not in any outward display. There had been no violence or fighting. He contemplated his walk through the vendors and their stalls… yes, there had been ale and even rum available. And, while he hadn't noticed anyone in a state of drunken debauchery, some of the men and women around the rum stall had been imbibing and enjoying what was being sold.

He pictured in his mind the female dwarf companions who had walked him to this spot. Each of them, while dressed in bizarre bodiced getups with leather and feathers in places the ladies in his native England might find offensive, sported colorful rings like the one Phineas Silas, the dwarf who had tended to him on the Balsa Robin, had worn. He was now more curious than before about what type of device those rings were: what they were, how they worked, and so on.

"Lord Greene, I presume?"

Parker turned slowly toward the voice that addressed him. There, standing less than a foot from him, was Headmaster Peter Swoonry. Greene wondered how all of these men from college had found their way to these four small islands in the middle of the ocean—how they were all working together on this project of Admiral Baki Frogs. "Hello, Mr. Swoonry."

"Oh, you're an adult now, and a Lord." The older man puffed out his chest. "Very impressive, even if it was because of your late brother."

"Sir, I will kindly thank you to refrain from pronouncing Cecil dead. He got away from you and your kind. He knows the world better than any man living. He could be anywhere."

"Quite right, quite right," Peter Swoonry repeated. "Let's begin again, shall we?" Swoonry held out his soft hand to Parker. "Please, call me Peter."

Parker didn't take the man's hand. He wanted to remark how much Peter looked like Dickens' Mr. Bumble in Oliver Twist: Big belly, red nose, soft features. Instead, he nodded and bent slightly at the waist. "As you wish, Peter."

The older man ignored the rebuff. "I'm to show you the final option. I have to tell you, the Admiral has never to my knowledge done this before, shown the new arrival all the outcomes before asking the question. You should feel honored."

Parker didn't feel honored. He was growing tired of being traipsed around the islands. He wanted to know what the question was. And, he wanted a hint as to what the "correct" answer might be. He had to survive all of this, figure out more fully what was going on, and then find a way to stop it, and, of course, escape. There was a great deal to figure out and plan.

"Please, Parker, walk with me."

The men went right up the great stone stairs of the Magistrate's home.

"You are the Magistrate?" Parker couldn't hold back the chuckle that bubbled from his throat.

Peter Swoonry led the way, and together they walked the full length of the mansion's balustrade porch, turned, and entered through a door, not a formal entrance, but rather a servant's access. They walked downward; they continued down for many, many flights.

"Where are we..." six-hundred paces. Parker was a little breathless; the air grew cooler. Occasionally, a wall was damp.

"Just follow," said Peter.

If Parker wanted to kill the man, it would be easy here. They were alone in this isolated stairwell. No one would hear or even know of the deed for some time. Yet, once again, curiosity about the outcome was stronger than his desire to dominate the situation. And, so he simply followed the headmaster-turned-Magistrate as they descended deeper and deeper into the earth.

Finally, they reached the bottom, and walked forward through a tunnel. There was no light at all. Parker Greene instinctively raised his hands out in front of himself to keep from bumping into anything in the utter darkness. All the while, he'd begun counting his paces.

The Magistrate took Parker's arm and guided him; he'd returned, emotionally, back to college, receiving help once more from the house master. After a hundred paces, Parker's eyes adjusted to the dark and he was able to make out the walls next to him and the open, unending blackness ahead of him.

A dim light appeared at a great distance.

After one-thousand paces, the men arrived at what seemed to be a dead end, yet the light that had called to them shone more brightly. As Parker inspected the lamp he could not discover the fuel source that kept it bright. It was not gas, nor wax candle. Instead, several strands of wire burned within a glass globe. Of course, everyone had heard of Humphry Davy's electric light, but no one had discovered a way to keep it lit without the filament burning out. Yet, here was a light that seemed to run by electricity, and yet, continued to burn and burn.

They stood at the electric globe for some time in silence. Peter turned a knob on the wall below the light and they began to ascend, as if by magic. There was no sound. He could see no pulleys or ropes. The floor they stood upon simply lifted them higher and higher into the darkness above.

Twenty-Two

"More peas, Edith," Gladys Wickliffe asked her daughter.

"No, Mother," said the young woman. "So, Father, tell us more."

Mr. Wickliffe looked from his daughter's sparkling eyes to his son's, who was looking more and more like him each day. "Well, the house is simply lovely, as I said. There are plants, paintings, and sculptures everywhere you turn. The young woman, Miss Greene, is a lovely pianist, although her technique is lacking, but we'll take care of that."

"I bet you will, Father. My knuckles are still sore after our last lesson together." Edith wrung her hands and offered her father a knowing wink.

"Don't tease so, Edith," chastised Mrs. Wickliffe.

"And, you there, you met the boy. What's he like?" Edith turned her full attention toward her brother.

"Rather standoffish. It isn't that he was rude exactly, but I do find it disconcerting when a man doesn't look you in the eye when he speaks to you," said Horatio as he pushed his face close to his sister's until their foreheads touched. That made Edith burst into fits of laughter.

The serving maid entered the room and paused at the scene.

"Mary, Mary, please take these plates and bring us the pudding, if you wouldn't mind," said Mrs. Wickliffe in her singsong voice.

"Yes, Mrs. Wickliffe," said the girl with a nod and a quick curtsey.

"Now, now. Please, call me Gladys. I've yet to grow comfortable with all these airs. I'm simply the vicar's wife, not the Queen herself."

The maid curtsied as she took away the plates.

Mrs. Wickliffe waited for the girl to leave the room, straining her neck to be sure she was out of earshot, before speaking in a conspiratorial whisper. "How they must live, the Parkers. All this 'Yes, Miss' and 'No, Miss' all the time."

The girl returned with a small cake that had already been sliced.

"Just one piece for me," announced Gladys to the table. "And, only one slice for Mr. Wickliffe, too."

Everyone at the table grew silent until the girl again left the room.

"Mother, you mustn't poke fun at the girl, or the Parker family for that matter. I just know that Mildred and I will be great, good friends. Horatio and Cole Parker, too. So, we must be very kind in all we say not only to them, but about them." Edith had more to say. She bent her head into the table and whispered, "Especially since our servants are on loan from them. Who knows what tales they'll be traipsing back with?"

All at the table nodded in agreement that they would always be kind when they spoke to or about the Parkers.

"So, tell me more, dear brother. Is Cole Parker very handsome? Will he make some woman a good husband?"

"You mean a good husband for you, don't you dear sister?"

"Heavens no!" she shrieked which delighted her brother.

Horatio reached across his sister and took up the plate of cake, helping himself to two more slices. "I can't tell you what sort of husband he will or won't make. But, I would say he is good looking. A bit shorter than me." Horatio indicated Cole's height with his fork. "But then, who isn't shorter than me?" He raised his fork to the top of his head.

"Stop talking with your utensils, Horatio," chided his mother. "There's little a man can do about his height."

"His hair is gold, not yellow, but gold. And, his eyes are green. He keeps himself clean shaven. Although, he does dress like a common farmhand instead of the son of a Lord."

"He's the nephew of a Lord," corrected Mr. Wickliffe.

"Looks, schmooks. What is he like?" insisted Edith, ignoring her father.

"Well, as I said, he didn't really say much to me. He was covered in grease because of something he was doing to their big, tower clock. Mr. Greene seemed rather preoccupied with that task. I did offer to assist—"

"You, get your hands dirty. How absurd!" chimed Edith.

Horatio continued as if his sister hadn't spoken: "…even though he could easily tell I had no interest in such an occupation."

"Father, you must take me there to call on them. You know I must be properly introduced before I can venture there on my own."

"Miss Canton has invited us there for dinner tomorrow evening. We shall all dress in our finest and be on our best behavior. After that, well, only the Lord himself knows what may occur." Mr. Wickliffe poured more wine into his wife's glass and then into his own as well.

"Edgar, you are right. Your father is always right, isn't he children?" Gladys patted her husband's hand. Neither of the children responded.

Twenty-Three

The floor continued to ascend in darkness. Parker Greene contemplated taking the older man's arm. Just as he thought that, he heard a snap and then a subtle pop. The two men were awash in brilliant, blinding sunlight. Peter Swoonry had prepared for the moment during the long ride up by placing a pair of goggles fitted with colored glass over his eyes. Parker shielded his face for a moment to allow his vision to adjust.

"Here we are," said Swoonry with a sweep of his arm.

"Where is here?" Parker lowered his hand to address the Magistrate, but then quickly raised it again to shield the sun, which beamed on him.

"Well, to you this will be the third island you've seen."

It dawned on Parker Greene in that very moment that he still didn't know where "here" was. "Where are we, sir? What is this place called?"

"I cannot offer that detail, Lord Greene. You understand, I'm certain, that revealing too much too quickly could be detrimental to our cause." The Magistrate looked away, then back at Parker with kindly eyes. "So, we're off."

With Mr. Swoonry leading by just a step, the two men traversed a wide avenue paved with flat, red bricks. A median with a canopy of trees blotted out the mid-day sun allowing the Magistrate to remove his goggles and Parker Greene to more easily see the vast setting. On each side of the street, stately homes were set on large grassy lots with well-established shade and ornamental trees.

Men and women, mostly of normal size, relaxed in the yards, parks, and porches of these homes. Even from his distance, Parker viewed many of them drinking from tall glasses that tinkled with ice and long, silver spoons. He licked his lips at the prospect of a cold drink.

"Where are my manners?" asked Swoonry who led Parker Greene off the street, up a long walk, to the porch of a great house. "Good afternoon, Lady Drake."

"Hello, Mr. Swoonry. May we offer you and your friend a cool drink?"

"If you'd be so kind." The Magistrate bowed to the lady dressed in a long, bright yellow dress. It wasn't frilly or full, but rather plain and simple. Nothing like the little women who had earlier accompanied him through the shop stalls.

The lady offered the two men drinks that tasted of lemons, limes, and rum. The clear glass was cold to the touch and inside, small, round pieces of ice bobbed. Parker Greene wanted to know how ice was available in this heat. He'd never had it before while visiting the places in the world that remained warm or hot all year round. Ice was something for the colder climates. Instead of asking questions, he enjoyed the cold, blended drink.

None of them spoke; they all sipped their drinks and looked off in different directions at the vast lawns with the bright flowers.

Swoonry placed his empty glass on the silver tray atop the little table. He watched Parker until Lord Greene placed his glass there, too. "Thank you, Madam," said the Magistrate.

"Yes, thank you," mimicked Parker Greene.

The two men stepped off the lady's porch, walked back down the path, and continued their stroll up the avenue.

"That was strange."

"How so, Lord Greene?"

He thought for a moment as their heels clicked on the paving stones. Parker stopped walking. He listened to the birds singing and the light breeze through the leaves of the lush trees. He breathed deep the smells of sea perfumed by exotic flowers. He realized it. For the first time since the ship had docked, there were no mechanical sounds. No equipment. No automatic horses or horseless carriages. There were no belts or gears or cogs turning anywhere here. Or, if there were, they were well hidden or buried. For the first time in a very long time, Parker Greene felt out of sorts in his location.

"Why have you brought me here, Mr. Swoonry?"

"This is the good life. This is what so many strive for. There is nothing to do or be done. Everything has been and will continue to be taken care of. There is nothing here but leisure time. Time to think. Time to read. Time to contemplate life from the comfort of a shady veranda with a pitcher of cold drinks. A place where silence really is golden. There are no young people, no children. There is nothing to attend to."

Lord Greene was confused. "And, you see this as perfection of some sort?"

"Well, yes." The Magistrate stopped. "Here, if you decide to join us, this will be your home."

Parker Greene turned toward where Swoonry had indicated. The house, while much smaller, was a lovely scaled reproduction of his home in England, Wickwillow Manor. The home was a replica not only in form, but in the patina of the bricks and the placement of the trees and shrubbery. Parker believed that if he were to walk behind this house, he would find a small walled garden, a workshop, and a barn. All that the place lacked were island versions of his young wards, Mildred and Cole. At the thought of them, tears formed in Lord Parker Greene's eyes.

Swoonry took on the air of confidence, like that of a horse auctioneer: "We shall offer you perfection. We shall provide you with time. You will have the workshop of your dreams. You will have access to one of the world's most complete libraries. You will have as many people as you require to build anything you can imagine. Basically, you can have just about anything you want."

"In exchange for what?" asked Lord Greene. He felt indignant, angry. He feared he'd pull out his small pistol at any moment and quickly and efficiently kill the Magistrate of this place.

"In exchange for helping us discern the mountains of technical plans we have come into possession of."

"The stolen entries. You want me to interpret and build the contraptions imagined by the peoples of Her Majesty's Empire."

The two men were silent for a long moment. The silence was greedily filled by two birds, calling and responding between two trees near the Wickwillow Manor replica.

Twenty-Four

Mildred walked down the path toward the garden. She swung her arms akimbo as she walked while singing softly to herself the refrain that Mr. Reeves had performed so expertly at the music house several weeks earlier:

"Come into the garden, Maud,
For the black bat, Night, has flown,
Come into the garden, Maud,
I am here at the gate alone"

As she pushed the garden gate open, it creaked and she repeated, "I am here at the gate alone; I am here at the gate alone."

Mildred was alone, not only in that moment, but in life. She was becoming a woman, but no one around her seemed to take any notice, instead they continued to treat her like a small girl. Mildred, who usually went right to work along the main path, alternately took the outer path that followed the interior walls. She touched the statue in the first alcove and enjoyed the moss under her fingertips. Because of the early hour, there was still dew on the lush green mat. She drew her fingers to her nose and enjoyed the earthy aroma.

Continuing her walk, she reached the stone bench under the overgrown Japanese maple and withdrew the last remaining letter from her uncle that she hadn't read yet. From another pocket, Mildred produced an apple. She took a large bite, enjoying the crisp spray that was released.

Her Uncle Parker wrote:
My Dearest Mildred,
How I long to be with you and share the stories of my travels. Instead, we must make due with these words scratched out on paper.

Today was another amazingly hot day. All the men on the island wear only a cloth wrapped about their waist, and nothing else. No shirts, under linens, or shoes. They are all very dark, both from having dark skin and from being exposed to this great sun. The women are only slightly more modest, with full length skirts that cover them from their waists down to their ankles, but they wear nothing above. I dare say all of the women you have ever met would be very uncomfortable at the site. Many of our crew here aren't comfortable with it either. But, we must always be very kind to these wonderful people, for they help us in every way you can imagine.

I'm sad to say that this will be the last letter you'll receive from me for a long time. We are heading into the jungle and expect to be gone from our base camp for at least three weeks. In the meantime, please keep good cheer and follow Miss Canton's instructions.

Your Loving Uncle

PS. I've finally selected a new vicar for the old chapel. If you haven't met him yet, I assure you he is a kind and generous man. I ask that you, and those you "command," do all you can to provide comfort and ease to Mr. Wickliffe and his family.

As Mildred refolded the letter imagining a place where all the women went topless, Perry ran up to her.

"Good morning, Miss."

"Good morning, Perry." Mildred watched the young boy go immediately to his continuing task of cutting away the overgrown grasses and weeds that ringed the inside wall. He wasn't at it for but a few minutes when she heard him scream. Mildred leapt up and ran to him. "What is it, Perry? What is it?"

"Sorry, Miss. I didn't mean to holler out like that, but look." Perry pointed to a large alcove in the wall. This one wasn't like the others they had discovered that housed odd pieces of statuary. Instead, there was a large wicker structure with all manner of greenery growing through and out of it. But, that wasn't the amazing part. What was remarkable was that bees were swarming all around it.

"Perry, have you ever seen anything like it?"

The young boy waved away a bee. "No, Miss. Not in all my days."

That was one of the boy's phrases: "Not in all my days." It usually made Mildred laugh, since the boy was barely twelve-years-old and hadn't had many days to compare anything in life to, but on this occasion, she didn't laugh, mesmerized by the hundreds of flying insects that were coming and going into several entrances of the wicker.

"I think we'll need to get Isaac's opinion of what to do about this." She waited, but Perry didn't budge. "Off with you now, go bring Isaac down here."

After another moment, Perry ran out of the garden while Mildred watched the insects, mesmerized. As she studied, first one and then a second landed on her exposed arm. Instead of feeling fear from them, she felt overwhelmed by calmness. It had happened before, more so since she'd started working in the garden, but she could clearly feel the presence of another entity, a ghost if you will. And, as if that weren't amazing enough, she knew with great certainty that the ghost was that of her mother. Whenever she felt it, whenever the spirit was near, Mildred immediately felt an overpowering calmness come over her. She knew she was healthy, well, and tremendously loved. Lately, moments such as those were the only time that Mildred didn't feel alone or lonely, so she treasured them and hoped they would stretch out for a long time.

While Mildred contemplated her mother's presence, more and more bees landed on her. None of them stung her or caused the girl any discomfort. By the time Isaac and young Perry returned to the discovery in the garden, Mildred was covered with bees from her neck to her boots. Not a single bee stepped upon her face. It looked simply as if she had upon her shoulders a full opera cloak, only it wasn't black fabric, but instead a moving, living collection of honey bees.

Her sensation was something you might call "out of body." Mildred was aware of her physical body, she felt perfectly centered and balanced. Yet, she didn't feel the thousands and thousands of creatures covering her. She was aware of the sunshine and the cool morning breeze, but could feel the weight of the massing honey bees.

"Miss Greene! Miss Greene!" Isaac shouted as he approached. "Holy Mother of God," he whispered. "Just like her mother."

Mildred turned to greet him. "Shh. Be quiet, or you'll upset them."

Isaac placed his wrinkled, leathery hand over his mouth. He held out his other arm to keep Perry at his side.

Mildred Greene knew something remarkable was happening to her. She felt a great connection to the earth and the heavens. Most of all, she felt a connection to her mother like she'd never experienced before.

She took a deep breath and, in her mind, asked the bees to return to their tasks. And, at first, one-by-one, the bees reluctantly began to take flight. And then, as more ascended into the air, they left her in a flurry of buzzing.

Isaac and Perry stood dumbfounded.

"Now, everything appears to be fine here. I'm certainly fine." She smiled and moved closer to the old stable master. "My question for you is what is this thing?"

"Well, Miss." Isaac removed a handkerchief from his pocket and wiped his brow. "It's an apiary miss, a bee hive. When your mother, god rest her soul, was alive, we kept several hives to pollinate the flowers and the fruit trees." He thought for a moment and scratched his head. "Will you come with me, Miss Mildred?"

"Of course," said the young woman who took up step after the man. They walked out of the garden followed by Perry, headed up the path, and into the storage shed next to the big barn. She'd never actually been into this out building before but knew it contained all manner of items. Some things, like certain tools, were stored there until they were required for a given season. Other items, like broken crates and milk stools, were discarded here; no one seemed ready to destroy them on the fire.

Isaac directed Perry and, with a large hook, the boy lowered an odd shaped wicker basket from a high shelf.

"This is an apiary. There was a woman in town, Miss, no Mrs.…." Isaac turned the basket around and around in his hands. "I'm sorry miss, I can't for the life of me think of her name. She was a widow and lived with her children on a small farm at the edge of the village. She made many of these hives for your mother."

"May I see it?" asked Mildred. She took the wicker container from Isaac, turned it over, removed the lid held by a rope, and looked inside. I don't understand how this works. Where do the bees make their home in this?"

"Well, Miss, they build a series of cells all linked together out of wax. Those, they fill with honey."

"How do you get out the honey?"

"Well, Miss, you…"

"Do you not know, Isaac?"

"I do know, Miss. But, I think it might upset you."

"Please, tell me." Mildred took a firm stance, hugging her arms to her chest. She'd dug in.

"We would wait for the bees to swarm. They do that when the hive becomes too crowded. Prior to that, we'd have placed a new hive in a nearby alcove, with the hopes that the swarm would take to it. Then…well we'd…"

"What?"

"The only way to extract the honey would be to break apart the apiary, Miss. And, to do that, we'd have to kill the bees that didn't swarm."

Mildred gasped.

"You mean to tell me you'd kill the bees, all that didn't move into the new apiary? Just kill them after they'd taken such good care of you." Tears rose into Mildred's eyes. "That's absurd and cruel. I just can't believe that my mother would have approved of such a thing."

Everyone was silent except for Mildred's stray sniffles.

"I'm sorry to upset you, Miss, but that is how it's always been done," said Isaac.

"Well, this simply won't do," she replied and waited for a new solution to appear.

"Good morning, Miss Greene," said Mr. Wickliffe from the top of his mechanical horse.

"Good morning, Vicar," she said, wiping a handkerchief across her eyes and then under her nose.

Mr. Wickliffe dismounted his horse, which Perry and Isaac were now closely inspecting. "Do you like, her, boys? Latest model. No more feed. No more manure. Just fill her with water, light the fire, and off she goes."

Mildred hated being ignored by all these men. "Who cares for a silly mechanical horse when there are bees being murdered."

"What? Who's being murdered?" asked Mr. Wickliffe in shock.

"Are you aware of how we get honey for our morning biscuits? They murder the bees." Mildred Parker was no longer in tears. She'd found a level of anger that was new even to her.

"It's how it's been done for centuries my dear. Maybe longer. No one has derived a better way." His voice was soothing.

"I won't be placated. And, I won't be able to play today. I'm sorry but there will be no piano lesson this afternoon."

"What's all the ruckus?" asked Cole who raced out of the workshop. "It's the new model? You have one? A Vicar?"

"Don't be rude, Cole," chastised Mildred. Even in her indignant state, she still did her best to maintain her brother's manners.

"Sorry, Mr. Wickliffe," offered Cole.

"Quite all right, young man. Yes, it is the latest model. And, you aren't incorrect. A Vicar's stipend hardly affords the luxuries such as this. It was a gift for service before we left the last vicarage."

Cole paid no attention to Mr. Wickliffe, instead running his hands over the solid flanks and body of the machine. "This is what I want to do," said Cole in a quiet voice. "I want to build and design such wonderful things."

"Children! Lunch!" called Lorain Canton from the doorway. "Children!"

"Won't you join us for lunch, Mr. Wickliffe?" asked Cole.

"I'd be delighted," said the vicar who guided Mildred and Cole along the path toward the door where the tutor waited.

Twenty-five

A little person came running at top speed toward Parker Greene and Magistrate Swoonry. The man, dressed like a medieval page, like the small men on the Balsa Robin, arrived, bowed with a flourish, and presented Lord Greene with his hat.

"Is the Balsa off again?" the magistrate asked.

"Soon. This evening."

"Tell Captain Flynn I'd like to speak to him before he departs."

The man bent at the waist. "As you wish, sir." He turned and ran off at break neck pace.

Parker put his favorite hat on his head, a custom made top hat with shiny black silk, and a small black feather, barely noticeable unless the sun shone just right. Yet, this hat made him feel home, a sensation he loved.

"Rather smart," offered Magistrate Swoonry.

"Thank you." Parker bowed slightly.

For a long moment, the men admired the wide avenue.

Swoonry produced a heavily carved, silver pocket watch, checked the time, and turned to his companion. "Well, Lord Greene, the hour is upon us. It is time for your next experience."

"I'm beginning to feel like Dickens' friend, Mr. Scrooge."

"How's that?" asked Swoonry, distracted by some thought.

"Charles Dickens? His Christmas story?"

"Sorry, I'm not familiar. I have to admit, I don't take time to read stories, novels...not even the penny dreadfuls that pass through here. Perhaps, if I had children...when you have children, you read stories to them around the fire and before bedtime. I live alone..." Peter Swoonry looked sad, maybe even forlorn. He worked his jowls up into a smile. "Well, we should be going."

"Where?"

"It's time for you to meet with the Admiral once again." Swoonry turned to lead the way.

They left the avenue, taking a series of streets, each one narrower than the previous, until they arrived at a dead end alley. As they walked, Parker Greene contemplated his options. He still didn't know what the question would be. He knew he'd have to offer an answer. It would be better to be dead than to suffer as the first men he'd encountered were suffering. It was impossible to think that he would be working for the pirates, even if that meant relative comfort and freedom. Yet, it was an intriguing idea that he would have access to the hundreds and hundreds of plans that had been submitted to the contest. If he didn't go through them, no one in Her Majesty's service might ever see them, know of them.

Parker wondered now, what might the pirates be looking for? Better ships? Better engines? Some other personal comforts? Why were they so interested in the plans? What were their goals? He had to find out. He had to stop them, or find a way to get word back to England about what was happening.

As they walked, Parker Greene realized, that in service to Her Majesty and his beloved Britannia, he must answer in such a way that allowed him to live another day. Even if that meant, in the short run, that he would appear to have joined the dreaded, horrible pirates.

Swoonry looked around in all directions. He stamped his foot several times and a trap door opened. Dirt and dust fell away as a wooden lift appeared. The men stepped onto it and it descended, just as the previous lift had risen out of it. Slowly and smoothly they were lowered once again and conveyed back into the ground.

Twenty-Six

Throughout luncheon, Mildred remained silent. When Lorain started her insipid questions, she simply ignored the tutor. Mr. Wickliffe, ever the peacemaker, took control of the conversation.

"Did I hear you correctly in the yard, Cole? You want to become an inventor?"

Cole, usually the one to remain silent by filling his mouth with food so he couldn't politely talk, said through his stuffed mouth: "Oh, yes. You know, Mr. Wickliffe." The boy swallowed hard. "I keep trying to build things, to take things apart and put them back together, but find that I'm always at a loss. It's as if, I don't know…"

"Yes," Mr. Wickliffe encouraged.

"Well, something goes askew in my mind, and I just can't manage."

"There are many things that can be learned, Cole. Perhaps, you could take an engineering track at university."

Everyone else in the room fell silent. The serving girl, who was making the rounds of the table with the fish course, stopped in her tracks and stared at the vicar, aghast at his sudden lack of insensitivity.

Lorain cleared her throat, but didn't speak.

"What have I said?" asked Mr. Wickliffe.

"I failed the exams," said Cole, his chin dropped low to his chest. "I've never been very good with books."

"Nonsense. Every young man who is well brought up, which you obviously have been, can master anything they attempt. It simply takes a little time and effort." He chose a piece of fish from the platter the girl held close to him. The beady eyes of the fishes staring at him, mimicked the treatment the humans in the room had just offered. "You know, I think it's simply because you haven't been passionate about the things you've studied. No offense meant to you, Miss Canton."

"Humph," escaped from Lorain's tight lips.

"Really, no offense. What I mean to say is that many boys don't do well at their studies until they discover what most interests them. There was a member in my last congregation who was a wonderful inventor and builder. He's the man who built my wonderful horse. Now, I'm certain that if I were to ask him, he'd be willing to offer you some advice. Perhaps, a list of books to read or maybe the two of you could visit for a bit."

"You would do that for me?" asked Cole. It was the brightest anyone had ever seen the young man.

"Mr. Wickliffe, if Cole's to take on a new line of study, don't you think we should get his uncle's approval?" Lorain's face was red.

"Of course, of course. Although, I should tell you that Mr. Parker, in his letter offering me his vicarage, also asked that I spend some time with his children and be of whatever assistance I might be. So, that is all I'm doing, fulfilling my duty to my patron." There was no malice in his voice. He spoke evenly and with a preacher's kind conviction.

Despite Mildred's feelings about the murdered bees, she couldn't help but smile at Mr. Wickliffe for once again putting Lorain in her place. She contemplated what it was about the vicar, about his tone or style that allowed him to take over any conversation. And, like the parting of clouds that allows sunshine to bathe a meadow, Mildred realized and understood. He was a man. Just that plain and simple. He was a man and, without another adult man in the room, he took over, took the authoritative tone. While Cole might be the age of a grown man, he had reached his majority to be sure, her brother, and she did love him dearly, was still only a boy. Here, Vicar Wickliffe arrives and is, just through the nature of being, a man who can command a room. And, more importantly, the room has easily, comfortably, allowed itself to be commanded.

"It's good to see you feeling a little better, Miss Greene," said Mr. Wickliffe as he sucked the last of the flesh off of a large fish bone.

"Well, I'm still concerned about my bees. I don't want them murdered."

"Bees? Murder? What story telling are you about, Millie?" asked Lorain.

Mildred didn't even know how to begin telling the story once more. Just the thought of it all brought tears to her eyes once again.

Mr. Wickliffe interceded on her behalf: "Mildred learned some sad, but real facts about animal husbandry this morning; she's rather upset."

"I see," said Lorain, still oblivious to her young charge's problem.

"Mr. Wickliffe, there must be a better way. A more humane way to care for our bees and reap the benefits of their talents. Although, I've come to a decision that we will no longer partake of any honey in the Parker home until a solution is arrived at."

"What are you talking about, Millie. We will not go without honey!" exclaimed Lorain.

"Miss Canton, that's my decision and as lady of this house it is also my decree." Mildred raised her eyes toward Lorain.

The tutor's eyes were stern and to be feared. "As you wish, Miss Greene," said Lorain.

"Perhaps, Mr. Wickliffe?"

"Yes, my dear?"

"Perhaps, when you write to your engineer friend you might ask if he could create some new apiary design?"

"I'm quite happy to oblige you, Miss Greene."

"Mr. Wickliffe, I told you yesterday, you must call me Mildred."

Twenty-Seven

After being handed off to several different dwarfs—each one, both the men and the women, wore the pointed little rings—Parker Greene found himself back in his own cabin. He wanted to ask about those rings, to better understand the protection they offered the wearers, beyond the obvious point, but he refrained.

He went to the basin and washed his hands and face. Parker Greene toweled dry; looked around his room, noted the time on the wall clock, two o'clock, surprised at how early it was. He discovered on his long table a pot of hot tea, a plate of fancy sandwiches, and that the fruit bowl had been refreshed. He sniffed at the contents of a crystal flask to discover whiskey. A ceramic pitcher held fresh, cool water. He looked again; it remained at two.

Parker took the timepiece off the wall, brought it to the table, and, as he enjoyed his refreshments, he took the back off the thing and surveyed the contents. He tinkered with the cogs and springs and thought fondly of the tower clock back at Wickwillow Manor. And, as all thoughts of home did, he was reminded of his young charges on their own in that faraway land. He hoped and believed that somehow or someway Cole would find his way, that the boy, now a young man, would discover a love or passion that would begin to more fully and successfully take charge of his journey. Greene chuckled to himself as he envisioned his nephew, hunched over the workbench, doing more harm than good to just about everything he tried to fix. Yet, Parker knew Cole's visions and ideas were remarkable.

Parker tightened a spring. Mildred came next to his mind, with her lovely charms and abilities. If she were not a young woman, but instead a man, Lord Greene knew that because of her mind Mildred could do as she wished. She'd be the head of a company or a great inventor in her own right, or perhaps a doctor or scientist, even. Really, there were no ends to her possibilities, except one: she was and always would be, a woman.

Greene tinkered with the clock. His only tool the dull knife he'd used to spread butter on his crust-less sandwiches. But, by the time he was enjoying a dram of whiskey, the clock once again ticked away. He rummaged through his belongings, found his pocket watch, and was about to set the clock when he realized his small watch was still on England's time, on Wickwillow Manor time. If that tower clock actually worked, it would be chiming the children and their horrible tutor to dinner. He'd let Miss Canton stay too long. Their mother's illegitimate half-sister, she was difficult to release. So much history there, so many memories.

He wondered now if the new vicar had arrived; if Mr. Wickliffe would offer the guidance and direction to his parish and Greene's charges that would aid all along their journeys.

Back in the moment, Parker thought about the Balsa Robin. He wanted to stop the ship from departing, but had no resources. He had no friends or compatriots. There was no way yet to know who he might trust, beyond those captives withering away to nothing in their outdoor cage. He'd save them if he could, but none that he met or saw were fit for any sort of rigorous action or deed.

It was in that moment of contemplation and realization that Lord Parker Greene knew what he must do. For now, for the moment, he must go along and participate in whatever scheme his captors had in store for him. He must work for them with all outward appearances of being a willing, cooperative, gentleman of his word. He must gain the trust of those he could, formulate a plan, destroy this island and the pirates upon it, and escape to freedom with as many as he could save, while returning all the blueprints and plans to Her Majesty. For, he must not only serve dear Queen Victoria, but he must return home safely to his charges and familial duties.

Twenty-Eight

The Wickliffe family stood at the grand entrance to Wickwillow manor. "Now children, please do be on your best behavior. Remember that these children are without a mother or father, and their uncle has been traveling great distances around the globe and is not much at home. It is our duty to offer them friendship and kindness, not only as their new friends, but also because their uncle is our patron. Everything we have at the moment is because of this family."

"Yes, Father," said the dutiful Edith.

"Horatio?"

"You've told us a million times, Father."

Mr. Wickliffe pulled at the bell, but nothing seemed to happen. The family waited, but no one answered the door.

"Edgar, why don't you try that knob," said Gladys Wickliffe as she pointed to a brass knob protruding outward, next to the door.

Mr. Wickliffe eyed the handle and touched it. He smiled at his wife and children before pulling on it. Upon its release, a series of whistles were heard from within the house. They played a popular tune of the day.

Edith clapped her hands with joy. "Pull it again, Father!"

Before he could have had such an opportunity to pull it again, a tall man in tie and red tails opened the great front door, which creaked.

"Good evening," said the servant.

"Good evening. The Wickliffe's."

"Very good, sir. May I take the gentlemen's hats?"

Mr. Wickliffe and his son removed their tall hats, removed their gloves and placed them inside the hats, and handed each in turn their headwear to the butler. Once everything had been stowed appropriately on the side table, the butler led the Wickliffe family down a corridor and into the conservatory.

There was an awkward moment as they entered. There was no man of the house to do the duties of welcome and introduction because Cole was not present in the room. The vicar's family stood at the doorway as the butler announced them to Miss Canton and Miss Greene. Mildred began to take a step forward to greet the guests, but Lorain gently placed a hand on her elbow, holding her back from the intended movement.

"Miss Greene," said the vicar, "since we've already met several times, I think it would be appropriate for me to make the introductions of my family to you."

Mildred allowed the vicar forward with a nod. "Yes, I do think it best. I'm not sure where Cole has gotten off to, and if we had to wait for him, why, we might be standing here awkwardly all evening." As she spoke, Mildred ignored Lorain Canton's glare.

"May I first present my wife, Mrs. Gladys Wickliffe."

"So lovely to meet you Mrs. Wickliffe," said Mildred with a brief curtsey.

Mrs. Wickliffe curtsied in return.

"This strapping lad is my eldest son, Horatio."

Horatio bowed as Mildred turned her eyes to the floor and curtsied.

"And, finally, my youngest, the jewel of our house, my daughter, Edith."

The two young women smiled at each other and offered the appropriate depth of curtsey. Edith offered Mildred a quick wink, which caused a broad smile on Mildred's face.

"And, this is my tutor, Miss Lorain Canton," said Mildred finally. She looked about the room, but Cole had not appeared. So, it was for her to become lady of the house. "Won't you please come in and make yourselves at home."

The Wickliffe family spread out a bit in the conservatory. Mildred whispered something to a nearby serving girl who disappeared and just as quickly reappeared with a tray of iced teas and lemonades.

"I must apologize. Without a man about the house, our offerings are a bit tepid when it comes to spirits. Our lemonade is the best in Wickwillowshire," said Mildred.

There was another long, awkward moment of silence among the assemblage each in the room eyeing up the others around them.

"Oh, please, feel free to sit or wander as you will. The room is filled with specimens that my father and uncle have collected on their travels."

"These flowering trees are marvelous," said Mrs. Wickliffe.

"I wish I paid better attention when he explained what was what and where it's all come from."

"It matters not the geographic location of beauty, for all things beautiful come from God," said Mr. Wickliffe with his wrinkle-eyed smile.

"Miss Greene, your dress is lovely," said Edith, sidling up to Mildred.

"Oh, thank you so much. I must say though that I detest all this formality. You are our friends and neighbors, and I would thoroughly enjoy it if you would please call me Mildred."

Edith looked toward her parents for advice. Her father nodded approval. "Very well, then, if I'm to call you Mildred, you must call me Edith."

The young women shook hands, as if creating a pact.

Cole burst into the room, his shirt collar unbuttoned. "Hello. Hello. I'm sorry to be so late. My sister abandoned me, and I wasn't able to get this blasted thing right."

Mildred quickly moved to her brother and got him properly buttoned and tucked.

"I'm sorry, Millie," said Cole.

"I can't believe you've left me alone to greet our guests," Mildred hissed at her brother.

Cole stepped away from his sister and shook hands with the Vicar who once again made the formal introductions. Cole smiled kindly and bowed toward Mrs. Wickliffe, shook Horatio's hand, and bowed, without making eye contact, in Miss Wickliffe's general direction.

Another awkward silence ensued, only to be broken by the arrival of the butler, and the announcement of dinner being served. Cole and Mildred led their guests and Lorain into the adjoining dining room.

Twenty-Nine

Parker Greene slid into bed. Through the wooden walls of his cabin cell he heard laughter and talking. It wasn't so clear that he could make out the words or conversation, but near enough to feel that he was left out of something. He'd waited all evening for someone to come and retrieve him and deliver him to the Admiral. No one had come. No one had brought him dinner, either. Of course, they'd replenished the large bowl of fruit over and over, so there was plenty of nourishment.

He heard the minutes tick by on the clock, still set to English time. Parker imagined his wards, Millie and Cole, at dinner alone at that large table with the horrid Miss Canton. He considered re-reading some of Mildred's letters, but felt sad enough already.

Lord Greene blew out the candle and snuggled down under the soft, warm comforter on his bunk. While the day had been balmy, the tropical night air felt cool and a bit damp. He imagined the bustle around the massive Balsa Robin as she prepared to depart under the moonlit sky. He was impressed by the airship. Who wouldn't be? He longed to know how those propellers worked. It was such a chore for them to keep a small schooner aloft; he simply couldn't imagine how they kept the massive, heavy Robin in the air.

Thoughts of the grand air ship led him to the army of dwarfs who served at the pleasure of Captain Flynn. As he imagined Flynn, standing tall and joyous, directing his charges as they loaded his ship for a thrilling voyage, Parker felt a stirring in his loins. Ever since they were boys together at school, Greene had had strong desires for Flynn.

Those memories led Greene to think of Able Currant. Their almost kiss earlier that day; and his scent, that blend of musk and coconut. He wondered if his tongue might have tasted of mango or some other exotic fruit. That did it; he was erect under the soft sheets. Parker cast his covers aside, took himself in hand, and as he stroked, imagined Able touching him, caressing him, dropping to his knees and…

The door burst open. For the briefest moment, he wondered if his fantasy had sprung to life. Instead, he realized the person at the door was far too short to be Currant. Parker pulled the sheet back over himself, not really hiding his previous actions, but at least adding a semblance of decency to the occasion.

"Dress." The voice was that of Phineas Silas.

Greene stood, unabashed, and in a few moments had himself tucked in, buttoned up, jacketed, and booted. "Am I to speak to the Admiral?"

Silas didn't answer. Instead, he hopped up onto the bench, turned Greene around, quickly replaced the bandage, and finally, jumping back to the floor, Silas pointed to Greene's right and the two men walked down the lighted hall and through a maze of corridors. The dwarf remained silent throughout his actions and along the journey.

Thirty

Out of protocol, Cole sat at the head of the table with his sister to his left. When the servants arrived for instructions, they wisely stood between the two siblings so that Mildred, who was better versed at formal dining could chime in with looks, nods, and when necessary, whispers. Cole, while acting as head of the family, gladly deferred to his sister in such matters.

To Cole's right, sat Mr. Wickliffe, next to him his wife. While next to Mildred sat Miss Wickliffe; Horatio Wickliffe and Lorain Canton sat across from each other furthest from Cole, with Miss Canton sitting next to Mrs. Wickliffe and Horatio next to his sister.

Mr. Wickliffe did his best to spur conversation for the whole group, but to little avail. It wasn't long before he and Cole were deeply engrossed in conversations about the great inventions Mr. Wickliffe had seen both in his living arrangements and his travels.

Mildred turned to Miss Wickliffe and studied her face for a moment. She was a beautiful young woman, nearly the same age as her. Her dress was a lovely pink with many ribbons and bows, yet her hands seemed terribly sturdy for someone considered in the nearly leisure class.

"Miss Wickliffe—" Mildred began.

"Edith. You must call me Edith," her dinner companion offered with the kindest smile she'd ever seen.

It was in that moment, and because of that smile, that Mildred decided the two of them would be very good friends.

"Edith, do you study?"

"Well, I've never had a formal tutor, such as you have." Edith ignored Mildred's eye roll. "But throughout my life, my father has selected books for me to read. He's taught me French and a bit of Latin, although I must admit I dislike Latin. And, of course, he's also taught me to play the pianoforte. Mother has shown me the womanly arts of sewing and cooking, but," here she lowered her voice to a whisper, "I'm not very good at either of them."

"It's as if we're sisters!" exclaimed Mildred. "Our educational likes and dislikes align perfectly. Perhaps we could help each other by studying our Latin together?"

"That would be lovely."

Their conversation paused as the servant offered them a selection of delicate cakes for their dessert.

Mildred looked around the table. Cole and Mr. Wickliffe were quite engrossed in conversation. Mrs. Wickliffe was suffering some diatribe from Lorain. And, poor Horatio, looking handsome and fit, was seemingly alone in his thoughts sitting as he was away from all the groupings.

"Edith, should we engage your brother in conversation?"

"No. He'll simply bore us with his boyish ways. He cares not for anything that interests me. We do laugh a lot together, but we rarely hold any stimulating discussions. In fact, I can't really tell you what interests my brother, beyond being witty and self-amused."

Mildred considered that. She found her own brother dull in social settings, but enjoyed spending time with him when they could be alone. And, no matter how she was feeling about him at any given moment, she would never speak disrespectfully of him to another, as Edith had just done of her own sibling. As she continued her contemplation, she again looked around at their guests and familiars only to realize everyone was staring at her.

"Do I have sugar on my face?" she asked, touching a napkin to her lips.

"My dear sister sometimes becomes lost in her mental machinations," said Cole with a warm smile offered toward Mildred. He leaned closer to her. "The question at hand is how we shall break up our party. Shall we all go to the parlor, where you and Miss Wickliffe shall entertain us on the piano, or shall we men retire to Father's study for brandy and you ladies enjoy coffee on your own."

It was a decision that he should make, Mildred thought to herself. Why was this falling to her? She could feel the heat of a blush rising toward her ears. "Why can't we all adjourn to the parlor for brandy, coffee, and music?"

"Excellent choice." Mr. Wickliffe stood and helped his wife from her chair with an offered hand.

Mildred watched as Mrs. Wickliffe, with some difficulty, stood up.

Within a few steps away from the table, she again walked fine, without any noticeable limp or infirmity. But, those first few steps were awkward. No one made any outward comment. Mildred, noticing that her dinner companion was standing, followed her lead, and stood up from her chair.

The dinner party walked down the long corridor, past the main entrance, and entered the parlor.

"What a lovely room, Miss Greene," said Gladys Wickliffe. The entire group stopped at the doorway, just inside the room to admire the gas lights, paintings, rich tapestries, grand fireplace, and artwork. At this time of night, with all the lamps lit, the room glowed.

"Thank you, Mrs. Wickliffe. Please, please, make yourself at home." Mildred took Edith's hand and led her to the piano. She liked the feel of Edith's fingers intertwined into her own. They were soft, yet strong. At the thought, a lovely chill that she'd never experienced before ran through her entire body. Mildred whispered into the other girl's ear, "I don't want this to become any sort of competition."

"Agreed," Edith whispered back.

They stood at the piano. Mildred pushed a button and the thin shelves of a tall case began to rotate. After a few moments of movement, she again hit the button to stop the rotation and removed several books.

"What is this? It's wonderful!"

"Oh, just something Cole and I played at last year. It's fun, isn't it? Sadly, it's only spring loaded, so this handle must be cranked occasionally to keep up the tension." Mildred showed Edith the side of the tall box with the crank. "I really wanted…" her thoughts trailed off. She wasn't ready to divulge her aspirations of creating a steam driven drive shaft for the whole house that would allow for all sorts of moving inventions she'd envisioned. So, instead, turned back to the music. "Do you know any of these duets?" Mildred asked as she held books toward the girl.

"I've played through a few of the Mozart pieces before, but I've never perfected them."

"Well, instead of performing, why don't we pick something neither of us have ever played before so we'll be on equal footing."

"Mildred, do you think that appropriate. It's a dinner party," Lorain said.

"Well, it's only just our families. Here, hold on." Mildred turned toward the small assemblage. "Would you mind if Edith and I simply play something new together, rather than performing for you?"

"Do as you wish, dear Sister. We won't really be paying any attention to you anyway," said Cole with a broad smile.

"Manners, Mr. Parker," hissed Lorain to her charge.

"I agree, do as you wish," said Mr. Wickliffe, again smoothing the edges of the relationships of the tutor and the Parker children.

"There," said Mildred. "It's settled."

The young women put their heads together as they turned the pages of the book and selected Mozart's Sonata for Piano Four Hands in C-Major. It took them nearly an hour to get through the twenty minute piece. As they played and laughed together, to each other they became the only people in the room. They laughed, they played, they nudged each other with their closest elbows. As they reached the final chords, with great flourishes, they fell to laughing so hard together that it took several moments and large gulps of water to regain their composure.

"So, you'll be here to help me in my garden early in the morning."

"I'm so looking forward to it. I just knew, from the moment we met, that we would become the best of friends," said Edith as she hugged Mildred goodnight. Her family was already out of the front door and waiting for her near their carriage and mechanical horse.

"Good-nights" rang out from those inside and outside the house.

Mildred stood with the big door open and watched the Wickliffe family's departure all the way down the long lane.

"Close the door!" shouted Lorain at Mildred.

Mildred waited a moment longer, still able to see the back of the carriage, and then obliged Lorain.

"What were you thinking this evening? Making such a ruckus with guests in the house. Not doing your duty of performing for the party and encouraging Miss Wickliffe to run off the rails with you? What were you thinking?"

Mildred turned toward her tutor. She felt emboldened by now having a friend. "Miss Canton, you are only our tutor here, not my mother. I made a decision of how I wanted the evening to be and everything was quite fun."

Lorain strode up next to her charge. "Listen, little miss. While your uncle is away, I've been tasked with raising you and your brother. It is my job to teach you both how to behave in society. And, what you pulled tonight…"

"Teacher or not, you are not my mother. Cole is the man of this house while my uncle is away, and I am the lady. It is for us to decide what should and should not be done when we have guests and when we don't. Please do remember your place, or you won't have a position any longer in this house." Mildred stood firm, her hands clenched in fists at her sides.

"How dare you speak to me in such a way." As she spoke, Lorain raised a hand to slap Mildred.

"Whoa!" shouted Cole, who appeared as if from nowhere. He grabbed Lorain's raised hand and closed his own around it. "Miss Canton!"

Lorain Canton struggled to regain her hand from Cole. Once he released her, she lowered it to her side.

"You will pack your things and leave in the morning."

"What?"

"You heard me, Miss Canton. My uncle would never agree that you should hit my sister for any reason. I think it's time that you leave us. I will have your final salary available to you in the morning, and you are to leave this house."

"Who do you think you are? You are just a boy. A failure."

"Don't move." Cole strode out of the entrance hall.

Lorain and Mildred stood, a few feet apart, in awkward silence. Neither woman making eye contact with the other.

Cole returned with a small velvet pouch.

"This is about double what salary you are due from my family. Kindly take it and remove yourself from our home this instant." Cole stood taller than Mildred had ever seen him before. He looked broader, too. His hair wild from this exchange with Lorain. He looked…he looked…he looked like a man.

"What about my things?"

"I shall have them sent around to you wherever you end up."

"How am I to get into town?"

"Walk. That is how you arrived at our house, of your own steam and volition, and that is how you are to go." Cole opened the front door. "Go!"

Lorain slowly exited the house, stalling just outside the door near the rut caused by the Wickliffe's carriage.

"You'll be sorry, Cole Parker." Lorain glared at the children.

"Go!" Cole once again shouted.

As Lorain turned, he slammed the door so viciously Mildred feared for the glass panes.

"Are you okay, my sister?"

"Yes. I'm fine."

The siblings stood, not looking at each other.

"What are we to do now?" Mildred asked.

"It's late. Take yourself off to bed. I'll write Uncle a letter and let him know what I have done. And, starting from this moment, while father is away, I am the man of this house. You are its lady."

"But, Cole…"

"No buts about it. Now, off to bed." Cole kissed the top of his sister's head and then, with a nudge, guided her to the staircase.

When she arrived at the first landing, Mildred turned to look back toward her brother.

Cole was watching her. He smiled and offered in a very soft voice, the voice she knew, "Go, Millie."

She turned her attention back toward the stairs, lifted her long skirts, and ascended to the upstairs hall. She wanted to think beautiful thoughts about her new friend Edith, but instead could only wonder what their future held now that they were alone in the world, without an adult to guide and care for them. Yes, they had a house filled with servants, but none of them were of their class, could train them properly. She resolved that they weren't really ready, but also believed that something or someone would appear to aid them along their journey.

Thirty-One

The Admiral sat at his desk as Lord Greene was ushered into the room. Silas bowed toward the man, unacknowledged, and left Parker standing in the middle of the Admiral's cabin. A stream of dwarfs came and went. Each one delivered a note, added more wine to the man's glass, or deposited fabrics, goods, and spices on a side table. The small space was a hive of activity.

Moments passed. Greene, still standing where he'd been left, began to feel uncomfortable and exposed. He imaged he felt much as Gulliver did in the land of the Lilliputians.

The unmistakable sound of the great doors opening brought all the activity around him to a pause. Everyone listened to the repeated click-clack, click-clack knowing that the wooden slats were exposing the Balsa Robin to the night sky and her next adventure.

Just as quickly as they'd stopped, each little man and woman moved quicker and quicker, accomplishing tasks at double time. It was obvious to him. Decisions had to be made if they were to be included in the new journey. If not, they would be left behind. The admiral, with a slight smile on his face, continued to sign papers, point at choices, and drink his wine, all the while never once making any sort of eye contact or other acknowledgement in Parker Greene's direction.

The room began to hum. It was a soft rumble in the floor. Parker looked around and noticed the portrait of the Queen rocking rhythmically against the wall. Their harnessing of power was impressive and Lord Greene once again longed to know and understand what these pirates had done to bring Tesla's ideas to such successful fruition.

It was during this moment of contemplation that he heard his name, not once, but twice.

"Greene?"

"Sorry, sir. I was a million miles away in my thoughts." He looked at the admiral who, now the only other person in the room, was focused squarely on Parker.

"It is time." The Admiral's tone changed. He wasn't the cordial host. There was the strain of a tired leader, but a leader, nonetheless.

Lord Greene squared his shoulders. His memory flashed on those poor souls withering away to nothing and the heads upon the spikes, knowing the latter were better off.

"My question is a simple one, and it is time for me to ask it of you." He opened a great, leather bound book on his now empty desk.

Greene wondered how and when the chaos of materials had been cleared away and how he had missed their being removed. The man nodded toward the Admiral. "As you wish, sir." Lord Greene raised himself up to his full height.

"It's a simple matter, really. You've seen the outcomes. I ask you now: will you relinquish your loyalty to Queen Victoria and England and swear your allegiance to us, Lord Parker Greene? Will you join us in our fight for justice?"

Greene's muscles tightened. He was instinctively ready to defend his beloved Queen to his own death and demise. He loved England. He loved his charges and his home. And, he was totally devoted to Victoria, his Queen and employer. Yet, he knew what must be done. He knew that to bring down these rogues and pirates he must become one with them, understand them, infiltrate their nest and destroy it from within. Parker Greene knew that if he ever hoped to see his home again, he must lie with all the sincerity he could muster in this moment. He must agree to their terms.

"Well, man? I must have your decision." The Admiral had grown harsh. It seemed to Parker that he was just as disturbed in the asking as Greene was in the responding.

"I shall join you, Admiral."

"Raise your right hand and repeat after me." The Admiral read a brief oath from the great book:

I, Parker Greene, swear allegiance to the Admiral and to the Statute for his Kingdom. I release and relinquish all other oaths and loyalties from my past. I swear that I will faithfully perform the duties my office lays upon me and respect the Pirate's Oath while upon any journey away from the Kingdom. This I declare and affirm so help me God almighty!

Parker said the words during the Admiral's pauses. He found himself wondering which Pirate's Oath they used, what Statutes were written, and what his office and duties would be. But, while he wondered these things, he kept his spoken tone even, relinquished his oath to the Queen, and became a pirate.

The Admiral turned the great book in Parker's direction, pointed to a blank space, and Greene signed his name, just below that of Ablest Currant. His breath quickened at the thought of being below that man on this list, or anywhere else.

Thirty-Two

For the first morning of her life, there was no one to greet her when she descended the grand staircase, except the servants, all of whom kept their heads down and avoided eye contact. Mildred entered the dining room and there were only two place settings, one at the head of the table and a second to its right hand. She knew it was proper for her to take her place at the right, so she did.

Mildred sat in the silent room. There was no more Lorain to play mother. On the one hand it's what she'd secretly desired for most of her life. The woman was a bore. She nagged and cajoled both her and Cole mostly into doing things they didn't want to do. And, what success had there been? Mildred knew she was awkward in social settings, and that's something that a good tutor would have taught her. And, Cole, he'd failed his university entrance exams. That was a massive failure in her eyes. What was that poor boy to do now? He had no prospects of any accomplished future. Although, being the male heir to her father's fortunes, not to mention those of her uncle, what need did Cole truly have of a formal education?

On the other hand, she now had her time free to pursue her own directions and ideas. If she had the opportunity, which she wouldn't, she already knew, even at her young age, that she could pass university exams if they were placed before her, except maybe for the Latin portion.

Through the closed windows she could see the leaves outside flutter to the morning breeze and hear the slight sounds of birds chirping through the leaded panes.

With determination, she rose, moved to the great windows, and with some effort, successfully flung two of them open. Immediately, the room cooled some. The air smelled fresh and sweet compared to the closed up house air that was stifling. Her effort to open the windows was great and she contemplated how window opening could also be assigned in some way to the great drive shaft she envisioned for the manor. As she began working on getting the third window open, a servant entered the room.

"Miss? What are you doing?"

"Opening the windows and airing out this house." She felt emboldened, empowered. If Cole was now officially the man of the house, then, by extension, she must be the lady. And, in all the homes she knew of and had read about in books, and Mildred had read a great many books, dealing with things inside the home fell to the lady.

"But, Miss, the instructions are that all the windows—"

"The rules are changing. There will, I suspect, be a great number of alterations that shall be undertaken in the days, weeks, and months to come." She thought for a moment. "First, I would like my breakfast."

"But Master Cole has not come down from his room."

"Well, I'm hungry; I no longer wish to wait. And, in the future…" How did one go about creating new rules for a great manor house? She quickly realized that speaking to a serving girl was not at all the proper approach. "Please bring my breakfast."

"Yes, Miss."

Mildred watched the girl rush from the room and realized she didn't even know her name. She knew few of the servants' names. They came and went, ran the house, and Mildred had been oblivious to all of it. They never seemed to be the same girls two days in a row, so she'd never invested the time. If she were to become the Lady of this manor, or any other house, she realized she'd need to know the names of the people who worked for her. Not just their names, but the jobs they did.

She got the hang of the windows and the sixth one she attempted opened easier than the others. The room was now filled with fresh air and the songs of the chattering birds.

Two girls returned to the room with trays and plates. Mildred took her seat to the right, placed the napkin on her lap, and nodded to the girls who served her morning meal.

Alone again, Mildred began working in her mind her next steps. She liked the windows open in the cool of the morning and the cool of the evening. Yet, they must be closed against the heat of the day. Was it acceptable for her to request this? She detested those horrible portraits in the bedroom hall. She would prefer gayer paintings. Was that a change she could make without anyone's approval? The piano required tuning, who would take care of that?

Her questions caused a realization that Mildred knew little of what it took to be the lady of the house. This notion infuriated her. Hadn't that been the tutor's job? To prepare her to be a wife some day? While she'd already decided she would never be a wife to some horrible man, she still felt slighted in her education. What good was it to be able to conjugate a thousand French verbs, when she didn't know how to open a window, change a picture, or have her own piano tuned. And, not knowing the names of the servants, she didn't even know who to ask.

Mildred split apart a muffin and spread soft butter on a piece before popping it into her mouth. "Well, it's obvious, isn't it?" Mildred asked to the empty room. "I must speak to someone about this. I must ask someone how to become the lady of my house." She ate a bit more muffin and washed it down with the cooling tea. "But who?"

"Who what?" asked Cole. He had arrived at the very end of his sister's questionings. "You couldn't wait for me?" He slumped into his seat at the head of the table as if it had always been his position. He pawed through the mail and papers on the silver tray next to his place.

"Brother, I'm no longer going to wait breakfast for you." She looked at his rumpled hair and wrinkled clothing. "Did you sleep in your clothes?"

"Yes. It took most of the night writing the letter to uncle about what transpired with Miss Canton. And, I just crawled into bed and fell asleep when I was finished."

"Well, as I was saying, I won't be waiting breakfast for you. And, there are many things that we need to work out."

"Please, let me have some coffee before you barrage me with questions and ideas."

Mildred didn't wait. She was anxious to move forward with her day now that her own breakfast was completed. She watched her brother poor himself a cup of coffee and take a long sip.

"This is tepid," he said, but took no action beyond drinking more of it.

"We don't know how to run this house. Lorain was the one who did that."

"You would defend her? I won't have her back in this house."

"I'm not defending her. And, I want to thank you for saving me from her blows."

Cole nodded toward his sister.

"What I am saying is that she took care of the details of this house."

"Nonsense, the servants take care of the details."

"And, she instructed the servants. Don't you see? It was her choices we ate for our meals. She made sure things were in good repair because she instructed the servants on all manner of details."

"Why are these windows open?"

"Cole, are you listening to me?"

"Who has given instruction that these windows be opened?"

"There was no instruction. I could see the breeze outside so I stood up and pushed the windows open myself." Mildred was defiant in her words. Would Cole be an even worse tyrant than Lorain? That would be a great disadvantage, because Cole could be uneven in his temper.

"Oh, fine."

"But that illustrates my example. I think we should have the windows opened in the morning and in the evening, but closed in the afternoons against the midday heat. How does one go about getting the servants to do that? I don't like monkfish, yet we frequently find it on our plates at dinner time. Who do I tell to no longer serve that at my table?" Mildred looked at her brother imploringly.

Cole held his head in one hand while he sipped coffee at an odd angle.

"You had too much port last night. Did you even write Uncle the letter?"

"I will not be questioned by you. I am, while Uncle is away, the man of this house, and I shall do as I please without question from you."

Mildred's eyes opened wide. "Will you now?" She stood up, but instead of slamming something, she simply turned and left the room.

"You'll be helping with the clock today, right? Come back here and close these windows." Cole called after her.

Mildred did not acknowledge him. Help him with his blasted clock after he talked to me worse than Lorain? Nonsense. He could close the windows if that's what he wanted. Without hat, gloves, or bag, Mildred left the house through the front door. She thought about leaving it open, just to make some unknown point, but thought better of it. She started walking, and walking, taking a direction toward the little duck pond. She wanted to clear her head and think more about her choices and options and a brisk walk around the pond would allow her to clear her energy.

When she arrived at the little bridge that crossed over the stream that left the pond and rejoined the Wickwillow River, she did not cross. Instead, she followed the stream to the river and the river path toward town. Her pace slowed. Mildred wished she had worn different shoes, but didn't want to go back to the house to change. She didn't want to see her brother at this moment for fear she'd say dreadful things to him that could never be taken back. So, she walked a little slower and thought of things other than her feet.

Among the first of her thoughts were the bees that had covered her the day before. She thought about the sensation and the weight of the small creatures as they crawled all over her. She hadn't suffered a single sting or moment of discomfort. She never felt scared or terrified, although the look on the faces of Perry and Isaac was startling. Thought as she did of that experience, not a single notion came to her as to the cause. And, while she certainly wouldn't seek to recreate the experience, it thrilled her that something like that had happened to her.

The river path was well worn. Lorain walked it several times a week from their home into town. It was a lovely path following the river's tree-lined edge. Their overhanging branches provided shelter and shade from the heat of the day.

Mildred breathed deeply of the verdant green, damp air. She listened to the babbling of the water and the songs of the calling birds. Instead of discovering answers to her questions or solutions to the problems at hand, she lost herself in thoughtlessness. She simply enjoyed the morning.

"Well, hello!"

Mildred looked up, for she'd been scuffing her toes in the dirt and enjoying the puffs of dust that lighted from her activity. "Edith!"

"I was to come to your garden this morning, wasn't I? Wasn't that the plan? Yet here you are headed on some other errand or task."

"Oh, my friend." Mildred took Edith's hands in her own. "I so dreadfully forgot our appointment. So much has happened since last I saw you." Tears rose into Mildred's eyes.

Edith took out her own handkerchief and dabbed at her new friend's eyes.

"My friend, what has you so upset?" She took Mildred's arm and gently guided her to a large rock near the path's edge. Together they sat upon it and Mildred relayed the events of the evening and the morning.

"Well, I have a wonderful solution. You must come and speak with Mother. Why, she's run a household with and without servants for most of her life. We've also been guests at some very grand homes many, many times. I know she'll have perfect advice for you."

"Really, she'd help me."

"My dear, she'd gladly offer any aid and assistance that she can to you. Your family are our patrons, so we are obliged to be of service to you."

"Edith, you're being ever so kind to me."

"Come, dry the last of those tears. Our house is just around this bend, and Mother is already in the sitting room working with her threads and needles. That's how she spends most midmornings. She loves company while she makes her needlework pictures." Edith took up her friend's arm, helped her stand, and gently pulled her along the path.

Mildred felt a bit lighter. By the time they reached the vicar's home, she once again had a spring in her step. She would learn all the requirements of being the great lady she was destined to be and had new friends to help her.

Thirty-Three

Lord Greene was led out of the Admiral's quarters. At the end of a short hallway, he hadn't been in before, the floor lowered Parker and the gaggle of small women who escorted him down to a deep tunnel, similar to the one he'd been in before. They arrived back at the island with the miniature version of Wickwillow Manor.

"Home, Sweet Home, Lord Greene," said one of the little women as she opened the great door and then stepped aside to allow the master of this home entry.

As he stepped inside, Greene's spirits fell a bit. It wasn't at all like the interior of his actual home. There weren't any portraits or fine marble floors. Instead, all was freshly painted wood and plaster. Everything was stark white, devoid of character, history, or charm.

The floor plan was also quite different. The first floor consisted of four rooms: a sitting room, dining room, office, and bedroom. The grand staircase led to a balcony that surrounded the entry hall.

Only two women had entered the home with Parker Greene. They were the ones who offered the tour in silence. And, now, with slight curtsies, they left him alone once again.

While he seemed to have the freedom to go where he wished, there was, sadly, nowhere he wished to go. He knew no one. He didn't yet know if there was anyone here he could trust. He opened the rear door which led to an open yard. An out building emitted smoke from a single chimney; he assumed it was the kitchen.

The night sky was filled with stars. The temperature was perfect. Night birds called to one another among the trees. And there, in the distance, was an airship moving silently away. The Balsa Robin had begun her voyage.

"Lord Greene?"

The voice saying his name caused Parker's knees to momentarily weaken. He took a moment to enjoy the swoon before responding: "Yes?" Greene turned to find himself facing Able Currant. His breath quickened.

"The Admiral has assigned me to be your aide and assistant. I've sorted and stacked all the plans into categories. I'd been in charge of the work, but truly, I don't have a head for mechanics. I'm just not able to see things in my head...."

Parker Greene stood, a blank stare on his face. He'd not heard a word Currant had uttered. "My what?" he managed to ask.

It took Currant a moment to figure out what Lord Greene was talking about. "Oh, your assistant. I'm to serve you as you wish."

"Why are you not there?" he pointed toward the barely visible airship.

"I never ask. None of us ever ask. We go where we're told. We do as we're told." Able Currant said these words in an off-the-cuff manner, not seeming bothered at all by their meaning.

"And, now I'm to tell you what to do, where to go?" Shivers passed over Parker Greene's flesh at the thought.

Able's smile was wry, a bit seductive. "To a point, sir. There are some commands only the Admiral may give."

The conversation had quickly turned into a game of cat and mouse. "I look forward to discovering the boundaries," said Greene.

The handsome men had moved close to one another, like metal to magnet.

Greene raised his hand, placed it on the back of Currant's neck and pulled the man those few remaining inches toward him. Able didn't resist. Just before their lips met, Able said: "As you wish, sir."

Thirty-four

Cole slammed a variety of items, one after another, on the workbench. A metal can suffered multiple blows, mostly because it was empty and fit well in Cole's long-fingered hand. After the banging, he strode around the tight space kicking anything that wasn't nailed to the floor. The tantrum did little to assuage the anger he felt toward his sister. Who was she, the younger of the two, to question him, his abilities, or his decisions? He was eighteen after all. He was a man. If it weren't for his uncle's high position or his father's connections, he would be halfway through an apprenticeship, or already toiling each day in the fields somewhere or other, or laying bricks from sunup to sundown. He was the son of the Lord of Wickwillowshire and would one day become Lord of the Manor himself.

With their uncle frequently away, away more than home, he'd always been the master of the house. He'd simply never risen to the position, instead allowing Miss Canton to maintain the role of caretaker and decision maker.

He liked the idea of being in charge, but had to admit, at least to himself, that he had no idea what the job entailed. No one had ever instructed him how to handle the house or the properties. There was a manager his father had hired long ago, a Mr. Eastlake, who handled all manner of things, from collecting rents for the lands surrounding the house, to overseeing arguments and debates among the tenants. He was the one who also oversaw all the financial dealings for the house, including providing the monies for the servants' wages, the general maintenance of things, and the generous allowances that he and his sister received each month, but rarely had opportunity to spend.

For Mildred's part, she never actually handled any of the money. Miss Canton took care of getting any personal items, music, and whatnot that his sister might require. And, in similar fashion, the butler took care of most of Cole's needs. Although, he also made a point of leaving pennies and stray shillings for the boy in small dish on the desk in Cole's rooms.

Cole rarely touched them, so there had grown a great heap of copper and metal in that bowl.

He trusted that in time, his uncle would write and offer him advice. But, that might take weeks, or even months, depending on where in the world the man currently was exploring.

Cole resolved, as he considered the situation, that he should spend some time with Mr. Eastlake. Make the rounds with him perhaps when he collected rent from the tenants. Or, peruse the man's account book to see what went on there.

He stomped on a spider scuttling across the roughhewn floor. It felt good to kill something, to take out the wrath he felt toward Miss Canton on something. He didn't know how best to handle his sister. He needed her help with the clock. He'd tried to piece things back together, but he didn't know where the gears, cogs, and springs belonged. Yet, he also wouldn't be managed by her, not when it came to being the man of the house.

Cole stopped for a moment and thought about Mildred, her sweet smile and bright eyes. Her intelligence and book knowledge overshadowed and overwhelmed him. Cole felt nothing but love toward her for these accomplishments. She was smarter not only than him, but everyone he'd ever met. Certainly all the other children he'd ever met. "How is that I can feel such love for her and such hatred?"

"Who do you love and hate?"

Cole spun to see who the intruder was. "Horatio, what are you doing here?"

"It's like a henhouse at our place between my mother and sister and now your sister as well. I was feeling terribly outnumbered and decided to get some air to clear my head. As I rode along, I decided to stop here and enquire about your clock. How goes your task?"

Cole considered his intruder, backlit as he was, looking all dark and shadowy dressed in black trousers, waist coat, jacket, and hat. Only his white shirt offered some break to the great amount of black the boy wore. His suit fabric shone with a similar quality as his great mane of hair and for a moment, just a moment, Cole wondered if his clothes weren't actually constructed from those locks. It was a silly notion, of course, and the time for childhood silliness was now done. It was time to become a more serious man about town.

"Well, there have been a few other things going on, and I haven't gotten the blasted thing ticking again. But, I will."

"I'm certain of your success," said Horatio, stepping backward out of the doorway as Cole moved forward.

"How can you be so certain?" Cole himself was rather uncertain. His certainty resided in the fact that it would be his sister's instruction and guidance mixed with his own brawny might that would be the combination required to bring the clock back to working order.

"Just making conversation, but don't men complete the tasks they start and end with success?"

Now, that was something new for Cole to consider. Men are successful at the tasks they undertake. His uncle always appeared successful at his tasks, always finding new, amazing plants, flowers, and trees to fill the private gardens of the Queen and her friends. Wasn't his sister—while not a man—also always successful at her tasks? Even the hired old stable master, Isaac, always seemed successful in his tasks, although there was a great amount of repetition in the work he completed over and over year after year.

"Is it always this hot here?" Horatio asked, giving a gentle tug to his shirt collar to allow a little air in.

"We're having an exceptionally warm summer."

"I was thinking it might be nice to have a swim. In the river, perhaps? Or, maybe, there's a pond or lake nearby?"

"The river is the only choice. There is a place where we built a rope swing a number of years ago, but I haven't been there in a very long time." The idea of an afternoon of bathing in the cool waters of the river appealed to Cole. He eyed up his companion, who, while a bit taller, was slighter of build than him. He could certainly use his brawn to hold the man's mane of hair under water and most probably win any other games they might find themselves at in the water.

"Well, let's go."

Cole looked around. "Where is your horse?"

"He threw a shoe and the farrier had two other jobs before our horse. That's the downside of being a vicar's son; we don't always get top attention from those in service."

"Well, it's worth the wait if you're speaking of Avon. He's very accomplished with all things related to horses and will do a good, solid job for you. But, what of your mechanical mount?"

"Father is making the rounds, meeting his parishioners. While he prefers the living beast, he took the other today."

"So you walked?"

"I'm quite capable of walking," said Horatio, indicating his long legs. "Although, Father, who had an errand, did allow me to ride with him on his mechanical horse for part of the journey until his turn was different from mine to come here."

It made Cole feel good that the new neighbor had sought out his company. They hadn't said very much to each other when they met or at dinner the previous night.

"So, what about that spot with the rope swing?"

"Come on."

They walked together toward the river in silence. A few times they bumped elbows and on one of those occasions, Horatio playfully added an extra, intentional bump to the accidental occurrence which made both young men smile.

Cole finally led them off the river path, over a small stone bridge, and into a proper wooded area. The canopy created by the old trees cooled them quickly. Old leaves and moss crunched under their feet and silenced the birds, creating an eerie calm. They walked a few hundred yards more over fallen logs and around large ferns, still not speaking.

"Are we almost there?" Horatio asked.

When Cole turned to look at him, he noticed that his companion was drenched in sweat. "I thought you said you could walk," Cole offered playfully.

Horatio didn't respond, instead breathing heavier and heavier, his breaths causing a wheeze to emanate from his lips.

Cole stopped and placed a hand on Horatio's damp chest. "There's something wrong here."

"I…sometimes…have…trouble…breathing."

The effort it took for Horatio to string together the sentence pained Cole. He surveyed the forest floor and discovered nearby a very large fallen tree. He took his companion by the elbow and gently supported him until they reached the log. "Sit here and I'll run and get some water."

"How will you gather it?" Horatio's words remained overtly difficult, but his breathing was a little easier now.

"I can use your hat or…"

"No, just let me catch my breath. I'll be fine if we don't have far to go?"

"Not much further. It's just over there." Cole pointed a long finger into what seemed to Horatio to be a random direction. There wasn't even the sound of moving water.

After a brief time, Horatio's color improved, and he stood up with a sprightly smile. "Let's go!"

The two young men finished the walk, and as they reached the crest of a small rise had the view of the river where it bent inward and created a pool. Cole pointed at the tree they were standing near. "See, there's still a bit of rope there, but it's all rotted."

"I see," said Horatio as he began unfastening the hooks and buttons that held him captive in his clothes.

Cole watched as his new friend began, bit by bit exposing his white flesh, made all the more stark against the black of his garments and the shadows of the forest. He began laboring over his own buttons, only his skin was darker having spent time shirtless working out of doors on his projects. As he watched Horatio he suddenly grew aroused. It wasn't an odd thing or out-of-the-ordinary thing for his cock to suddenly become erect at the slightest thought or brush of a hand, but this felt different somehow. As he looked at the tall, thin, yet handsome man now undressed down to his socks and undershorts, a thrill shot through him and his erection grew hard. It embarrassed him so he quickly threw off his drawers, ran to the end of the water, and threw himself off the bank into the cool, black pool that in the past had been very deep.

Much to his dismay, he struck a spot with a painful splat into nearly a foot of thick, rich, mud and crunchy leaves.

Horatio heard the splash and then the sucking sounds as Cole extricated himself from the deep mud. He laughed heartily until Cole, anger flaring, hit him in the head with a handful of mud.

Not to be undone, Horatio, now naked, ran to the edge, but instead of jumping in, bent down, took up two handfuls of the sticky, gummy earth and threw it with all his might at Cole who, backing up to avoid the hit, suddenly went under the water. He came up, tossed his wet hair, and laughed, more out of relief that his excited body was hidden, than by the experience of falling in the water.

The boys spent the afternoon romping and playing in and around the deep river pool. Frequently, Cole found himself aroused. He wanted to take care of it by stroking until he ejaculated, feeling that might be enough to calm him down, yet he was far too embarrassed to do such a thing in front of another person. He considered getting into the deep water and quickly stroking to success, but, as he placed his hand on his dick to give it a quick try, Horatio wrapped his arms around him from behind and dunked Cole under the water.

So, for the rest of the playful afternoon, the two boys frolicked, searched the bank for rocks to skim, and generally and frequently kept their backs to each other.

Thirty-Five

Lord Greene sat at the large desk sifting through plans for objects and devices. So far, they ranged from mundane kitchen aids to elaborate personal flying contraptions. He hadn't yet deciphered Able Currant's filing system. Why, for example, had the man chosen to group a device to toast breakfast bread with another that would, according to its inventor, allow for time travel?

With each device he contemplated, his mind went easily to work, seeing each spring, cog, and wire in multiple dimensions. He knew within moments of watching the puzzle pieces of a device dance in his head whether it was feasible to construct, whether the design would work, and how useful it would be once built. Parker Greene had always had this skill, this gift, this ability, to see an object in multiple dimensions within his mind's eye. He could always tell how objects and creations were put together and why and how they worked. At times, his mechanical mind felt itself to be a curse, and at others he appreciated it for the great gift that it was.

Even with such a gift, he'd never finished his education. He dropped out of university, feeling it was a waste of time. Instead, he'd desired adventure and took the first opportunity he could to join his older brother Cecil as he explored the world looking for plants, trees, and flowers for their Queen.

At the thought of Victoria, Parker winced. He'd signed an oath against his beloved Queen. He reminded himself that it was necessary, required even, to do this great job for her and her kingdom.

What a surprise it had been to discover, rather by accident, that his brother wasn't only a plant hunter, but also, and more impressively, an agent of the great Victoria. Traveling the world, both within and beyond the empire's vast borders, to thwart evildoers as the Queen requested and required. And, at the same time, discovering new plant species to bring back to England, cultivate, and make an ongoing living from selling them into the gardens and conservatories of all the royalty of the land. Here he was, like his lost brother, on one of those secret missions, too. He wished Cecil were with him. His brother quickly contemplated situations and developed vast, yet workable plans. It took Parker a bit longer to arrive at similar types of decisions and conclusions.

As the morning progressed, a series of small women brought him all manner of treats, teas, and even coffees. It was nice to feel cared for by these little women, and yet, it seemed that the hourly parade of scones, biscuits, and beverages was less about his sustenance and more about them getting a look at the latest captive. Parker thought he heard whispers and laughter coming from the hall both before and after these visits.

"You there!" he called out to one of the girls as she placed a tray with some sort of cake and a cup of steaming liquid on a free table.

The woman cast her eyes downward before responding: "Yes, sir?"

"How many of you are there caring for me?"

"Well, Lord Greene, there aren't any of us permanently assigned; we are working in shifts as volunteers. You may choose among us if you have a preference."

It seemed to Parker that the woman blushed a bit. He eyed her. She dressed in the same, odd manner of others he'd seen with strange shades of soft materials in layers, some of which reached the heels of leather boots, with a bustier of sorts holding it all together on the outside. It seemed like the outfits were somehow backward or inside out. And, like the dwarf men he'd met on the airship, each of these women also wore a pointed, dangerous looking ring.

"Is Mr. Currant around?" Greene asked.

"He has stepped away for a bit, but said he'd return before luncheon. Oh, if you have any preferences or favorite dishes, I'll let Cook know." Still she kept her face turned down, away from Parker Greene.

"I shall speak to Cook myself once I've sampled her food." After a pause, "Now, off with you. I've work to do."

The serving girl left, and Parker returned to sorting through the hundreds and hundreds of inventions that had been submitted to the Queen. Some of the plans were written in a rough hand, the notes and instructions poorly spelt. Others were obviously from educated and upper class sorts, with exacting drawings and descriptions. Among the stacks, some of the gruffer designs appeared the most useful and feasible. While not as advanced in concept as their intellectual counterparts, they were suitable, practical, and doable. Several of these, mostly farming implements, he tossed into the trial pile.

Parker took a moment to look through those devices and realized what he'd been instinctively doing. The trial pile filled with tools and gadgets that could be quickly and easily built and used against these pirates to bring their scourge of terror to an end. Yet, he'd require an army of helpers if the now budding plan was going to come to fruition.

Thirty-Six

Mildred, who had received a friendly welcome in the Wickliffe's parlor, was now seated next to the vicar's wife who immediately put Edith and Mildred to work balling periwinkle blue yarn from a large skein she had recently purchased from a nearby village sheep farmer. The girls laughed when they momentarily became tangled together.

Once their work was easily underway again, Mrs. Wickliffe asked: "So, to what do we owe your visit, today?"

Mildred looked first to Edith, then at Mrs. Wickliffe, and finally allowed her eyes to settle once again on the ball of yarn that was growing larger and larger with each spin of her hand.

"It's okay, Mildred. You can talk to her. Really you can," Edith prompted her new friend. She would have patted Mildred's hand for encouragement except both of her hands were occupied as a spindle for the skein.

Mrs. Wickliffe lowered the knitting needles she'd been manipulating with a steady click, click, click into her lap and offered her complete attention to the young woman so fearful of speaking.

The silence turned deafening to Mildred who blurted out: "Last night, after your family left our home, my brother turned Miss Canton out of the house. Now, I find I'm without a caregiver." She kept her eyes on the ball of yarn that had grown misshapen at her lack of attention. "That's not really the issue. We have a house filled with servants to care for us and I'm not a little girl anymore. What I need help with…"

Mrs. Wickliffe did not speak while Edith lowered herself to the floor so that she could attempt to make eye contact with her friend. Those eyes offered great encouragement, and when she added a nod and "go on," Mildred smiled at her.

"Oh, Mrs. Wickliffe," Mildred implored, thrusting her tear stained face upward, "it all seems to be falling apart. It's all a mess. As if losing Miss Canton isn't enough, Cole and I had a terrible row this morning over breakfast and our windows. It's all falling apart. I want to run our house, but don't know the first thing about it."

"Now, now, young one, it isn't as bad as all that." Mrs. Wickliffe's voice was motherly and soothing. "We shall unravel everything together, just as you girls are unraveling the yarn. These moments in one's life are simply the raw material that you'll make something wonderful out of."

"Just like the yarn becoming a scarf, Mother's making me a scarf with this," Edith chimed in with her singsong voice.

Mildred placed the ball of yarn in her lap and looked around the room. The walls were freshly painted. The fireplace was sparkling clean. She could actually see her own reflection in the high polish of the wooden floors. As she admired the cleanliness of the house one of the serving girls arrived with a silver tea service on a platter.

"Place it there, please, Sarah," said Mrs. Wickliffe.

The girl, who looked familiar to Mildred, placed the tray, curtsied, and left the room.

Mrs. Wickliffe took a cup from the tray, filled it with hot tea, added a bit of sugar, and handed it to Mildred without asking if she wanted it. Next, after Edith had freed herself from the yarn, she gave a cup to her daughter, and finally poured one for herself. "So, what is it that I can do to help you?" It was obvious from the tone of her voice and the language unspoken, offered by her body language, that Mrs. Wickliffe was sincere in her offering.

Mildred was steadier now. The tea and sympathy had helped her find a familiar voice. "I realized this morning, as I sat at the breakfast table waiting for Cole, who is always late, that if he was now the man of the house, until Uncle's return anyway, that that made me the Lady of the Manor. Yet, I've received no instruction in how to be that or do that. What are my tasks? How do I talk to the servants? Do I have to plan meals and the like, or does the cook take care of that?" Mildred only stopped because she'd grown flush and out of breath.

"Well, it seems we have a great deal to discuss." Mrs. Wickliffe smiled, not only with her lips, but with her entire face. "And, as we help our dear friend, Mildred, you, too, Edith, shall receive an education about how one becomes the lady of her own home. Neither of you are too young for this training. I have to admit that I'm a little surprised that Miss Canton…" she stopped herself. "Well, it matters not how you have found yourself in desire of this knowledge. What does matter is that you have come to me and I will be more than happy to help you."

"Really? You won't find it a bother to teach me these things?"

"A bother? Certainly not. A girl of breeding and class, such as yourself, and you, too, Edith, must learn how best to run a household so that you will one day make the perfect wife to some lord or barrister."

"See!" Edith exclaimed brightly. "I told you Mother would help."

Thirty-Seven

Parker Greene's eyes ached; his temples pounded and the pressure built inside his head. He checked the clock and realized he'd been reading plans for five hours straight. He stood from his desk and looked out the window at the green lawn and flowering trees. Parker put on his coat, found his hat, and headed out of his office, down the staircase, and out into the afternoon air. He breathed deep of the exotic floral scents.

He walked down the lane, nodding to those he encountered sitting on their grand porches, or under the shade of massive trees. These weren't common folk, but obvious elite with manners and grace. Everyone seemed calm and comfortable, even happy to be where they were. All of them must have answered the question correctly. What might they be offering to this land of pirates and thugs? Lord Greene chose not to engage any of these people in idle chatter, there was no way to know who he could trust. So he continuing his walk along the avenue, breathing deeply as he went, clearing his head of the clutter of gears, cogs, and spinning contraptions.

A little assistant in his head now worked, filing each plan into a cabinet or cupboard. Greene knew he could recall anything he desired easily as each puzzle piece was cataloged and filed in his magnificent brain. This certainly wasn't the most elegant analogy, but Parker had devised the method as a small child. It worked to clear his mind, so he'd kept it all these years. It dawned on him, as his heels clicked on the cobbled walk, that the little assistant in his mind didn't have a name.

"Lord Greene? Is it really you?"

Startled out of his thoughts, Parker looked up to find a tall, thin man he and his brother had served with more than a decade ago. "Rifle Helms!"

The two men started with a handshake that turned into a hearty hug with playful pounding of hands on backs, laughter, and camaraderie.

"What on earth are you doing here?" Greene asked as they lessened their grip on one another, but continued holding hands for a moment longer.

"The Rover was taken. Most of my men were killed."

"Your men?"

Rifle Helms smiled. "I'd been promoted to captain of the Rover after our last mission together." At the word "mission," Rifle looked around.

"Well, congratulations."

"I'm still not sure why they kept me alive or brought me here. Life has been good though for the past few years. Plenty of food. A nice home. Servants."

"So, you answered the question correctly."

Rifle searched Parker's face. "So did you."

Lord Greene understood the tone. They'd used those same inflections when they'd been captured by cannibals in Indonesia. "We should have supper together tonight."

"That would be wonderful. I'm sure your home is better equipped than my own. Shall we say eight?"

"Eight it is, Rifle." Parker couldn't contain himself and once again gave his tall friend a hearty bear hug.

"Can't breathe!" Helms spewed out.

As Greene released his grip the two men laughed in a comfortable, familiar way. It was obvious from Rifle's tone that Parker had found at least one person he could trust and count on. That was a start.

Thirty-Eight

Mildred sat alone in her garden, looking at the work that had been accomplished. She felt, while there was still a great deal more to do, that she and her young companion, Perry, were making remarkable progress. They had cleared and cleaned nearly a quarter of it so far, exposing the paving stones down the central walk all the way to the old fountain and from the main gate to the side gate along the east wall to the honey bee hive.

She ran her hand along the stone bench feeling the deep carved edge filled with soft green moss. The stone was cool to her touch, even as the morning warmed. Perry had been called away for some big barn cleaning that her brother had ordered.

Cole. Mildred did love her brother. He'd always been her friend and protector. Her heart warmed even more toward him as she contemplated the actions he had taken to save her from Lorain's violence. Yet, something had altered. He had changed somehow. And, with his modification, their relationship had somehow distorted, as well. It had been many nights since he had visited her in her rooms in the evening. They had a constant battle going about whether the windows around the manor should be opened or closed and found themselves at times following each other around the place opening or closing the windows behind the other.

Meals had been awkward, so much so, that Mildred was now taking most of them in her room, in the conservatory, or with the Wickliffe family just to avoid his silence.

That's what bothered her most, Cole's silence. He simply would not speak to her. When they did attempt to talk it always ended up in a row of some sort with one or the other of them stomping off, which only prolonged this already too long fight between them.

A hummingbird flitted in front of her and then moved on to the recently uncovered flowers. The "L" shaped portion of the garden that had been once again exposed was now awash in purples, pinks, yellows, reds, and whites. The small bird took advantage of the exposed blooms to nourish itself before flitting away again over the wall.

Mildred inhaled deeply and enjoyed the scent of flowers mixed with moss, dead leaves, and freshly cut grass. It was good, this earthy smell. It reminded her of her father after he'd spent a morning in the greenhouse filling its rows and rows of racks with stone and peat to prepare it for a winter of growing and budding. It caused her to wonder whether he would be home in time to begin the process in the late fall. And, then she remembered that her father was lost to them.

She took out one of her uncle's letters that she'd been carrying with her. Its paper was now stained and the edges had grown a bit ragged. She read her favorite line aloud: "I love you my darling niece and wish nothing but joy and happiness for you. I so long and look forward to the time we will once again be together." The words and sentiment brought a mist to her eyes.

"Stop!" she commanded herself. "How have you become so sentimental?"

Mildred didn't have an answer. But, for some reason, over the past few months, she had grown rather melancholy about a great many things. At times she was despondent for no reason she could discern. And, at other times, fits and bursts of anger rose to the surface seemingly from nowhere and without cause.

"Hello!" Edith called from the gate. "I've taken you up on your offer, finally, and have come to see your garden." Her friend didn't enter the garden, but instead stood at the gate.

Mildred wiped her eyes with a handkerchief and then went to greet her friend. "Hello! I'm so glad you have come to visit me." She took Edith's hand. "May I show you around?"

"Please do."

The girls took on the airs and manners that Mrs. Wickliffe had described to them over the past few days.

"Oh, Mildred, it's wonderful. And you've done all this work yourself. You've pulled out the weeds and cut all this grass on your own?"

She was pleased her friend was impressed. "Not all by myself. Little Perry has been a tremendous help. He's carted so much debris away and cut all this grass." She stopped at the head of the paving stone path. With a sweep of her arm she indicated the portion that was her accomplishment.

"I've cleaned out all of this so far. Aren't these roses lovely? This morning I saw a hummingbird taking advantage of these big red flowers. I don't know what they're called." The words tumbled from her mouth. No one, beside herself and Perry, had shown a lick of interest in the work she'd been doing.

"It really is marvelous!" Edith, still holding on to Mildred, began walking down the path. "And, these other little paths?" She pointed into the roses. "Will you work on them, too?"

"Of course. My goal was to arrive at the center, which I think the fountain indicates." They moved to the stone basin, filled with weeds. No water flowed, so what was present was black and muck-filled. "I'm still a afraid to climb that little wall and get in there and clean it out. The water was black muck and there were weeds and leaves growing on top of the muck. Vines had taken such a strong hold of the enclosure as to totally obscure the statues.

"Well, there's plenty to do before you have to face that," said Edith who turned around, bringing Mildred, who was still clamped to her arm, around with her. "Remarkable accomplishment already."

The two girls fell silent, surveying the garden. From their vantage, the right side represented the before image and the left the nearly finished.

"I would like some lunch. And, I thought I might meddle my way into your table," said Edith with a wink.

"Well, if I weren't such a lady, I would tell you how rude you're being." Mildred took on a matronly voice. "Is it really time for lunch already?"

Edith held her lips together tight, but furiously and playfully nodded her head up and down.

"My dear, Edith, won't you please join me for luncheon?"

"I would be most pleased to do so."

Together, the girls skipped out of the garden, up the path, and toward the house running smack dab into Cole and Horatio.

The foursome was quiet, a little stunned to see the others. It was Edith who finally shattered the moment: "Horatio, I've been invited to join Miss Greene for luncheon."

"I have, too, dear sister, by Mr. Parker."

Cole and Horatio allowed the girls to enter the house first and then followed.

"I'll be just a moment," said Mildred as she stepped out of the group, walked down the little hallway, and entered the butler's pantry. There, she discovered one of the serving girls folding napkins. She tried to remember the girl's name, but couldn't. "Please let Cook know we'll be four for lunch."

"Yes, Miss," said the girl with a bowed head and a curtsey.

Mildred returned to her guests and brother, trusting that when they entered the dining room together the table would be properly set. She'd had talks with the serving girls and the cook about how the house would now be run. Although, she'd also learned that footmen should be serving at table and they didn't have any of those. She didn't know yet how to hire staff, but she would ask Mrs. Wickliffe.

Thirty-Nine

Parker Greene heard the chimes announcing Rifle Helm's arrival. He bound out of his chambers only to find a little woman opening the door and welcoming his dinner guest.

"Lord Greene!" Rifle called, dropped his hat with the girl, and approached the master of the house. The two men hugged once again, holding each other for a long embrace without words but filled with information.

"I'm so pleased to see you." They broke their hold. "I have given the women the night off, once the meal is served. We'll have the whole evening alone together." Parker couldn't stifle his broad smile and was happier still to see it reflected on Rifle's face.

"Excellent."

The men stood for a long moment assessing each other. Through their open faces and relaxed posture, they knew already they were on the same page. "Here, I brought this for you." Helms handed Parker a bottle of wine.

"Thank you." Greene inspected the label. It was a French vintage. The date was the year Parker's brother had disappeared. Parker looked expectantly at his guest, but Rifle only continued smiling.

A maid joined them near the entry where the two still stood. "Would you enjoy drinks in the parlor before dinner?"

"No, let's get right to it. Please lay out the meal on the buffet, and then you may all take your leave. We will be just fine on our own. And, we will have this with dinner." He moved to hand the bottle to the maid.

"Perhaps we should save that for after." Rifle's tone was, once again, filled with coded nuance.

Greene pulled back the bottle toward his chest. "As you recommend," he replied, with an acknowledging tone.

"As you gentleman wish. Give us just a moment." She rushed from the room, skirts sweeping the floor around her.

"Where do they get all these dwarfs?" Rifle asked. "I've been here for years, and still don't understand it."

"They do seem to be everywhere, don't they? And, those pointed rings. Each one of them wears one." Again the two stood staring at each other until it felt a bit awkward. "I'm the master of this strange house. Let's just go in." He led the way into the small dining room to discover a stream of women, like a line of ants, entering the room, each depositing a dish, glass, or tray in its perfect location, and departing in a merge-like dance out through the same door they arrived, alternating one arrival, one departure with a perfectly swinging door.

With the table set and a line of steaming food on the buffet, the men set about filling their plates and sitting down at the table. Rifle took the initiative and filled glasses for both of them, one of water and another of wine.

A girl entered, stopped close to Parker. "Will that really be all, sir?"

"Yes. All of you should now vacate my home. All of you."

The girl curtsied so low, her head dropped below the tabletop.

"We have so much to discuss. What is your plan?" Rifle Helms launched immediately into the discussion.

Parker, with a raised hand of caution, spoke: "Let us take a few moments to enjoy our meal before we embark down that path. These walls still have ears." As he spoke, the two men heard the scurry of small feet nearby. In silence only broken by noises of approval, the two dug in joyfully to their meal.

Forty

While they dined, the girls with their heads together talking, and the boys in the same position, a wind swept through Wickwillowshire bringing a sky of heavy dark clouds. When the girl offered Mildred her bowl of pudding, she whispered to her: "Please have the servants close the windows against the storm."

"Yes, Miss," said the girl. She finished her task of serving and left the room in a rush.

As the foursome finished lunch they could hear the windows, one after another, rhythmically closing throughout the house. Cole turned to his sister and offered a smirk. She knew what he was thinking, that if she hadn't ordered all the windows to be opened, they wouldn't have to be closed now. But, he didn't speak a word to her. He hadn't spoken more than the most minor of pleasantries to her since their breakfast argument a few days earlier, and it was getting on her nerves. She missed her brother and his kindnesses. And, didn't know how to change the situation.

After lunch, with rain pounding against Wickwillow Manor, the girls retired to the parlor and the boys disappeared somewhere else into the house.

Edith plopped down onto a sofa, her limbs akimbo on the richly upholstered cushions. "What shall we do now, Mildred?"

Mildred looked around the room. "We could play the piano together. Your father chastises me because I don't practice enough."

Edith shook her head. "No."

"I have some new yarn that we could ball together. That would be a great help to me, because I don't like to ask the servants to help me. I never know what to say to them, but it's terribly difficult for me to do it by myself." She missed Miss Canton. Of course, while the tutor had resided in their home, she'd resented having to help her with the menial tasks, like balling yarn, but now that there wasn't anyone to look after her, she sometimes felt lost and alone. Especially in the evenings after dinner, and now even more so since her brother wasn't speaking to her at all.

"Fine," said Edith.

Mildred gathered up the three skeins of yarn, their soft pastel colors a great contrast to the rooms darker décor. Together, with Mildred holding the first skein of yarn in her two hands after having found the free end, gently rolled her hands as Edith formed the ball. They quickly found a rhythm. While silent in the moment, Mildred liked the feel of working together with Edith. She watched her friend as she focused on forming the ball, turning it expertly in her small hands forming the most even ball of yarn Mildred had ever seen. She wanted to ask her how she managed to do that, keep the thing so even, yet she didn't want to break the spell that had formed in the short minutes that had passed.

"What will you make?" asked Edith, her eyes still firmly on her task.

"What?" Mildred felt confused in the moment and that embarrassed her.

"With the yarn. What do you plan to make?"

"I was thinking of crafting a light shawl. Something I can put over my shoulders at night while I sit at my desk and write to Uncle. Sometimes, even in the dead of summer, the house grows a bit chilly in the evening."

"May I see your room?" Edith asked as they started on the second skein of yarn, this one a contrasting and lighter blue than the first.

"I suppose so. I've never had anyone in there before, well other than Cole or Lorain." She thought for a moment, "or the servants, of course."

Edith didn't speak, but nodded her head as she listened. The girl didn't make eye contact with Mildred, keeping her focus on the perfectly forming ball in her hands.

Again, Mildred wanted to ask her how she did that, kept the form so regulated. Her own balls of yarns always were misshapen and lopsided. But, once again, embarrassed by the question, she refrained.

"I guess we could go up there once were finished here."

Lightning brightened the room with a flash and a long roll of thunder followed.

Edith jumped at the sound. "I hate these storms. I've lived all over England because of Father's work, and nowhere I've ever been have the storms been as violent as here."

"I hadn't noticed that there had been any storms since you arrived," said Mildred, her hands rhythmically rolling to allow the thread Edith worked slip as easily as possible from the source.

"Oh, there was a horrible storm a few nights ago, in the middle of the night. Woke me up from a wonderful dream. We were sitting in your garden, it looked much different in my dream because, of course, I'd never seen it before today. Anyway, we were having a lovely time walking along the paths, feeding fish in the fountain, and so forth, when this horrible storm came up."

"In the dream or for real?"

Edith looked up from her work, her hands stopped their motion. She tilted her head ever so slightly to one side. "I don't know. I don't know if the storm was in my dream or if it woke me from the dream."

Another crash of thunder caused Edith to let out the smallest of screams.

Mildred, tethered as she was with her hands full of yarn, moved a bit closer to her friend and pressed her shoulder kindly into Edith's. The two shared that moment of intimacy and then, as if nothing had happened, Edith's face calmed and she returned to her work.

Rain now pounded against the glass. The sound was deafening.

When they'd finished the second skein and before moving to the third, Mildred turned up the nearest gas lamp in an attempt to counter the darkness brought on by the storm. They sat in the small circle of light and quickly went to work on the third skein. Rapidly, without any further conversation, the girls galloped through the chore bringing it quickly to completion.

Edith dropped the finished ball of yarn into the sewing basket and then slipped closer to Mildred who placed an arm around her friend's shoulders. Together, they sat in the gloom in silence. Mildred listened to her friend's labored breathing. She wanted to console her, but as she tried out phrases in her head, "It's going to be all right, dear," and the like, they sounded trite. They sounded fake, like the sentiments Lorain had expressed to her when she awoke from a bad dream, or found herself frightened by a spider. So, she chose not to speak, instead just holding one arm around Edith's shoulder and taking up her friend's hand with the other.

Edith folded into her embrace.

The air in the room grew thick and humid from the frenetic storm. Mildred felt her face grow warm, then flush, then damp. But, her hands were occupied touching Edith. There was nothing she could do but suffer the slight discomfort, or remove her hands and cause discomfort for her friend.

Mildred thought for a moment. She realized that she liked holding Edith in her arms. She'd never felt the sensations in her chest, or the sensation in her nether regions before. Nothing like this. She suddenly had a strong desire to kiss Edith. With pounding heart, she moved her head closer and in very slow motion lowered her lips to her friend's cheek.

Mildred's eyes were closed. She had thoughts about Edith she'd never experienced before. She longed for Edith to return her touch, her kiss. She wanted to feel Edith's lips against hers.

Edith turned toward Mildred. She brought her lips to meet those of her friend and hostess. For a long moment, the girls simply let their lips rest together without movement or breath.

Mildred's emotions grew violent. She wanted to push hard into her friend, pin her beneath her and hold their lips together forever. She felt hot and sweaty and rain poured harder and harder against their home. She wondered if her actions and thoughts, which seemed both so perfect and so wrong at the very same time would cause God to release his fury through the storm and destroy the house around them until the two young women were killed violently and buried in the rubble never to be discovered again.

As her thoughts raced, Edith rose her hand to Mildred's cheek and cupped the moist flesh in her small fingers.

It felt like the thunderbolts that had been clashing outside now ran through Mildred's limbs, body, and soul. She responded to that gentle touch with more pressure of her lips on Edith's. As she did so, Edith darted her tongue into Mildred's mouth. She'd never felt that before. No one had ever done that to her. What was just a breath ago lightning coursing through her, now included thunder as her whole body shuddered. She felt in that moment that she had no control over anything. Her body ceased to exist. She saw green meadows covered by all manner of red flowers gently and easily moving in the soft breezes.

Mildred copied her friend's actions. First she raised a hand to Edith's cheek, and then she slipped her own tongue into the girl's mouth. The sensation was beyond description. She lost track fully of where she began and where Edith ended. They had somehow become a single entity.

Just as it had started, from a loud crack of thunder, a fresh jolt of lightning flash and a whip crack burst of thunder, jolted the girls apart.

Mildred felt excited and embarrassed and began to turn her head away from Edith, but her friend, with a knowing in her eyes that belied Edith's age, held Mildred's head in place and looked deep into her eyes.

Forty-One

With a sense of joy and satisfaction, Parker Greene, still seated at the head of the dining room table, exhaled a great cloud of cigar smoke over his head. He slogged down the last of the brandy in his snifter. While he puffed on his cigar some more, he smiled as the tall, handsome Rifle Helms filled both their glasses with more liquor.

"So, then, she removed her wooden leg and beat Burbank senseless shouting, 'Take advantage of my whore? Take advantage of my whore?'" Helms sipped brandy through his laughter, snorting a bit. "It took three of his mates to break them up and drag him out of the whorehouse. He survived, but was never really right in the head after that."

The two men's laughter died down. "Oh, my friend, I've missed you. You tell a story better than anyone." Parker tamped ashes into a saucer, among the remains from dinner.

"I feel like we should tidy this mess up." Rifle stacked a few of the dishes nearest him without much enthusiasm.

"Should we retire upstairs?"

The two men looked from the dirty dishes and silver toward each other.

"I didn't think…I…"

"Like magic, you appear before me today. A bit of the past. An important bit. I don't care what they think or know at this point."

As Parker spoke, something in Rifle Helms' eyes softened. He reached a hand toward Parker's and rested his atop his friends.

A shudder ran through Parker Greene. He felt the blood shift in his body as his erection formed fast and hard and tight against his trousers.

"Park, we have to be careful. This isn't just us on a deserted island. I've seen men, and women, too, hanged for what you're suggesting." Rifle didn't remove his hand. Instead, he rubbed his index finger along the length of Parker Greene's.

"I don't care," Lord Greene proclaimed, standing. Rifle followed his lead and the two men, with an easy, comfortable step, were entwined in each other's arms. Any onlooker could tell that this wasn't the first time these two men had embraced. There was a comfort and ease, mixed with longing and desire in the way their arms came around each other; in the way their chests pressed together; in the way their lips crushed together, before parting enough to allow hungry tongues to wander and explore.

Greene's erection was matched by Helms' own. The two began stripping off each other's clothes. Layers and layers of coats, vests, cravats, ruffled shirts, boots, trousers…it felt endless as their clothes intertwined and undulated easier than the two men.

Finally, the two stood naked, still groping and exploring each other's bodies with hands and tongues and knees and feet. Greene enjoyed again the broad chest of Helms, its thick black curly hair growing damp with a mix of perspiration and wet kisses. Helms kneading Parker's ass with his large, thin-fingered hands. Both men breathing shallow and quick, their cocks pushing into each other's flat, muscled stomachs, growing wet and slippery from pre-cum.

"I can't wait any longer," Parker panted as he wrapped his arms around Rifle's broad shoulders, pulling him even closer.

Rifle Helms, without a prompt, dropped to his knees, took Lord Greene's pulsing cock into his mouth, and with rapid movements bobbed his head up and down, taking all of his lord and lover into his throat.

Parker's hands dropped into Rifle's sweat matted locks, directed the movements of his friend's head, as he thrust himself deeper and deeper until Rifle Helms let out the smallest of choking sounds as his lover released his passion inside of him. Simultaneously, Rifle shot his own manly passions over Parker Greene's shins and feet.

Rifle suckled and cooed until Parker softened and begged for his friend to stop. He dropped to his knees and once again they smothered each other with kisses, kisses that now tasted intimately of Parker Greene.

"I'm so glad we've run into each other," Rifle murmured into Greene's neck.

After a few moments of recovery, Parker stood and pulled Helms up with him. "Grab those clothes." Greene collected the brandy bottle and the remains of a sugary apple pie and led his guest up to his comfortable bedroom. He took a moment to be sure he'd locked the door, before they settled into the four poster bed.

As he watched Rifle sleep, Parker hoped he could trust his old friend.

He was desperate to tell someone of the plan he'd developed that would allow destruction of his pirate captors and his own return to his beloved England. Risking your life for sex was one thing, but risking it for treason was another. He only had until the Balsa Robin's return, and he didn't know when that would be. But, he had the workings of a plan. All he needed now was a second and a crew to help him.

Forty-Two

Mildred started at the abrasive knock at her bedroom door. She pulled on her robe, suspecting that the intruder was a house maid. Now that she'd taken a more active role in the household duties, giving instructions on meals, having pictures moved, and noticing when a grate hadn't been cleaned properly, the women who worked in the house were a constant bother to her, coming to her, as it were, with all manner of troubles, both related to Wickwillow Manor, and their personal lives.

She opened the door a crack, ready to send the intruder away. Certainly, any problem of the moment could wait until morning. Standing before her was her brother looking wet and disheveled.

"Cole!" She eyed him from his mud splattered boots and pants legs, to his open shirt, to soft brown curly hair plastered to his head. "What on earth has happened to you?"

"May I come in?"

"Of course," said Mildred as she held the door open further to allow his entrance. "But, please don't flop yourself down on my couch. You'll dirty it." She moved to her closet and retrieved a towel, which she placed over the old chair that no one liked. "Sit here," she instructed. Next, she moved toward the fireplace and gave the coals a stir which brought the fire up. It had been a cool several days with the rain and wind and she'd had fires lit in the most used rooms, including her own bedroom.

Before sitting where instructed, Cole moved to the fire and held out his hands.

"You'll catch your death wandering around all wet and damp. Why don't you go change your clothes and come back?"

"This can't wait," said Cole, but he went no further.

"Shall I ring for some tea?" Mildred offered. Their days and days of not speaking made this moment awkward for both of them.

"No." He turned, not really to face her, but to warm his backside nearer the low flames. "Something horrible has happened. I shouldn't even tell you, you being such a young girl, but…"

As his words trailed off, so did his eyes. For a few moments, Mildred didn't think he was in the room, not in his mind anyway. First, he simply looked distanced, as if he was thinking about some past memory, a haunting past. Then, his face contorted into something almost grotesque. From the look of him, Mildred softened her mood and attitude. While they'd had their squabble, they were, nonetheless, still brother and sister. More than that, they were friends.

Steam began to escape from Cole's damp clothes and Mildred did worry for his health and well-being. She urged him back to her. "Won't you please tell me what's happened, Cole? It can't be bad as all that." Mildred took him by the arm and guided him gently to the chair next to the fire. He allowed himself to be arranged in the chair and, just for a moment, Mildred saw the child in him, the innocent boy who was her friend.

She pulled the chair from her desk close to him, near enough that their knees could touch, although because of his muddy state, she avoided that contact.

Mildred allowed him his silence, watching him while navigating her position close enough to take his hands into hers if the need arose. She was taken back to when they were both very young. It must have been twelve or thirteen years ago. Father, as usual, was away. It was very late at night, or possibly very early in the morning. Christmas morning. Cole looked similar as he sat in her rooms confessing that he'd discovered that Father Christmas had been there. Instead of waiting, or even waking his sister, he'd opened all the presents on the tree. After the joyful moment of ripping open every single package, not only those with his name on them, he'd gone into a panic and had awoken Mildred. Together, they'd gone down to see the destruction and she'd done all she could to help him rewrap the gifts and retie the ribbons. In the morning, when Lorain finally awoke, the two of them were on the floor, opening their gifts so that it looked like it had only just happened. Lorain was suspicious of them, but no one, not a single servant, offered them any grief.

Mildred knew, that just like that early morning so long ago, she would do all in her power and abilities to help her troubled brother. "Cole, if I'm to help, you must tell me what has happened."

He looked up at her. He'd returned to the moment; tears stained his face. "Dear Sister, how can something that seems so right in the moment, feel so terribly wrong later?"

Mildred thought for a moment and decided that Cole's question must be one of a rhetorical nature. She chose not to offer a response.

"I've done something horrible."

Mildred was growing unnerved. "You simply must tell me."

"Horatio and I were riding. It was wonderful. My horse was able to keep up with his mechanical one. We were riding out over those open fields well back beyond our home. You know, that rising meadow where you like to go and gather flowers in the springtime?"

Mildred nodded both to acknowledge the place and to offer encouragement.

Cole's tone remained calm, even. "Well, suddenly, out of nowhere, a storm came up. Just like it did the other day, remember, after we'd had lunch with Horatio and Edith. Well, Horatio and I have become friends and it's so nice to have a friend. It's been so long since there was a boy around for me to, well, play with." Cole scoffed at the words. "I'm acting like I'm eight-years-old."

"It's so good to have friends to share time with," encouraged Mildred.

"Oh, Sister, I'm so sorry about how I've been acting toward you. I'm feeling so lost in my role as man of the house. I'm trying my best, but feel such a failure."

"Cole, come back to the horse ride with Horatio."

"Yes, yes. Well, the storm came up and ahead of us was that old stone house, you know the one. It's been empty our whole lives. We tethered my horse, there was nothing to do for the mechanical one, it had to remain in the rain, and we got inside. Most of the roof is gone, but there were a few corners that provided a bit of cover from the torrent."

"Well, that was helpful."

He looked at his sister again as if he didn't know her. She took his hand and he pulled it away.

"So, we were sitting there and sitting there and the rain wasn't letting up. So, I gathered up some debris and managed to get a fire going."

"That was good thinking," said Mildred, trying to picture the scene in her head of the old stone house without a roof.

"We sat close to the fire, trying to keep warm and dry. Our knees were touching. I, I don't know why I did it, but I placed my hand on his leg, just above his knee. He felt so warm to me. Before I knew it, his arm was around my shoulder and we huddled together. It seemed less about the cold and rain and more about something else. Desire, perhaps."

As he talked, Mildred remembered with fondness and discomfort the kiss she'd shared with Edith on the day of the first storm.

"Are you hearing me?" Cole's voice was louder, but only a little bit.

"Yes, Brother, I'm hearing you."

"I don't know why I did it, but I leaned into Horatio and kissed him. At first he didn't respond, but then before I knew it, he kissed me back. Oh, it felt so nice. I'd forgotten in that moment that it was wrong to do such things. Men don't kiss men, not in that way. This wasn't like Uncle kissing the top of my head good night. This was ardent, amorous. I was excited and aroused.

"We'd been swimming a while ago. We'd stripped down at the river, you know, the place Uncle built for us with the rope. We'd stripped out of our clothes and, when I saw him naked, I imagined kissing him and holding him and making love with him. And, here we were, trapped by the rain, pulling at each other's buttons and ties until we were naked, making love on the dirty floor in front of the fire in that wretched little house. Oh, Sister, it was wonderful to be with someone, to know what it feels like to touch and kiss another person…"

Mildred blushed at the image of her brother naked and writhing with the vicar's son. Yet, momentarily, changed the scene's players into her and Edith. The little house once again had a roof and clean floors, flowers on the mantle, and comfortable furniture for she and her lover to enjoy, rather than being on a stone floor in the dirt debris.

"That's when I hit him."

"I'm sorry, what?"

"Not Horatio, some man who was standing in the doorway watching us. I was startled by him when he whistled and uttered a vulgarity I can't repeat to you. I stood, and socked him hard. He fell back and then ran away across the field toward town. I'm sure he's already told everyone that Lord Greene's boy is a queer. That the vicar's son is a pervert."

"What happened next?"

Cole looked hard at his sister.

"What did you and Horatio do?"

"We could hardly look at each other from the shame of the scene. It was no longer a magic time filled with love and tenderness, but we became fully aware of the horrible acts we'd committed and the fact that everyone would know about them before we arrived back home. We dressed with our backs to each other. We went out to get on our horses and return home, but his mechanical horse wouldn't start, I guess from the wetness. I gave Horatio my horse to ride home, but he insisted that we both ride her together. Which we did. Me in front, him in the rear holding on to me. Oh, the touch of his hands on me, his arms around me, his body warming my back as we rode was both the most amazing thing I've ever experienced and the most horrifying."

"Come with me," she said, helping him stand. She wrapped her arms around her brother. He resisted at first, but then slowly took the kindness and crumpled into her arms. He sobbed as Mildred cooed in his ear. She thought nothing of the dirt and grime that would cause her to have to change bedclothes and simply did all she could, which seemed very little, to soothe her brother. She wanted him to bathe. She wanted to get some warm tea into him. She wanted to somehow change the sequence of events and keep her brother safe from the scorn of others.

She realized as he sobbed, that he'd fallen in love with Horatio. It was just like a scene from one of the pot boiler novels she'd read, only the actors in this scene weren't a man and a woman, but instead two men. And, she reasoned with herself, what was so terribly wrong with that. She herself had strong, loving feelings for Edith, why couldn't or even shouldn't Cole have similar feelings for Horatio? They were both strong, handsome men. They were from good families. Why shouldn't they be allowed to love the one they wished?

"Come, brother." Mildred guided him out of her room and into his own. They were met in the hall by Marcus, the houseman who was going through the halls and turning down all the gas lamps. "Marcus, please have hot water brought up so Cole can bathe. Have some hot tea sent up quickly, as well."

"Yes, Miss. Is the master well?"

Mildred thought for a moment. "He'll be fine. He got caught in the storm, that's all. Now away with you and hurry please."

She didn't look after the houseman, but instead steered Cole down the hall. It had been months since she'd been inside her brother's rooms which, despite the best efforts of the maids, were a cluttered mess of books, papers, drawings, and clothes strewn about. She wanted to chastise him, but thought better of it. He didn't need any more trouble this evening. Instead, she played mother. She acted at being Lady of the Manor and offered her time and attention to getting her brother cleaned up, into fresh dry clothes, and drinking a mug of hot tea with a little brandy. As she helped him undress, bathe, and put on a soft nightshirt, neither sibling offered any shyness or discomfort. It all felt medicinal to Mildred.

After settling Cole into bed, Mildred returned to her own rooms and lay in bed exhausted from the day. She thought of Cole, finally asleep. She'd heard about similar scandals, of men doing things with other men and upon discovery being run out of town. Those stories, while shared widely, were always shared in hushed tones with darting eyes. She wondered what would become of them, what would become of the Wickliffe family. She'd become fond of all of them. But, surely, as those below their own class, it would be easy enough to place the blame on them, freeing her brother from scrutiny and scorn. That was her role, certainly, to protect her family and its standing in society.

Yet, as she considered how to protect Cole, her thoughts drifted again and again to her kiss on the parlor couch with Edith. Had anyone seen the two of them? Some house girl perhaps? Shudders ran through her causing goose flesh to rise on her arms and neck.

Mildred sat at her desk with the intention of writing. She absently played with the mechanical toy rabbit. She longed for her uncle's return. She longed even for Lorain, who would at least provide information from what those in town were speaking of. She feared there would be some knock on the door and people with fire and pitchforks would run them out of town. With these thoughts drifting through her head, she gave up trying to write and fell into bed for a restless night's sleep.

Forty-Three

The sun was high when Lord Greene awoke with a start at the soft rap at the door. He opened his eyes, having momentarily forgotten where he was. There, next to him, uncovered, naked, chest rising and falling evenly in sleep, lay Rifle Helms. Parker smiled at the remembrance of the previous night and morning, so glad to have a friend and compatriot literally at his side.

Again, a louder rap at the door. "sir?" It was one of the ever-changing house maids.

"Yes," Parker said, hoping not to wake the beautiful vision lying next to him. That taut flat stomach, hairy crotch offering a nest to the now soft, but perfect cock. Greene felt a pang of desire in his ass.

The wench at the door attempted its handle, but he'd taken care to secure the lock.

"Mmmmm," Rifle murmured. With eyes still closed he softly scratched himself, from muscled thighs over furry balls, up that V-shaped torso, to his strong, in-need-of-a-shave chin. "Is there breakfast, sir?" he asked as his eyes opened revealing a sparkle that melted Greene's heart. "Tell her breakfast for two in the dining room in ten minutes. What's gotten into you, Parker?" Rifle playfully poked his friend's side, shifted, and took Greene's stiffening cock into his mouth once more.

Lord Greene murmured approval. He also repeated Rifle's command to the serving girl.

"Yes, sir," came through the door.

Greene and Helms sat at the table, consuming huge mounds of foods and cup after cup of strong, black coffee. The staff of women who served them showed no shock or dismay at Lord Greene's company. In fact, from Greene's perspective, it seemed that all the women showed signs that they knew his guest well.

Parker swallowed a mouthful of pancakes with a syrup he'd never tasted before, sweet and thick and rich. In a whisper he asked, "Do you know these women?"

Helms leaned forward. "Well, very well." The man looked around to see if anyone was within hearing distance and he whispered. "We've been working on a plan to help them escape from the island. We've figured out how to shut the place down with minimum death and harm. We just haven't got the leaving part. My little women could never overpower the crew of the Balsa Robin. And that's what we'd need. There are thousands of them to get off the islands."

Greene thought for a moment. He pondered if he truly could trust his old friend. He'd been questioning that all night as they'd once again consummated a very long friendship and love affair. They'd been lovers on many of Her Royal Majesty's missions. They'd joked repeatedly that if they were man and woman they'd have wed years ago. In fact, the joke reemerged last night. He chose trust. "I've worked out that plan; I just require a crew of knowledgeable men to fly it."

"That ship is filled with little men. The pages know every nook and cranny of the air ship."

One of the women entered with a platter of fresh, tropical fruits. The men fell silent. She placed the tray between them, curtsied, and received a wink and a nod from Rifle Helms. There was a broad smile on her face as she retreated from the room.

"I'm ready to hear more, Parker. Don't keep me in suspense."

As his last word hung in the air, Ablest Currant strode into the room. "What have we here?" he took a slice of watermelon from the tray without invitation.

Greene looked from a white-faced Helms to a red-faced Currant as he felt a bit of the blood drain from his own head.

Forty-Four

Mildred sat quietly at the breakfast table. The newspaper rested next to her brother's place setting. She wanted to pick it up and read it. She instead sipped tea from a delicate cup and waited for her brother's arrival to ring the bell for service of her breakfast. Her feelings of helplessness, while less in the morning light streaming through the open dining room windows, persisted. But, it was nice to have sunlight instead of storm clouds and she longed to eat and get into her garden to see what all the rain had produced. She knew the flowers would be happy to have the return of the sun and hoped they might be putting on a show for her.

Yet, she didn't rush. She didn't have breakfast alone. She waited for her brother to emerge from his room and for them to find some form of normalcy between them once more, at least in their routines. Mildred thought of his haggard look as she tucked him, clean, dry and warm, into his large bed. While he'd been in the bath, she'd tidied his room a bit by moving stacks of belongings and folding shirts and trousers. She'd had the serving girl take away his soiled clothes, so they could be cleaned and pressed. She'd taken Mrs. Wickliffe's advice and had not spoken about any of what had happened with Cole with any of the servants. She did make one small comment as the young girl with wide eyes looked about Cole's room: "Not a word about this to anyone." The girl didn't speak, but curtsied and hurried away.

So, now she sat, thinking once again about the improvements she would make to this house once she was able to have installed the steam powered drive shaft. She envisioned that it would run not below the floor, but instead under a drop ceiling of ornately carved wood panels. They would add elegance to the house, while also allowing simple access to the mechanisms they concealed. The shaft, behind secret walls, could be connected to all manner of items she'd design and have built.

Mildred, sometime between working in the garden and dreaming in her bed, had decided that she didn't want to become a builder of inventions, but simply the inventor and the overseer of their construction. She'd realized that there was some level of enjoyment found for her when getting her hands dirty with the rich soil, but yet she drew a line at having her hands covered in grease and oil.

"Good morning, Sister," said Cole.

Mildred looked up from her thoughts to find her brother, tall and handsome, smiling as if nothing had happened in his life.

He sat at his spot at the table, glanced at the day's headline, and pushed the newspaper aside. He reached for the tea pot, "I thought there would be coffee."

Without a word, Mildred rang the bell and placed a hand atop her brother's. The servant girl arrived. "Please, bring our breakfast and a pot of coffee for Mr. Parker."

The girl removed herself from the room with a "Yes, Ma'am."

"Well, look at you, playing Lady of the Manor."

She smiled shyly at her brother.

"It suits you well," he said, taking the paper in hand and opening it.

The siblings sat in silence, Cole reading the news and Mildred simply and patiently waiting for her food to be served. She wanted to speak again of last night. She wanted to assure Cole that she loved him and stood behind him no matter what might come of the recent events. But, she held her tongue and willed her stomach not to make a sound as her hunger grew.

While she waited, she contemplated, too, telling Cole about her own romantic encounter with Edith. But, once again decided there was not reason or need at this time to share such a story. It might only serve to upset her brother and it was nice to see him so calm and even in his tempers.

Two girls arrived from the swinging door and placed plates in front of the Parker children. The taller of them poured Cole a cup of coffee and placed the silver pot on the table. They ate with gusto, while remaining silent. It was only after he'd finished his first cup of coffee and the meat from his plate that Cole, while pouring a second cup for himself asked: "So, what plans do you have today?"

Mildred contemplated her options. "I was planning on spending the morning in the garden."

"I think it might be too damp from all the rain we've endured. Perhaps, instead, you'd consider spending the morning in the tower helping with the clock?" He hadn't made eye contact with her; instead his head was still down, with eyes focused on the newsprint.

Mildred studied her brother's face. It was soft without line or wrinkle, except for the slight crease between his eyebrows, just like their father. She didn't know when that had appeared and tried to think back. She hadn't even noticed it last evening when she'd done all she could to focus on her brother's face instead of his naked body as she'd helped him in and out of the bath. Yet, she didn't remember that line being there.

"I'd be happy to work on the clock with you," she said, eating the last of the scone slathered in soft butter and honey. She'd eaten honey, without even thinking about it. She thought of her bees and placed the sticky treat on her plate. "I do have to speak to the staff about lunch and dinner for today, and I do want to at least take a stroll around the garden to see the state of things there."

"As you wish." He pushed the paper away, took a last gulp of coffee, and stood. "I'll be in the clock tower, you join me when you're ready." His tone wasn't like the old Cole, there was a lack of playfulness. Yet, it also was much better than the bitter angry boy he'd been over the past week. There was a solid strength that was new.

Mildred watched him leave the room. His shoulders were square, he stood to his full height. It was as if nothing out of the ordinary had happened between them. It was as if the fight that had filled the last week with a combination of silence and sudden outbursts had never occurred. It was as if last night, their closeness and support of each other was something out of a dream instead of being a reality that they'd shared.

Entering the garden, Mildred discovered Edith sitting on one of the benches along the wall. Perry was at work with a scythe cutting the tall grass well beyond the honeybee hives. The boy was making remarkable progress, much more so than her.

"Mildred! You've arrived." Edith bounced up from her spot and joined her friend close to the gate. "Look at all the color today!"

"Hello, Edith." The girls, arm in arm, walked the main path and admired the brilliant reds, yellows, and pinks of the gnarled rose bushes. "The book says these must be cut back and trimmed," said Mildred sharing the knowledge she'd gained about roses from her father's books, "but, I do love them in their current form, overgrown and a bit out of control."

"They seem natural," Edith agreed.

They reached the end of the path, well, not really the end, but as far as Mildred had so far cleared. The large fountain, after the days of rain, was now filled not only with overgrown plants, but water and a mucky soup, too. A group of gnats and flies hovered above the rank reservoir. Mildred guided her friend back the way they had come and they arrived at the gate.

"I do not wish to be rude, but I have promised my brother that I'd help him with his clock this morning."

"Can we speak for a few moments first?" Edith seemed suddenly agitated.

"Of course," said Mildred, still tethered to Edith, their arms entwined together. The girls went back to the stone bench and sat.

Edith looked around to discover Perry's location, and, feeling he was sufficiently distant enough she began: "Now Mildred, I want to share a story with you. Please don't interrupt me. I want to get it out quickly." Her tones were hushed and her eyes were wide.

"I'm listening," said Mildred.

Edith removed her hand from the crook of her friend's arm. "We have moved several times in recent years. We sometimes don't stay more than a few weeks in any one location. For a long time I didn't understand our moving about so, but father assured me, when I asked, that this was the life of a vicar. That we must go where God calls us. But, the last time, we left in the middle of the night after packing in haste. That was right before we came here. Our house was very small and the walls were thin. I heard my father telling my mother that Horatio had been buggered by a stableman. I hate that word, 'buggered.' Anyway, I heard my father and mother last evening and there's speculation that he's done something like that again. I don't know where or with whom, but he came in very late last night, drenched to the bone and shortly after there was a knock at the door. I don't know who it was or what was said, but I heard my mother ask my father if we'd be moving again. He said not right away, but most probably." Edith sat with her back against the stone wall.

"Sit forward, Edith. You'll soil your dress on the mossy wall." Mildred guided her friend.

"That's all you have to say?" Edith wouldn't make eye contact, instead she focused on a thumbnail and a piece of skin that was hanging there.

Mildred wanted to share what she knew, that it was Cole that Edith's brother had been with last night. She wondered if their own actions might have been discovered, too. She mourned that people weren't allowed to care for and love those they wanted. She hated that her brother's activities had such terrible names such as "buggered" and "perverted." But, she also knew that it wasn't her lot in life to change all of society and the way that society thought. Yet, she cared deeply for Edith and hated the idea that she might lose her friend to the scandal, should one emerge.

"I care so much for you," said Mildred. "I'd hate to lose you so quickly."

Edith finally looked up at her friend. There were tears in her eyes, but a smile on her face. "That's all you have to say? Nothing in judgment about poor Horatio."

Again Mildred contemplated her options. "Oh, Edith, I so want to tell you something, but I fear the knowing of it, or my saying it aloud, will in some way…"

"What? You must tell me anything you think is relevant."

"Horatio was with my brother last night."

"Oh, so the stories aren't true then." Edith's smile grew larger.

"They were together last night and the story you suspect about your brother is also true."

"Cole and Horatio? How could they?"

"How could we?" Mildred asked.

"Oh, our," she hesitated. "Our encounter was nothing so horrible as that."

"I fear it is exactly the same," said Mildred.

The two girls sat in silence. Mildred wondered how life went from being a childhood filled with laughter and tantrums, to speaking of such grownup topics without any grownups even around to prompt the conversations.

"You mustn't tell anyone else of what we've spoken this morning," cautioned Mildred.

"Do you really think that's best? Should I tell my father at least so he knows what Horatio has been up to? He should at least speak to my brother."

"No. Don't tell anyone. You and I are going to come up with a solution, so that you don't have to move away again. I can't fathom losing you after knowing you for such a brief period of time." Mildred hugged her friend for a long moment. "Now, I have to go meet Cole in the clock tower.

"Please," she said as they stood from the bench, "not a word to anyone."

Forty-Five

"Would you care to join us for breakfast?" Parker Greene stood to greet his guest.

"No, thank you. I ate hours ago. It's nearly lunch." Ablest Currant looked from Greene to the food on the table to Rifle Helms. "What is he doing here?"

Without hesitation, Parker pointed to his friend, "We've known each other for years. I was walking down the grand avenue yesterday afternoon and was so surprised to see him there."

"And, you invited him to breakfast?" Ablest asked. His shoulders rolled forward, his chin dropped down to his chest for a moment. He sighed, as if ready to cry, but then quickly recovered, squared his shoulders, and looked Parker Greene in the eye.

"What can I do for you this morning?" Greene sat back down, leaving Currant standing awkwardly. Parker sipped from his coffee cup and then turned his attention back to his plate of food. In that moment, he'd made the choice. Flirting with Ablest Currant had been fun, but Rifle was back in his life now. One man was plenty for anyone.

"You have a week."

"For what?" Parker asked through a mouthful of ham steak.

"To choose all the useful plans, especially the weapons. And, then you have another week to build all that you can as examples. Your life depends on there being helpful tools and new weapons for the Balsa Robin. It will return in ten days, be refurbished and outfitted with the latest you've found, and head back out." Currant picked up a piece of thick, crisp bacon and took a bite.

"Two weeks? Impossible!" Greene stood again. "Some of those inventions, well, we'll have to create tools to build them. I don't…"

"Two weeks." He ate the rest of the bacon. "It's obvious you haven't seen the workshop." Ablest turned to Helms and smiled. Rifle ignored the man. "Your friend works there. After your breakfast he can give you a tour." Currant looked once more at the two men, eating, and then turned quickly and left.

"What was all of that about?" Greene asked. "You were silent."

Rifle turned to Parker and looked him square in the eye. "Ablest and I, well, we had a brief relationship. It was just after I answered the question. He'd, well, persuaded me…"

"I understand." Greene thought back to the almost-kiss he'd had while imprisoned in the cabin.

"Really? Just like that?"

"Don't look so…however it is you look. We're not married. We've both done things over the past few years…listen to us, like two old married… finish your breakfast and take me to this workshop."

Rifle turned back to his food, satisfied. He scooped big forkfuls of eggs and pancakes into his mouth while speaking. "The workshop. Wait 'till you see this place."

Parker Greene and Rifle Helms, with hats and walking sticks, strode down the grand avenue together. Rifle waved this way and that at others who offered greetings on the street and from their verandas.

"You seem to know everyone," Parker remarked.

"It doesn't take long. This is an island of busybodies. Us taking this walk together is confirming all your neighbors' thoughts that you are queer. They all know that we spent the night together. You can tell from some of their looks that they're imagining what it is two men might do together in bed."

Greene laughed. "I'm still trying to figure that out, too."

"Always happy to help with your exploration of the male anatomy."

"You're in a good mood." Greene was aware his own step had a spark to it, too.

"I'm so glad we're together again. I've missed having someone I can trust and love in my life. I've missed comfortable moments over meals. I've missed you."

Greene stopped and Rifle did the same, turning to him. Without warning, Parker pulled Helms to him and kissed his friend hard on the mouth. Somewhere nearby a neighbor or passerby let out a catcall.

Rifle didn't pull away, but when the kiss ended, he said in a whisper, "It's one thing for everyone to know what happened with us, it's something else to show them. You can still be hung on this island for what we did last night...hell, for what we just did on the street. We don't need to change the world here, just defeat it."

It was the first mention of taking down the pirates. Over the past few hours, Greene had decided to trust Rifle, no matter what the outcome of that decision meant. It would be better to go down loving someone than never trusting anyone again. And, his statement of desire to defeat their captors cinched the deal. He felt desperate to be alone with Helms, not only to enjoy his body, but to share with him the plan that had been brewing for several days. But, there wasn't time now.

"Here we are."

They'd arrived at the avenue's end, the water's edge. It was at the fully opposite end as how he'd entered this island with the Governor. Rifle pressed the lever, the ground opened, and a platform appeared. Without prompting, Greene stepped upon the platform, Helms followed. Another shift of the lever and they began to descend underground.

Amazed by the technology around him, Greene remained silent as his eyes adjusted to the dim electric lights and the damp air. He knew, as they left the lift and walked forward, that they were now under the ocean. The walls here were pressed with sea shells. This tunnel wasn't as well kept or comfortable as the others he'd experienced. But, it was bigger, much wider, much taller.

They traveled with only the crunch of their feet on a mixture of shell and stone. Both silent. Had too much been shared or said? No, it was what was coming next. The anticipation of this workshop silenced Greene. Again, they reached a dead end. They turned 180 degrees.

Helms hit a lever. "Just wait."

Greene loved how excited his friend was. A buzz grew louder and louder as the lift rose. Finally, they emerged into the middle of a raucous, busy workshop. This wasn't a mere, dark room with a few benches. No, this was the largest room Parker Greene had ever seen. Hundreds and hundreds of dwarfs, mostly men, worked at fantastical projects and inventions. It reminded Greene of something. Suddenly, the room around him grew silent, all eyes turned toward him. Santa's workshop. It's the vision he'd always had. Everyone was dressed differently. Instead of red and green, some wore elaborate plumes and great coats, others sported grey dusters covering overalls. But, to a man, they were all dwarfs. And, as he and Rifle stepped off the platform, he felt like Santa, as each small man offered him a bow or head nod.

One of the men, older than the rest, a pencil behind his ear, rushed up to him. "Lord Greene, we're so pleased you have come to visit us. We are great admirers of your work and inventions. We are great friends to you." He bowed deeply, still clutching Greene's hands.

Parker couldn't help but notice he, like the small women, wore the sharp, pointed ring. "Thank you," he offered, dumbfounded.

"We are at your service, sir. We know that you will be bringing us new plans and we are to build them as quickly as possible. Anything you desire, we can create. We might be small, but our little creative army is powerful."

"I have no doubt."

"My name is Nate, Nathanial Butler by birth. Not the famous sea captain, sadly. Don't have the height for that job." He laughed good naturedly. "Whatever you desire, Sir, come to me and I'll assign it to the best man for the job. I've been here twenty years now. I'm in charge when there isn't another to be in charge. I know every nook, cranny, and conversation that happens here."

"Well, it's good to meet you, Nate. Good to know you." Parker looked into the man's eyes and liked what he saw. There were messages shared in that moment that had nothing to do with words or language. He knew… well, that knowing would be handy later.

"This," said Rifle," is the Workshop."

Rifle and Parker, led by Nate, spent the afternoon on a tour of the benches and projects. Parker took note of anything that would fit well in his own plan, beyond knowing that he not only had an army of women, but a sizable army of little men to add to his growing idea. Life was getting better and better.

Forty-Six

Mildred and Cole stood at the top of the clock tower. A light breeze brought in the hint of summer flowers while a few pigeons, escaping the afternoon heat, roosted and cooed above them in the tower's steeple.

"Which next?" Cole asked, looking at the collection of gears and cogs leaned against two walls of the little room.

Mildred looked into her mind where a perfectly working clock of exactly this type took itself apart and placed itself back together. Once together in her mind, the clock hands whirled in perfect order and harmony. She enjoyed the vision, but, because there was work to do, she reversed the order of parts, looked around at those not yet placed, and pointed. "It's that thick one next." Cole took up the small, thick metal cog, its teeth softly gouging his stomach as he lifted the heavy part, Mildred turned back toward the clockworks, studied the slots, grooves, pins, and other pieces already in place and pointed. "It needs to fit on this pin and align with this other piece, the teeth need to align." She watched as her brother struggled to get the piece in place. He required help and, much to her dismay at soiling her hands or clothes with the oil and grease required for smooth movement of the parts, Mildred leaned in and gently pushed the aligning piece into a position that would accept the return of its playmate.

Cole, pulling his hands back, drew a rag from his back pocket and wiped his hands. He offered the thing to his sister who took it, even though it seemed like it would make the dirt on her hands worse.

They continued to work in this manner with several more pieces. They didn't speak of the previous night or of Mildred's conversation with Edith earlier that morning. If Mildred's mind was any indication, the choice to not speak was deafening. Her own thoughts were constantly churning the problem of how to keep the Wickliffe's in Wickwillow while also keeping her brother's honor and respect intact. Of course, the biggest problem seemed to be outside of their circle. Did the man who saw her brother and Horatio naked together know who either of the boys were? If he didn't know, it wouldn't really matter who he told. Although, both Cole and Horatio were quite distinctive looking, and if he got a good look at them, through his description of the boys to others, those others might be able to surmise who was there. If they went in search of the man, they would most certainly draw attention to themselves and in the process, if the man didn't know who they were, they might tip him off.

Cole had insisted the night before that he had never seen the man before. But, he had only recently started making rounds with the land manager, Mr. Eastlake, and hadn't yet met all the tenants. Wasn't it also possible that the man was only passing through the shire? Wasn't it possible that he might already be gone from their lands, having been simply a traveler? Although, Cole said he hadn't seen the man carrying anything other than a gun and basket. He might have been a poacher getting an early start on the grouse season. And, if the man were a poacher, would he be so daring as to say what he was doing on the grounds? The little stone house, after all, was on Wickwillow Manor's grounds, which their uncle did not open to hunting by his tenants. This thought caused Mildred to breathe a sigh of relief.

"What is it, can't you figure out the next piece?" asked Cole. He'd been watching his sister's expression, waiting for instructions.

"Oh," said Mildred, simply. She looked at the clockwork in her mind and pointed out the next piece and its proper location. She didn't want to speak about this subject to her brother until she had a better grasp of it or a possible plan. There was no need to upset or agitate him again.

So, the siblings continued placing piece after piece in its proper location until everything Cole had removed from the clockworks had finally been replaced. The clock was not in motion.

"What now?" he asked.

She looked hard both in her mind and at the actual clock. Everything appeared to be in perfect position.

"We must regain tension on the spring and that is done from turning that crank there," Mildred said indicating the handle. "Move around to the front side and set the time."

Cole looked at his sister. "What time is it?"

The two laughed. Neither owned a pocket watch of any sort. The only other time piece in the house was the old mantle clock, and that one hadn't worked properly for many years having been knocked off its base during a scuffle between the siblings over what neither could remember.

Cole stuck his head out the little window, attempting to judge the time by the sun. "It must be nearly noon."

"We can't just decide on some random time," insisted Mildred. She tried to think of another way. After all, she wanted to see if her instructions had brought the desired results of fixing the old clock. She could see the pendulum swing again in the lower reaches of the clock tower. She envisioned the heavy weight making its two-day journey from where they now stood down the tower's several flights, the action propelling the pendulum, which propelled the gears and cogs. The anticipation of success, which she fully believed would be achieved, was being held off simply because they didn't know what time it was.

"Can't we just start it up and set the time more correct later?" asked her brother, his hand on the crank handle.

"NO!" shouted Mildred. "We must be correct about this. It's an important thing we've done here together, fixing this clock. And, if we are successful, we'll want to know the exact time of our achievement so we can share it with Uncle Parker. This is the sort of accomplishment that legends are built up from."

Mildred liked the idea that they would fix this clock today. It was the day after her brother's troubles, so he would be redeemed in some way by the accomplishment.

They simply stood there looking at each other. The unspoken "what now?" remained in the air between them.

"Hello!" came the call from below.

Once again, Cole stuck his head out of the little window. "Mr. Wickliffe. Hello!" he called down.

"I knocked at the big door of the house, but no one answered," he called up.

"Do you know the time?" Cole shouted down.

There was a pause in the shouts between Cole and Mr. Wickliffe. Mildred's heart began beating faster. What would the vicar say about last evening? Would he be offering a tendering of resignation, isn't that what such things are called?

"Eleven fifty-two," shouted Mr. Wickliffe.

Cole quickly moved to the clock hands and after some effort, set the time to eleven fifty-three. He jumped back to the handle and tried to push it forward. It didn't budge. "Help me, Mildred."

Mildred placed her hands atop her brother's and together, with all their might, they moved the crank a half turn.

"Oil it, Cole," she said.

Cole stepped away, took up the oil can, and squirted the black lubricant into the base of the crank. He set down the can, and once again, with their two sets of hands intertwined, they pulled up on the crank handle. It moved easier. And, as they turned and turned the handle together, the going grew easier still. When they let go of the crank, they both held their breath. Nothing happened.

Mr. Wickliffe, breathing heavily after his quick journey up the staircase, looked over their shoulders at the clockworks. "Impressive," he remarked and, reaching past them, pulled a small lever neither of the children had noticed. The clockworks gave a small groan, and within another beat, the wheels and gears began to turn. "Impressive," the vicar said again.

"Cole, you've done it. You've fixed the old clock!" Mildred hugged her brother who had a self-satisfied grin that spread across his whole face.

Mr. Wickliffe clapped his back and shook his hand. "Good job, Cole. Very impressive indeed."

In that moment, Mildred thought about saying that she had helped. She wanted to tell someone that it was her doing, her seeing all the pieces in their proper place, that guided Cole to this success, but the look on her brother's face stopped her from speaking. She loved to see him so happy. She couldn't remember the last time she'd seen him smile so. His shoulders were back and straight. He looked taller than she'd remembered. He was happy and proud and Mr. Wickliffe was so proud of him. It was almost like having Father there. Almost.

Together, the threesome enjoyed the victory for another moment, mesmerized by the spin and whirl of the gears of the clockwork as the arm of the clock face moved to record another minute in the passage of human existence.

"Sister, you've soiled your dress. You must change before lunch. Mr. Wickliffe, you will, won't you please, you will join us for lunch once my sister changes her dress."

"Of course," said Mr. Wickliffe.

All three made their way down the stone stairs and back out into the sunshine of the day. It was a glorious summer afternoon with a high, full sun, bright and shining, the scent of flowers blooming in the air, and birds soaring on the breeze.

"Run, Mildred, please. Change into something more suitable."

Cole's tone had resumed that of fatherly advice. It annoyed her; he wasn't her father, Cole was her brother. She was smarter than him. She should be in charge. Mildred rushed into the house through the nearest door, the servant's back entrance. She advised Cook, who was bent over her oven, that there would be three for lunch and that it was the vicar so to be sure to offer him the best cut of meat. The cook nodded with a simple "Yes, Miss," and Mildred raced up the servant's stairs, down the hall, and into her bedroom where she quickly pulled off her top frock and chose a different dress to slip into. She rushed not only because she was indeed quite hungry, but because she didn't wish to leave Cole and Mr. Wickliffe alone for too long. She didn't want to be left out of whatever discussion had necessitated the vicar's arrival.

Forty-Seven

Nate Butler led Parker Greene and Rifle Helms toward a bank of small rooms and stopped at the one in the middle. "This one is yours while you are here. You may use it as you like."

"The coveted middle office," said Rifle good-naturedly.

The room was larger than the others, with glass on all sides making it easy to see what was happening in the workshop, the other offices, and beyond the building.

Parker stepped into the room and was drawn to the window that faced outside. It offered a framed view of all four islands; their shapes, sizes, and positions now made sense to him.

"We know about the deadline," said Butler.

Parker had gone somewhere else, the escape plan consumed his mind. Two ideas he'd had were in conflict. And now, with the thought of adding all these little men to his plan, but getting them into proper position…he realized Nate Butler was watching him, waiting for him. "What?"

"Sorry, sir. I didn't mean to interrupt your process. But, I said, we know about the two week deadline you've been given."

Greene thought about Able Currant. How the man burst into his home at will. How he'd tried to seduce him, had seduced him. Parker felt the heat of a blush cross his cheeks. He knew now, in his gut, that the handsome Currant was not to be trusted—why had he let his guard down? Because Able was handsome. Greene found his senses. Trust was now off the table, and it was time for those tables to be turned, so sex used against Able wasn't out of the question.

"Rifle, would you mind?" Parker pointed to the door.

Lover or not, the dependable man knew his place. Helms ranked under Greene, probably always would.

"Not at all, sir." There was no malice in his tone. Rifle stepped outside the office and closed the door.

"Nate, I need to spend some time here. I want to know everything you've been working on. Everything." Greene watched the little man's eyes for signs and clues. He so desperately hoped he'd picked up the coded language earlier.

The dwarf's eyes twinkled. "Everything?" he repeated.

"We understand each other?"

"In two weeks, there will be a rebellion. With your help, our clan of little people will finally find liberation! And, you will lead us there?"

Parker Greene was taken aback at how blunt Nate was being.

Butler continued without waiting for an answer: "We've been waiting for one of the Queen's leaders to arrive. We thought we'd gotten it when Helms was captured. But, we were quick to discover, as much as we liked him and as talented as he is, that Rifle is not a leader."

"No, but he's a brilliant follower." Parker's mind whirled. Could this little man be trusted? Was he being set up? Or, was this what he'd been thinking and hoping, that the dwarfs, so many of them, were here against their will.

Nate continued quickly, "Exactly. But, you. You're the real leader. There's so much for us to discuss and we can't do it here, surrounded by glass in the light of day."

"You shall dine with me." The only way to find out the truth was to talk to the man, to hear his story, and to take the risks related to building an army large enough to defeat the pirates and yet still escape. "Lunch will tell."

"Sir?" Nate asked.

Greene was content. "I have a stack of plans at my home that we must begin working on at once. Can someone please accompany me? We'll need a wagon or transport, too."

"Of course, Lord…uh…Mr. Greene." Nate flung open the door. He barked out names and commands and before another minute had passed, Lord Greene, accompanied by six small men, was headed back into the tunnel and toward his home.

Forty-Eight

The vicar's conversation over lunch was light and easy. He spoke with Mildred and Cole about the clocks he'd seen in his travels. He shared stories of a light nature from the daily newspaper as well as polite gossip about their neighbors and friends. He really was a charming meal companion and his presence provided the siblings a little time with an adult, which both, whether they were to admit it or not, enjoyed.

It wasn't until after the rich, chocolate pudding that Cole asked: "So, Mr. Wickliffe, to what do we owe the honor of your company for lunch?"

"Well, your cook is very good, and the conversation is pleasant, so that keeps me coming back." He chuckled lightly and the infectious sound caused Mildred and Cole to laugh. "But, I have come on a mission. Horatio told me that my mechanical horse, which he'd taken out yesterday, became water logged and stopped working. I was hoping that you might help me retrieve it this afternoon. Horatio would have come as well, but after being soaked to the bone yesterday, he's come down with a little cold."

As the vicar spoke, Mildred kept her attention not on the wise man, but on her brother. She was watching his face for some sign related to the previous day's events. But, Cole sat with a blank look on his face that she couldn't read.

At the mention of Horatio's illness, Mildred said: "I do hope your son will quickly recover. Perhaps we could send around some soup or some of our special salve?"

"Special salve?" asked Mr. Wickliffe.

"I've been told that it was our mother's recipe. One of the house girls keeps several jars, just in case a cold sets in."

"It works quite well," said Cole, his tone was conversational, but he seemed guarded.

"That would be very nice of you, Miss Greene," said the vicar.

Mildred didn't correct his formal address to her. "No trouble at all, Mr. Wickliffe. Anything that might soothe Horatio we will gladly offer."

Cole's eyes shot from his sister to the empty dish in front of him. He murmured something Mildred didn't understand, but seemed to offer his consent.

"May I come along? I might be of some assistance if the horse is not working." Mildred looked hopefully toward the vicar.

"Well, I don't know."

"Mildred, it's some distance from the house," said Cole.

"I've traveled to all edges of our shire at one time or another, Cole." She huffed.

"It is fine with me. The more hands we have the better," said Mr. Wickliffe, looking from one sibling to the other.

His eyes were kind. It did not appear, from Mildred's perspective, that the vicar knew anything about the events of the previous, rainy day.

"So, it's settled." Mildred rang the little bell that now sat next to her place at the table. Before she set the bell back down, one of the housemaids appeared at her side. She whispered an instruction about having both her horse and Cole's saddled. The girl nodded, and then cleared the empty desert bowls form the table.

"Shall we step outside and see how your clock is doing?" asked Mr. Wickliffe.

"Let's," said Mildred who stood up from her chair.

As she stood, both Mr. Wickliffe and Cole rushed out of their own chairs. The clamor made Mildred smile. She loved chivalry, mostly because it usually caught her brother off guard and it took some effort for him to catch up.

The threesome stood outside, some yards from the clock tower. The vicar removed his silver pocket watch.

"Still running on time," he pronounced.

Mildred noticed that Cole's chest puffed out a bit with the news that the clock was running on time.

"Just remember to crank up that weight every day or two and you should be fine."

Mildred thought for a moment about that night's letter to her uncle. She'd always told him everything, but she wondered if she shouldn't let Cole write to him about the clock once again working so that he may receive the credit for the activity. She also knew that she would not, could not speak of Cole's recent troubles. It didn't seem her place to tell the tale.

Something had changed in her. She saw her brother as the man of the house now and it just didn't seem right or appropriate to tell his stories, be they triumph or failure.

"Mildred?" Cole said.

"Sorry, I was lost somewhere in my thoughts," she said and took several quick steps to catch up to Cole and Mr. Wickliffe who were headed toward the barn.

When they arrived at the long, stone building, Isaac and Perry had the three horses ready to go.

"We should take a rope, just in case," said Cole to Mr. Wickliffe, who nodded his approval. Cole walked into the barn. Isaac handed the horses' reigns to Perry and followed close behind Cole into the darkness.

"Your family's property is impressive," said the vicar.

"Thank you, Mr. Wickliffe." Mildred turned her full attention toward the vicar. "There are always so many things that require attention…" she allowed her words to trail off. She wanted to include "since Lorain has left us," but thought better of that. She didn't think it right to speak of her, more because she didn't want the vicar's input on the situation. As much as she liked Mr. Wickliffe, she had noticed that he had a tendency to share his opinion on any topic that was placed before him.

Before more could be said, Cole returned with a coiled length of rope over his shoulder. He asked: "Mildred, do you want my help?"

"No," she said and, with little effort, she placed a foot in the stirrup and a hand on the saddle, and easily pulled herself up onto the horse. She'd been taught to ride by her brother, and thus, rode like a man, astride the horse.

Mr. Wickliffe did his best to catch and curb his reaction, which Mildred politely ignored.

Cole and Mr. Wickliffe both mounted their own animals and, after giving a click of his tongue, Cole led the party down the long path, into the pasture, and then into the meadow. None of them spoke, instead enjoying the sunny beauty of the day. Occasionally, Mr. Wickliffe hummed the melody of a hymn, but he didn't sing the words, which pleased Mildred. The vicar had a nice sounding voice, but she didn't want the obligation of singing along. So long as the man only hummed, she knew it would be appropriate not to join in.

After a bit, they arrived at the dilapidated stone house. Mildred kept watching her brother for some sign or reaction, but, with the exception of a single moment when he stuck his head into the house and turned back, shaking his head ever so slightly, he maintained his full composure.

Mr. Wickliffe approached the horse and touched it, much like he did the horse he'd ridden to get there. He treated the mechanical version so much like the live one that Mildred wanted to laugh or make some smart comment, but she chose to remain silent seeing how serious the vicar was about his actions toward the mechanical horse. He mounted the metal beast and pulled on a knob concealed in the horn of the saddle. Nothing happened. He waited for a brief moment, and once again pulled on the knob and again nothing happened. Mr. Wickliffe slid down off the mechanical horse and moved around to the front of the animal. As he moved, his living horse neighed.

"I don't think he likes his clockwork replica," said Mildred.

Mr. Wickliffe opened a panel on the mechanical horse's chest. Both Mildred and Cole advanced to see the inner workings of the beast, but because the space was so small, Mildred held back to allow Cole to move close enough to see. She knew if she could get a look inside the animal, that she would quickly deduce the trouble, but there was protocol to follow. The men must come first in all things machine or mechanical.

The two men had their heads close together and were speaking, but Mildred couldn't make out their words. She hated being left out of any conversation, but especially conversations that involved steam, clockworks, or mechanics. Still, being a woman, she knew there was an expectation that she'd hold her place, away from the machinery and that she'd keep her opinion to herself. That's why what happened next caught her totally off guard.

Cole said, loud enough for his sister to hear: "We should have Mildred look at the thing. She's amazing at figuring out springs, gears, and cogs."

"Well, I'm sorry, Miss Greene. Why don't you step up here and take a look."

Mildred did as told and moved up to the front of the animal. She peered into the chamber that was the horse's chest. She followed the connections of each wheel, cog, and spring. Once she'd seen them, she closed her eyes and quickly envisioned how each cog and wheel aligned with the next and the next. And, while she hadn't yet seen the connections to the legs, it was easy for her, with eyes closed, to envision how the thing operated.

"Shall I?" she asked once she opened her eyes.

Mr. Wickliffe said: "Go ahead, we weren't able to find a solution."

She again closed her eyes, followed the diagram that appeared there, and then opened her eyes, located a single, small spring, and returned it to its rightful place. As she fixed the problem, she deduced that the cause wasn't the rain at all, but the jiggle and agitation of riding at fast speeds over uneven terrain. She wanted to explain her suspicions, but instead simply said: "Try it now, Mr. Wickliffe."

The vicar mounted the horse and pulled the knob. The thing clinked and clanked in an even rhythm. "Mildred, you're wonderful!"

"Thank you, sir," she said smiling toward her brother. Cole had his eyes focused some distance away. Mildred handed him the reigns of his horse and the Vicar, with a wave of his hat, set off for home.

Mildred wanted to talk to her brother. She also wanted to look inside the stone hunting lodge to better envision the experience Cole had had with Horatio, but she refrained. Instead, she mounted her horse and prepared to head back home.

"Are you coming?" she asked.

"You go ahead."

Mildred didn't move. Cole didn't make eye contact with her. She gave him another moment to do or say something, anything, but he didn't. She gave a solid kick to her horse, who took off at a lope.

Why, Mildred wondered as she rode over the pastures, did the men feel so…she didn't have a word for what she witnessed in her brother and Mr. Wickliffe when she fixed the automated horse. But, why was it such a surprise to them that she, a girl, had the ability to fix things? Did it threaten their manhood in some way? Did it threaten their perceived perception of their standing in society?

Of course, she had no answers. She wished her mother were alive. That would be someone to ask such questions. She didn't feel that Mrs. Wickliffe would provide suitable answers. Mildred didn't care how she fit in society, or how a lady was supposed to or expected to act. She felt a great fondness toward Mrs. Wickliffe. Her advice about running a house, about how to speak to the servants especially, had been a tremendous help. She still didn't know everyone's names, there were so many of them. But, she knew what tone to use when and that was very helpful. But, on matters such as these, about her wanting so much to be different from what was expected of her, that didn't seem appropriate to ask the vicar's wife.

Mildred slowed the horse when she arrived at the little stream that cut the side pasture into two great parcels and allowed her horse to drink. She liked that this stream appeared and disappeared based on the recent weather. With the rain of the past few days, the stream moved quickly. She thought of dismounting, removing her shoes, and walking through the water, but decided against it. Such things seemed childish and her mood was more adult at this moment. Instead, Mildred let the horse drink as she contemplated the difficulty. She was on her own now. There was no one to assist her. From the looks of things, she might never have another tutor. After all, the only reason that Lorain had stayed so long was because of her precarious connection to their family.

Mildred, being a girl, had no opportunity to go off to university. There was little expectation that she would pursue anything of an academic nature at all. She had been taught to play the piano, to sew and do needle work. She'd been taught how to pour tea and offer cakes to visitors. The fact that she was allowed to pursue French, Latin, and philosophy was more about her uncle's amusement that she found interest in such topics than his desire that his niece be well educated.

Her horse raised his head.

"What is it, Mr. Darcy?" Mildred had named her horse after her favorite Jane Austin suitor. She wanted to feel the way Elizabeth Bennet felt about a man, but that had never happened. She'd met few boys, but none of them caused the feelings of romantic love to invade her soul. At the thought of romance, she envisioned Edith Wickliffe, kissing her in the parlor as the rain pounded the house. As she remembered the kiss, her heart beat faster.

The horse neighed and stamped its right hoof, which caused Mildred to leave the memory of the kiss and look up again. There, approaching across the pasture was a person on a horse. She didn't know the horse or the rider, a young man who sat very tall in the saddle, with a stovepipe hat that made him not only look foolish, but even taller than he was.

Mildred took up the reigns and sat taller in her seat. She was both curious and excited that someone new was appearing, as if by some magic. In the distance, she heard a bell pealing. It rang twice and she couldn't for the life of her think what bell that might be, when she remembered suddenly the clock. It hadn't chimed noon or one, but here it was chiming two. She felt a sudden pride in her accomplishment, even if Cole took the credit. Mildred knew it was her mind and actions that brought the old clock back to life.

"Good afternoon, Miss. Would you be Miss Greene?" The speaker was tall and thin, he wore a navy uniform, but an incongruous hat. He was clean shaven, but his features were those that Mildred had heard others refer to as lovely.

"I am Miss Greene," stated Mildred in a reserved way.

She liked his eyes. They were green, like cat's eyes, and suggested a cunning and intelligence. Those were traits that Mildred did admire.

"Miss Greene, allow me to introduce myself."

Mildred nodded approval, even though she also knew it was inappropriate to speak to a strange man without the proper introductions. She was once again relieved that Lorain was no longer in the picture so she wouldn't be scolded all evening for committing yet another social faux pas.

The man removed his silly hat. "I'm Chief Petty Officer Roland Willoughby." He bowed his head.

"What does a chief petty officer do?" asked Mildred.

"I was chief steward on one of the ships that your father, Mr. Cecil Greene—"

"You know Father?" Mildred's indifference was wiped away. "When did you see him last? Is he healthy and well?"

"Your father wanted me to let you know he is well, healthy, and…" Mr. Willoughby scratched his head. "What was the third thing?"

Mildred knew and offered: "Hale. Well, healthy, and hale!" That was her father's favorite phrase. Whenever anyone asked how he was, he'd sing out, loud and jubilant, "Well, healthy, and hale." He'd said it was from a popular song from his own childhood, but he could never remember the rest of the words, or the melody.

Mr. Willoughby smiled. "Yes, that was his phrase, well, healthy, and hale."

The message, even from the mouth of stranger, made her feel safe and confident. "And, where and when did you last see him?"

The Chief Petty Officer relaxed his grip and allowed his horse to drink from the stream. "We sailed together for some time during an excursion of the islands of Indonesia. Your father, as you probably know, remained behind on one of the islands there and will return with a later ship."

Mildred grew excited. "He's on his way home?"

"No. The ship will return with the specimens he's collecting, but it will also drop him at a new location, I believe. You should have received by Royal Post the letters he sent with us."

Mildred thought of the stack of recent letters and the one, well creased and worn, that she'd been carrying in her pocket. "No, his letters did not arrive, only those of my uncle." She wondered why this man hadn't brought the letters. As much as she wanted to ask, Mildred also felt it was inappropriate for her to ask.

"Oh, I'm being a horrible hostess. Would you like something to eat? Our home is just over that little rise there." Mildred pointed in the direction of the house.

"Well, there's a bit more I'm interested in." Mr. Willoughby raised his hands to his jacket pockets and rummaged around inside his coat. He produced a letter. I'm supposed to provide this introduction from your father to Cole Parker."

"From whom?"

"Your Father, Miss."

"My…" Mildred felt the blood rush into her head. She thought she might feignt and grasped tighter to the saddle horn.

"Yes, I served with him on an exhibition; I was injured in duty and he offered me a position here at Wickwillow Manor."

She wanted to tear into the letter he still held in front of him. "When was this?"

"Oh, Miss, it's more than a year. It took some time to settle my affairs with Her Majesty's Navy and to then also heal from my injuries." His tone never wavered. "So, where might I find the young Mr. Parker?"

"That's my brother." She wondered what the letter contained, but guessed that it was an offer of a servant position for this man. Father's unique habit was to meet young men and send them to the manor to take on all manner of jobs and positions. When other people traveled they came back with art and sculptures, or jewelry or some other bric-a-brac to clutter their library shelves. Her father, instead, collected people. Nearly all the men who worked in the house and on the grounds of their manor were men and their wives that Father had met on his travels. "Let me take you back to the house," said Mildred.

They rode for a few moments in silence. Mildred wondered why the letter of introduction was only addressed to her brother and not to both of them. It added salt to the wound she still felt about fixing the mechanical horse. But, she decided that there wouldn't be a solution or resolution to her quandary between her current location and her return with Mr. Willoughby to the house, so she decided to leave off the thoughts for the moment.

Forty-Nine

"Nate, can you send them along and hold here for a moment? Perhaps have some luncheon with me?" Parker Greene asked a question, but it was clear that it was a polite order.

"Oh, of course, sir." The small foreman ran to his crew and after a moment he returned to Lord Greene. "At your service."

Greene led Nate into the dining room where the table was set for two. After taking seats, Greene poured a bit of wine into their glasses, he stared hard at the man, noticing the glint of sun off the pointed ring on his right hand. "Sir, time is short." Parker's voice was low and soft. "And, while this may cost my life, I must know, with certainty, are you with me?" His eyes never left his luncheon companion.

With his hand raised, holding the glass, he whispered back, "I am, my Lord." Nate's eyes held Parker Greene's.

"Then we must make haste. We'll skip through this meal and then adjourn to my workroom upstairs—"

A servant entered the room with a platter of steaming meats and potatoes.

Nate smiled brightly, his eyes twinkling like Ole St. Nicholas. "Oh, my Lord, you can trust all of us, to a one."

"Excuse me? I know there are those on these islands that can't be trusted. I have seen the heads on poles and the poor souls rotting and going to the rats."

"The pirates cannot be trusted, except perhaps your friend." Here Nate winked with a knowing turn of his head. "But us, the wee ones, your small friends, we dwarfs, that is the we I mean. We are to be trusted. And, we are to be rescued no matter what your amazing plan might be. We are an army. A force. We have been planning an escape for years. Without a leader and without the ability to truly take by force our means of escape, which can only be the Balsa Robin, we have been patiently waiting. But, we are ready and willing at a moment's notice to follow whomever might prove to be our leader, our savior. And, it is without doubt, that is you." Nate lifted his glass in toast.

"Share then, if you'd be so kind, what plans you have already made, and I shall then complete the details of our escape."

"Well, each of us is prepared to depart quickly. We have a signal in place and upon hearing or seeing the sign, day or night, we all know to meet at a point just beyond the great hangar where the Robin roosts when she is in port. We all are prepared to leave with only that which can securely and easily fit within the pockets of our clothing. It is why many of the women have taken to wearing so many layers and flounces."

Lord Greene thought back to the odd way so many of the women were dressed, with corsets on the outside of their garments, flowing skirts with many pockets, and so forth. He had to smile. "Go on," he encouraged.

"We have restrained ourselves and have had no children while on these islands. That has been a chore, to say the least, but we have agreed, to a one. We did not want choices to include wee babes. We have held back the greatest of the inventions, saying that we can't get them to work, so that we might use the magical weapons and devices for ourselves. We are quite well armed. And," here he held up his ringed hand. "And, we have all been trained to kill using just this point. It is rather messy, but can be done quickly, especially if there are two or three of us together. Our rings are delivery devices with a deadly poison inside. The points are sharp and can cut a man's arteries."

Greene sat back in his chair. "Is there more?"

"Yes, sir. I can go through each item and the order in which it will happen upon the signal if you wish."

"Our meal will get cold. We should eat first."

"And, you have begun to develop a plan?" Nate heaped enough food for two or three men onto his plate and dug in noisily.

"I have the beginnings of a plan, but it will be easier now and altered because of what you have told me. How many of you are there?"

"Two hundred and seven," said Nate through a mouthful of potato.

"And, can you fly the Balsa?"

Nate swallowed. "Not exactly. There are some aspects that we cannot master. We are not tall enough to stoke the furnaces that heat the water to steam the ship. We have tried several ideas, but the space really is designed for strong, tall, nimble young men."

Greene once again remembered the young stoker he returned to his post when the Barkley had been attacked and he wondered what had become of him.

"My Lord, are you okay?"

"Oh, yes, just thinking. Is there anything else?"

"Well, sir, rigging. We can't climb the rigging with our short legs and stubby arms. But, that is all. We have already worked into teams and crews. We have practiced. We know we can do everything else. We have all served on the ship at one time or another and know the passages and methods."

"Okay then. It is clear what must be done." He drank off his glass of wine. "Eat, eat. I have a stack of plans. Weapons and devices that will aid us. We will talk more. You will build me my tools. And, we will finalize a plan of attack to get all of us off of these islands.

Fifty

"Well, Mr. Willoughby. I must apologize, but I do not know where Cole has gone off to. May I offer you a glass of wine in the parlor while we wait for him?" Mildred was put out. She had wanted to spend time in her garden. She had wanted to practice the piano. She had wanted to accomplish a great many different activities that afternoon. Instead, she'd spent her time showing Mr. Willoughby the grounds of the manor. She had tried to engage him in conversations about her father and Indonesia, but he was a man, while charming to look at, who spoke very few words. She wanted desperately to read the letter of introduction, but that would have to wait until after her brother's return. Mildred considered that Cole might not show her the letter at all, but with two-thousand six-hundred and fifty-five favors due to her from him, including fixing the clock and the mechanical horse, she had decided that if he wouldn't show her the letter that she would call in one of her many chits.

"I do not drink wine, Miss Greene." He eyed the girl suspiciously.

"Then," Mildred thought for a moment. "Tea perhaps? Or coffee?"

"A strong cup of coffee would be nice."

Mildred pulled the knob that rang the servants. She watched Mr. Willoughby as he made the rounds of the parlor, considering perhaps that he would be more comfortable in her father's study. But, that was not a room she was comfortable in and, since she didn't know this man, Mildred had decided it best to stay with him while he was in the house.

A servant girl arrived and Mildred, in a quiet whisper, requested coffee and some sweets. She took advantage of the conversation to tell the girl that there would be three for dinner.

"Do you play, Miss Greene?" Mr. Willoughby caressed the grand pianoforte.

"I do." It felt good to give a short answer, even if it also felt rude.

Was it a request for her to play, Mildred wondered? Or, perhaps he played. She realized that with short answers came a great many other questions and a greater desire for answers. "Do you play, Mr. Willoughby?"

Roland Willoughby further molested the piano with his touch. He didn't look at Mildred, seemingly lost in his thoughts. "My mother played. She was a wonderful pianist. She wanted to be on the stage, but her father wouldn't allow it."

Mildred wanted to ask questions about his mother. She liked to ask others about their mothers, hoping to gain insight into what people thought of them, what these women who cared for children were like, and to better form the image she had been creating her whole life of what her mother would have been like, how she would have treated her and acted toward her, had she been alive. But, knowing it wasn't proper to probe in such ways, or feeling uncertain if it would be acceptable with a stranger to quiz him, she kept silent for a long moment to see if he would say more. It also bothered her that he hadn't answered the question she had asked.

The girl entered the room with a silver tray containing a pot of coffee, cups, sugar, cream, and a small selection of sweets.

Mildred indicated that she should place her burden on the table with a quick flick of her wrist. She was learning the ways of a woman's world from Mrs. Wickliffe and enjoyed trying them out. Each new gesture, such as this flick of her wrist, brought her joy and astonishment when they worked, as so many of the actions had.

"I'll serve," she said to the girl, and dismissed her with another hand gesture. She'd seen the sheep herders offering similar hand motions to their dogs and felt both dismay and excitement that the motions she produced created successful results with her servants. "How do you enjoy your coffee, Mr. Willoughby?"

The man took a long moment to answer, as he continued to fondle the piano. "Black," he finally said, still without giving Mildred any attention.

She poured two cups of coffee; into hers she added a considerable amount of sugar and milk. Mildred picked up Mr. Willoughby's cup and took it to him at the piano. He turned and took it from her, not tasting it. He moved to the stack of music in the cabinet next to the piano, placed his cup on top of the cupboard, and removed several books of music and thumbed through them.

Mildred watched his tall frame. With time to study him, since he wasn't speaking to her and his back was to her, she noticed that his head, which looked perfectly normal from the front, seemed rectangular and flat from the back. She wondered how he managed to keep a hat on his head, without it falling backward onto the flat slope. She noticed his hands as he turned the pages of a collection of Mozart studies. He had extremely long, thin fingers and decided that if he wasn't a piano player himself that he'd possibly missed his callings. Between the finger length and the size of his hands, which were almost grotesque in their lack of symmetry to the remainder of his build, she figured he'd be able to reach at least an octave and a half, possibly even two full octaves between the stretch of his thumb and pinky. She wanted to touch his hands, to inspect them, but believed that such actions would be unacceptable, especially with a stranger.

Mr. Willoughby sat down on the piano bench, opened the cover from the keyboard, and placed the book of Mozart studies on the stand. He rubbed his two large hands together before placing them on the keys. He launched, with great speed into Mozart. His hands were a blur over the keys as he played. Mildred became mesmerized. The delicate precision of Mozart captured her, bringing images as clear in her mind as the workings of the mechanical horse.

He finished the first piece and launched into the second. Mildred knew it required two page turns and she moved to his left side. Willoughby offered a slight head nod when it was time for the page to be turned. She knew it was more than eight bars ahead, but she turned the page at that barely imperceptible nod. He offered the same motion each time he wanted the page turned, but by the fourth piece she realized he wasn't really reading the music. He obviously had the pieces memorized, but had the music before him just in case he ran into trouble, which he didn't.

When he completed the last of the exercises, she applauded. "Mr. Willoughby, you're magnificent!"

"Thank you, Miss Greene," was all that he said. He offered no explanation. He gave her no cause to speak further. Instead, he selected a work by the Polish composer Chopin and played the nocturne in E flat. The melody was haunting and extremely well voiced. She missed his head turn prompt, lost in the music. He didn't turn the page either, simply playing the beautiful piece from within his own mind. To Mildred, it was as if Chopin himself were there in the parlor playing for her, as if Mr. Willoughby knew the soul of the great composer and was channeling him to life.

Finished, with the ring of the last notes still sounding in the room, Cole came in. "What have we here?" he asked in a lewd manner.

Roland Willoughby quickly stood. He made a queer motion, as if adjusting a tale coat that he wasn't wearing. Mildred didn't think Cole noticed, but she did. This action only added more questions to the list she was forming in her mind.

"Cole, this is Mr. Willoughby." Cole didn't respond and she added, "Father has sent him to us."

Her brother moved to the service on the table and poured himself a cup of coffee. He dropped a single sugar cube into the cup, but did not pick up a spoon. "Oh, one of Father's boys," he finally said. He still hadn't looked directly at Mr. Willoughby, who was still standing at attention near the piano. "And, what are we to do with this one?"

Roland Willoughby, for the second time that afternoon, removed the letter of introduction from his coat pocket, but he didn't move forward to present it.

"Father has sent a letter with Mr. Willoughby," prompted Mildred. She had grown extremely fond of the newcomer. She saw a depth of personality in his performance on the pianoforte and had decided she liked him. She wanted to take the letter from his hands and put it into her brother's. She wanted to chastise Cole for his rudeness. But, she remained still and silent knowing that if she contradicted him in front of the stranger that she might ignite another fight between them, and then she'd never have an opportunity to read the letter.

Cole popped a sweet cake into his mouth and washed it down with the coffee.

Mr. Willoughby finally moved. He turned, picked up his own coffee cup, which he had been given without a saucer, and approached Cole. Mildred watched the move she felt to be calculated. There was no way to expect his hand to be shaken, a formality which Cole had already ignored or evaded. Willoughby approached Cole and presented the letter.

Her brother took it from the man's hand and studied it. "Well," he began. "It's Father's writing. Here, Mildred, you read it." He held the object out toward his sister who nearly tripped over the piano bench to retrieve it.

She couldn't understand why Cole showed no excitement. This letter proved father was alive as close as a year ago. It proved it. Mildred hastily popped the wax seal and unfolded the letter. In his wonderfully neat hand, she read to herself:

Dear Cole,

Before you is Chief Petty Officer Roland Willoughby. He was the ship's steward on my recent journey. His years of service have come to an end. I like this man tremendously. I've found him to be well educated and well liked among all the ship's inhabitants and have hired him on as a man servant for you. It is time that you had someone to look after the details of your life.

His sister shall be arriving in a fortnight to serve as a personal maid for your sister.

Your loving father.

She offered the letter to Cole who turned away. He selected another sweet from the plate without offering any to his sister or their guest.

"What does it say we're to do with him?" Cole asked.

"He's to be your," she looked back to the letter. "Mr. Willoughby is to be your man servant. A personal valet. And, his sister is to arrive soon to be a personal maid to me." Mildred beamed. "Isn't that lovely?"

"I hope you haven't ordered dinner for three. It wouldn't do to have a meal with the help," said Cole. He drank off the last of the coffee, which was now sweet from the dissolved sugar cube, set the cup back on the tray, and strode out of the room.

Mildred wanted to apologize for her brother. She wanted to say a great many things, but she remained silent, fuming lightly about how her brother had treated Mr. Willoughby.

"Don't worry yourself, Miss Greene," said Mr. Willoughby.

It was as if he had read her thoughts. She smoothed her face. Mildred was not at all certain of the protocol required of her. She'd only ever dealt with the serving girls, cook, and housemaid. She didn't know what personal servants did.

"Is there a butler in this house?" he asked.

"Of course!" Mildred felt insulted.

"I meant no offense, Miss Greene. I simply inquired because that would be the appropriate person for me to speak to about my duties and the customs of the house."

In that moment, Mildred realized she'd been taken advantage of by Mr. Willoughby. By Willoughby. She remembered what Mrs. Wickliffe had instructed. It was suitable to call the girls by their first names. The cook and other elevated housekeepers and maids should be addressed by their formal names. All the male help should be addressed by their last names only, except for the butler, who warranted a "Mister" proceeding the name. She had told Mildred, that no matter how friendly she felt toward the help, that she should never treat them like guests within the house. That their lot in life was below that of the family living there.

She watched as Willoughby placed his cup of coffee on the tray. He hadn't consumed its contents. Mildred moved to the knob and pulled it three times. Her hand had barely left the thing before Mr. Chesterland entered the room.

"You've rung for me, Miss?" The old man appeared grumpy.

It was the first time Mildred had ever rung for the butler, having only recently learned the bell code of the house. "Yes. This is Roland Willoughby. He has been hired by Father to be the personal valet for Cole. Will you please show him the house and his room?"

"Of course, Miss. Is that all?"

"His sister will also be joining the house as my personal maid. She'll be arriving in a fortnight, according to the letter from Father."

"Very good, Miss Greene."

"That will be all, Mr. Chesterland." She avoided making eye contact with Willoughby. She slumped onto the sofa and drank more of her tepid coffee. She'd have to return to Mrs. Wickliffe's for a lesson about personal maids.

The serving girl arrived in the room without being summoned. She waited at the edge of the room, no doubt surprised that Mildred was alone.

"I'm sorry, what is your name?" Mildred had asked this girl more than a dozen times, but for some reason could never retain her name in her mind.

"Selina, Miss."

"Selina, we will again be only two for dinner. You may take this tray with you." Mildred placed her half-drunk cup on the serving tray.

"Yes, Miss." The girl picked up the tray and left the room.

Mildred considered the game Willoughby had played on her. It was upsetting to be treated in such a way by a servant. Yet, at the same time, she was enthralled by his abilities at the pianoforte. And, if he hadn't played the game, she might never have heard him play. She decided, for the moment, that the score for him was even and he thus deserved another chance. Plus, her father liked this man. That definitely was cause for her giving him a second chance. She looked at the letter again, running her finger over his signature at the bottom. She missed him so much. She wanted to talk to him, not just write letters that went weeks, sometimes months without response. She wanted to sit in his lap, even though she'd now grown too big for such things, and to hear him whisper in her ear, "I love you, Little Willow." She so missed hearing his pet name for her.

Fifty-One

Parker Greene kept his patterns. He was nearly finished sorting through the Queen's contest entries that filled his office. There were those of no use, those he hoped to use against his captors, and, finally, those that would appear to be weapons and tools his captors would find interesting, that would be easy to build, but would never work.

He gathered the papers into two great stacks and sent word via his house girls that he required help moving them to the workshop. He wondered how he'd ever get them all back to England.

Whenever he asked the women for anything, they were polite and coy, filled with joyous smiles and giggles. Parker worried that their mirth might offer a clue or sign to the pirates, but his neighbors seemed oblivious to the dwarfs. Those who lived in the houses around him kept to themselves, drinking away the days on their lawns and shaded porches. Those captives, he decided, would be left behind.

A group of little men arrived with two small wagons. They took the papers and transported them to the workshop. Parker tagged along, enjoying the journey through the tunnel where he did his best to explore the reddish-orange lighting. The bulbs in the tunnel seemed to burn bright, but there weren't wires inside the glass enclosures.

"Sir?"

"What is it?" Parker asked one of the small men.

"We have found a way to fill the glass globes with an inert gas. This, when electricity is introduced, glows brightly, without the need for wires or filaments. The bulbs at the ends do have filaments, but that's because we haven't been able to replace them yet."

"And why is that?"

"Both of our glass blowers died in a furnace accident." All the men bowed their heads for a moment before continuing on their journey.

They arrived in the workshop and, as when Parker Greene had arrived before, all activity in the shop stopped.

"What is this silence? There's work to do!" Nate barked at his crew. He came around the corner, discovered Parker Greene, and lowered his head. "My apologies, Lord Greene."

"No apologies necessary. Back to work." His tone was playful, but the small men at the many benches around the room went back to pounding, molding, and whatever other activities they were about. "Nate, come with me." He pointed to the men lugging the wagons and indicated for the ones pulling the escape plans to head into his office and the others to set the stack outside the door on a table.

"So, you are finished?" Nate asked, looking at the plans.

Greene dismissed the helpers. "Yes. These are tools and weapons I think might be useful. I've ordered them in desired preference. The stack outside the door are the dummies. There is another batch, still in my home, that are useless."

"Oh, I wish you had brought those, too. It is helpful to keep the majority of the boys working on things that hold no hope of aid to the pirates. Most of the benches out there have two projects going. One for show, that is rubbish, and a second that will be for our use to escape."

"I like your style, Nate." Parker resisted the urge to pat the little man on the head and instead he bent a bit and patted the foreman on the shoulder.

"If you'll come into my office, I want to show you the plan we've developed." The two moved from one small glassed cube to another. "Here." Nate pulled on a handle and the top of his desk flipped over to reveal a map of the four islands. "We're here." Nate pointed to a building on one of the brown circles. "Brown for land, blue water. Just for reference, here's your house. And, this is the Magistrate's island and the bazaar."

Parker Greene shuddered at the thought of the heads on the poles.

Nate continued to point out landmarks. "The Balsa Robin's hangar is there. And the meeting point for our people is here."

Parker estimated that the distance between the hangar and the meeting point were about fifty yards apart. "That's quite an expanse for folks with short legs." He didn't want to be insulting, but it was a truth that had to be addressed.

"I know," began Nate. "We've got a second meeting point here, just behind the hangar. And, we've added not only a trap door, but cover foliage here. Our plan is to have about a quarter of our folks go to the first location and the remainder arrive at the second. There is also a trap door in the middle of the first location with a tunnel that leads right to a staircase into the lower bowels of the Balsa. Our first goal was to get a flight crew onto the ship. The second wave of us, well, we're the fighters."

Nate flipped cards and showed the advanced weapons they'd built. Some used electricity stored in acid. Others, springs and cogs to fire repeated rounds of arrows, darts, and even bullets. There were other tools and weapons that Parker Greene didn't understand, but he could envision them working to subdue the pirates, or anyone else who might hinder the progress of this dwarf army. Most were designed to do their job from low angles and positions that compensated for the small stature of the men and women in the dwarf community.

Parker still needed to know how the Balsa Robin actually operated. He asked Nate for details, but the foreman didn't know. He'd never been below decks.

Nate went out into the workroom and climbed up on a tall stool. He looked around the room. "Kidd. Tow. Pell." Three small men made their way over to Nate and Greene. In a whisper, Nate asked: "Have any of you been below decks on the Robin?" All three men shook their heads. "Really? With all the trips you've taken?"

"Sir, they don't allow our kind below the third deck. That's where the machine rooms are and the boilers. Only the strong, tall, young men go there. And, they never come up."

"What? What are you saying?" Greene asked, his voice loud.

"The boys in the boiler and machine rooms are all prisoners. They've all been taken from the schooners. Once down on the lower decks, they never come out, not even when the Robin is perched in the hangar."

Parker Greene again was drawn to memories of the young, blonde airman stoker. He hoped the boy was still alive. "And above? On the rigging?" Greene asked.

"Those are only the pirates."

"I understand the rigging."

"Sorry, who are you?"

"Pell, sir. I've been on ships my whole life. Until I ended up here. For thirty years, I was the fool on one or another of Her Majesty's vessels. I learned the rigging and the sails just from being around them."

"And, you others? What skills have you?" Greene questioned.

"I'm a master navigator," said Kidd. "By the stars or the charts."

"And, I'm a cargo master. I handled the books on hundreds and hundreds of voyages. I understand weights and measures. I know what's required in food stuffs, water, ballast, and cargo, whether cased or human."

"Nate?" Nate was still on the stool so Parker and the foreman were eye-to-eye. "You obviously trust them?"

"With my life."

"So, you three will be in charge of what you know best. I want you all in the meeting point at the distance. And, I want you to build a team of ten to participate with you. I want every position doubled and tripled. If anything happens to one, I want another to step in and easily take their place. I don't want to leave anyone behind, but we'll only get one chance at this escape. Understood."

"Sir, while I understand the rigging, I can't climb or work it. None of us can. You have to be at least five feet tall or more to comfortably climb the nets and lines. Four and a half might make it, but none of us are that tall."

"Pell, can you quickly inform young, taller men? Once we take the ship, I believe the captives below decks will gladly do as we ask. Some of them may have experience."

Pell thought for a moment. "Yes. I'll need a dozen or more. But, yes."

"Excellent." Greene looked from one man to the next. "We shall plan to take the Robin."

"We serve at your pleasure, Lord."

"We serve at Her Majesty's pleasure, Lord."

"Very good, boys. You begin preparing. We will leave exactly twenty four hours after the Balsa Robin returns. We must be ready at a moment's notice."

"Yes, sir," all four men said in unison.

Fifty-Two

Cole walked through the woodlands alone with his thoughts. All around him, in the trees above, birds called out and sang. The forest provided a respite from the heat. As he ambled he considered recent events. He didn't understand his feelings for Horatio. He'd never felt like that with anyone he'd met. None of the girls from the town, or any of their visiting relations, had ever caused him to feel such a longing before. Neither had any of the men or boys he'd ever met or encountered.

He knew he was in love with Horatio. Cole knew that these things he was feeling, this longing and desire he struggled with, was like the love he'd read about in his sister's novels. Cole never told Mildred, but once she finished a book and discarded it to the tall shelves in the library, he would sneak them out, one at a time, and, under the gas lamp in his room, late at night, he'd read them. One after another he devoured these novels looking for some clue, some hint about what love was like.

Of course, he felt love for his sister. To him, that type of love felt like being her protector. Such feelings kept him going. Such feelings motivated him to see that no one harmed her. He also knew that it was the love that he felt for her and knew that she felt for him that gave him permission to tease and pester Millie.

He felt love for his uncle, the man who was rarely there with them. His uncle provided for their well-being. His earnings provided their food and home and the clothes that they wore. His oversight of their lives also provided servants to care for and educate them.

He felt love, too, for his long-lost father. As Cole thought of his father, a twinge of guilt ate at his stomach. How could Cole not be a disappointment to the great, educated, world traveler that was the person of his father? Cole again felt the sense of failure. His ineptitude at everything must reflect poorly on his family. Yet, it wasn't a relief that his father was gone and couldn't be shamed by him. No, his father being gone made it even worse. Shaming a memory was harsher than shaming a living man. No one had ever said it to his face, but he had heard of the whispers of just about everyone that if it weren't for being the son and nephew of wealthy men, and having a well-proportioned body and handsome face, he'd have no attributes or abilities to offer to anyone.

This made him think again of Horatio. That boy never made him feel guilty or sad. In the short time they'd known each other, Horatio had treated him well. He'd shown him kindnesses as no other. But, his feelings for the vicar's son were more than just those for a friend who supports another. At the first sight of him, Cole had felt his blood pump faster. He'd been sexually aroused, too. That had made him feel embarrassed the first time they'd been swimming together. But, in short order, he'd discovered that Horatio's body showed similar, unavoidable-to-hide physical signs.

Just the thought now of Horatio's cock being hard in his presence caused Cole to look around, and being sure there was no one near him, he pushed his hand into his trousers and adjusted his own hardening member. Again he looked around, stepped off the path and walked into the forest a few yards, and with his back braced against a tree, not facing the path, he unbuttoned his pants, took himself into his hands, and stroked himself to release, all the while remembering his cock entering Horatio that rain soaked night in the stone, huntsmen's cabin.

It wasn't just the act of sex, while that was wonderful, but feeling so very close to Horatio. Knowing that their bodies had merged into a single entity. That night had been different. They had already pounded each other at the swimming hole. It had been manly and rough. They'd been wrestling in the water, playfully attempting to dunk one another, when Cole had reached under the water, in a wrestling attempt to better Horatio while keeping the knowledge of his own erection from his new friend, that he discovered that Horatio's cock was also fully erect. He hesitated only for a moment, and then, because of some previously unknown animal urge, he grabbed Horatio's dick and held tight to it. Not in some cruel way, but with a gentle force. He wanted to see what would happen.

What occurred next became a blur. Horatio relaxed the grip he had around Cole's neck. He let go of the force he'd been using to try to push Cole under the water. But, he kept his hands and arms around Cole's naked body. And, as Cole fondled him under the water, Horatio had turned to him, his cheeks ruddy from their fight, he kissed Cole on the mouth.

Their lips held together softly at first. Cole felt as if he might explode from the feeling of this man's lips to his own. But, he didn't explode. He didn't die in that moment. And, as Horatio's lips parted slightly, as his tongue entered and flicked in and out of Cole's own mouth, he realized for the very first time in his life that he wouldn't die, couldn't die, but would now be willing to die, because he was feeling what all those heroes and heroines spoke of and felt in those novels.

That first time they'd made love, it wasn't really making love. They'd fucked each other with force and desire. They alternated fucking each other multiple times that afternoon. One or the other had their dick up the ass of one or the other for hours and hours that afternoon. In between, they dipped back into the water to cleanse themselves and each other. And, they kissed. Sometimes soft. Sometimes with brutal force. All the while, Cole believed and knew that he could do as he wished with Horatio.

But, what he remembered now, as he stroked his dick, more of release of tension than anything else, was their time in the cabin. They'd gone in to escape the sudden and violent storm only to discover, to both their amusement, that the cabin had no roof and it was almost as wet inside as out. But, there was a small area, near the old stone fireplace, where the rain seemed to be hitting less hard. There, they huddled out of the weather. It only took a moment to take advantage for a second time of their close proximity. They kissed, playfully at first. Before either knew what they were doing, they were naked. Cole had turned Horatio toward the wall. The boy braced himself there as Cole pushed inside of him. He was about to do so with force, as they had done to each other at the river. Instead, something came over him and he gently, teasingly, pushed himself inside that hot, welcoming respite. He didn't pound and pound with force, but instead, gently, ever so softly, he pushed his manhood into Horatio, and just as sensitively, he pulled it back out, not all the way, but almost all the way. Cole kept his hands on Horatio's hips and watched the man's backside with him entering and retreating. He gently kissed Horatio's shoulders. He reached around an arm and hugged his lover to him. And, with every choice he made, with each stroke and kiss he offered, Horatio responded easily, allowing. They made love together like that for a long time. It felt like a blessed eternity. And, as he was nearing fruition of this sensual journey, as he tightened his own muscles to keep from releasing his fluids, to prolong as long as possible this scene, as if it were a dream that he refused to let go of and wake up from, Horatio tightened his ass and pushed himself hard onto Cole. He let out a gasp that was unmistakable as his load emptied onto the stone wall in front of him. In that moment, Horatio was like a vice around his cock, Cole pushed forward with all his might and relaxed his own muscles until he exploded. Neither one moved, not wanting this moment to end, extending it as far and as long as possible. Until, finally, without any control, as if by mutual consent neither had agreed to, Cole slipped out of Horatio. Both knew that they wouldn't reciprocate the actions of the other, not right away, maybe not ever. Cole clung to Horatio, both his arms now wrapped tight around his friend. They breathed heavily, but even the violent breaths they gulped and released, even those, they did in harmony.

As Cole's memory reached the story's climax, he did also in this moment in the woods alone, spraying his jism over a clump of ferns. He stroked and shuddered, milking each virile drop of life out of himself. He tucked himself back together and buttoned up his pants. And, as he headed back to the trail, he tried to remember those moments that followed. He tried to see the man's face in the doorway when he turned, but he couldn't. It was all a blur of darkness and rain and shame.

Yet, it wasn't really shame. He hated the idea that because of the judgment of another that he might never again have that amazing experience with his friend. That because others decided that it wasn't the custom for two men to be together, that he might never again hear Horatio whisper "I love you," while in the throes of passion.

Was it wrong for two men to be together? He never read of such things in any of the books his sister read. But, was it really wrong? He'd heard men in the fields make jokes about it. The slang they used made it out to be something no one respectable would do, but what about unrespectable people?

For the past few days, Cole and Horatio had not seen each other. Cole wondered that the vicar didn't reference anything, even when they were retrieving the mechanical horse. He thought that maybe Dr. Wickliffe didn't know anything about it, but that thought faded when he and the vicar made eye contact that day. Cole saw the sadness on Dr. Wickliffe's face and knew in an instant that he realized the whole story. That which he might not have known was certainly supplied by the guilt that shone from Cole's eyes in his direction.

What if they ran off together? Cole contemplated. There was all that allowance money in the dish. That would get them started off in some direction. Maybe, just maybe, Horatio had a few pounds set aside as well. But, that would never work. If they were to run away, he'd be abandoning his sister. Cole knew that was impossible. Mildred, especially since he'd relieved Miss Canton of her position, was now solely Cole's responsibility, at least until his uncle returned. That would be many weeks, at least.

Cole felt sick to his stomach. I've always solved my problems before, he thought to himself and then stopped. No, it's always Millie who solves them, isn't it? That was a huge blow to his ego. He thought about the clock and the mechanical horse. Those solutions were Mildred's. Cole stopped and looked into the treetops. He tried to remember one single problem that he had actually solved without her. The only one, ever, that came to mind, was his stopping Miss Canton from striking his sister. "Any common brute could do that," he said to the leaves.

He started to walk again and stopped. "But, I can't go to her with this. I just can't."

Fifty-Three

Parker Greene stood at the tunnel entrance. He'd pushed the button he'd seen others push to activate the lift, but nothing happened. Greene looked around, but there was no one in sight. There was no way to get from his home island to the workshop, except through the tunnel. No boat sailed the water, no flying ship traveled the sky. He wondered about that and began walking along the beach. No one lounged or frolicked at the water's edge. He followed the shore for several hours and encountered no one. Most of the sands were pristine, except for his own footsteps and those of the birds who made a meal of the small fish, crabs, and creatures in the shallows.

Parker arrived back where he'd begun and a bit winded and tired from traipsing through the sands, loosened his collar and shirt, removed his hat, and reclined under a tree while using its strong trunk as a back support.

"You'll not want to let them see you inspecting the islands. They don't care for that."

He looked up at the feminine voice whose owner, with the sun to their back, was fully in shadow. Greene began to get up, but the woman raised a hand in protest. Instead, she first handed him a glass with a cloudy beverage inside, and then lowered herself to the ground, her skirts flouncing out in all directions.

"There," she said once she and the fabric that surrounded her had settled.

"Thank you for the drink, what is it?" Parker tasted the concoction as a way of avoiding the woman's voluptuous breasts that were now in easy reach of his eyes and his body as she thrust them out and toward him.

"Well, it's a homemade brew of ginger beer and fresh squeezed lemons. I have a prolific lemon tree." As she spoke of the lemons she leaned a bit forward, allowing Parker a view of her décolletage. "I'm so pleased that you enjoy it."

"I do. So, what were you saying about the pirates?"

"I'm Miss Ebony, by the way." She held out a gloved hand, and Greene politely shook it. "I was saying that you should be careful of your inspection of the islands. All those who have taken to those sorts of antics have mysteriously disappeared. One or two have had their heads appear again in the square. Some of them…simply gone."

"Thank you for the warning. But, I was simply taking a walk. I had hoped to go into the workshop today, but can't make the contraption take me down to the tunnel."

"Well, of course not. Not on Wednesday. The electricity doesn't run on Wednesday." Miss Ebony took up her fan, opened it with an expert motion that reminded Parker of a certain type of woman, and she fanned herself.

"Really? Everything in my home seems to be working just fine this morning."

"Steam. Our homes are powered by steam, not electricity. But, the lifts and the lights and the workshops and the lamps and so on are all powered by the electricity. The generator is not run on Wednesdays."

"Why is that?" Greene was intrigued.

"They give those little creatures the day off. The little ones, they sit on seats and pedal like mad for several hours straight. Shift after shift around the clock. They tried to build a larger version, but it never worked, for some reason, creating the grander machine didn't work. So, Every day but Wednesday. It's nice of the Admiral and the Magistrate to give them time off." Miss Ebony continued to fan. "Drink up. There's more where that came from if you'd like a refill?"

Parker Greene considered what the woman had said and wondered how it would affect their plans. His own arrival had been on a Wednesday. "So, the Balsa Robin never arrives on Wednesdays?"

"Oh, the beautiful Robin, she comes and goes as she wishes. There is always a look out and a call when the bird arrives. All hands on deck. Or," here Miss Ebony laughed behind her fan, "all feet on the pedals."

They were both silent.

So, that explained the dwarfs. They were the only ones who could fit into and work as part of the machine. Parker finished his drink and stood. If he took the dwarfs with him, he would further paralyze the islands by taking away one of their power sources. "Well, I guess I'll return home and work on my projects there." He offered his hand to the lady who accepted and stood up with Greene's assistance.

"Why don't you leave off work for the day and spend the time with me. I'm sure I can bring you pleasure and happiness." Miss Ebony continued to work her fan in a seductive way.

This was not the first time Parker Greene had been propositioned by a courtesan. "You are very kind, but I think I will spend the day to my own devices." His tone was flirtatious and seductive.

"As you wish, my Lord."

"Oh, Miss Ebony, I am no lord, not on these islands, for I serve at the Admiral's and the Magistrate's pleasure. Good day to you." He remained polite, trying not to become too entangled in the woman's game, especially since he didn't know what that game might be.

Returning home, he felt light headed and assumed the drink was either alcoholic or laced with something. He was sure to lock the front door behind himself. Greene settled in the office and rang the bell. When the small servant arrived, he asked for a pitcher of water.

He worked to clear his head as he contemplated the idea that there would be no electricity on the island once the call had been made to the dwarfs. He'd have to plan appropriately.

Fifty-four

Mildred, not quite ready to tackle cleaning out the fountain, turned her attention to the first major side aisle from the center toward the honey bee wall, as it had come to be known. She had not been molested again by the bees, although Perry had stopped working on that side of the garden and was now weeding his way around the opposite wall. She was on her knees sorting out weeds from desired plants. Mildred took cuttings of those items that were foreign to her with the plan of attempting to match them in a book in her father's study.

She hummed a tune to herself, not sure of its origin as she worked. It was a brilliant afternoon. Not too hot with a high sun and fluffy clouds dotting the sky. An earthworm, unearthed by her activity, was working its way back underground.

"Mildred!" called Edith.

Mildred gently untangled herself from under the thorny rose bushes and overgrown weeds. "Edith!" She was pleased to see her friend. "Do you care to join me down here?" she asked. The look on Edith's face made her laugh. "Well," she rolled around to face her friend, "help me up."

Edith extended her hand, which, after helping Mildred to her feet, was covered in dirt. She wanted to wipe that hand on her skirt, but thought better of it, being dressed in a flowery print that would show the filth. She held her hand aloft until Mildred took it in her own hand and brought them both to the dirty apron she wore over at her waist. The girls laughed as Mildred wiped both their hands in the cloth.

"It's so nice to see you," said Mildred through her laughter. She waited for the return of those deep emotions from the previous night, but felt nothing similar. She felt happy to have a friend, but the touching of her hands caused nothing emotional, nothing, sexual. Confusion flooded her for a moment and then flittered out like one of her bees.

"I've been wanting to visit with you, too. Might we have a cup of tea?"

"Of course." Mildred picked up her basket of sample plants and led the way to the center walk and toward the garden gate. "Perry, I'm going up to the house," she called.

Neither of them could see Perry, but from the rustling in the tall grasses heard: "Yes, Miss!"

"Do you mind if I look in father's books while we visit? I'd like to figure out what these plants are before they wilt too much."

"Whatever you would prefer." Edith slipped her hand into the crook of Mildred's arm, drawing herself close to Mildred; she'd seen married couples in the village do this, come close together; it didn't feel nice to her so she gently added space between them, careful to not actually push Edith away.

The girls walked up the path to the house just as the clock chimed three times.

"You've fixed the clock! Father told us, but I had forgotten. The bell sounds lovely."

"Shh. You must never say it like that. Cole fixed the clock. That is what you always must say."

Edith looked hard at her friend's profile, but tripped on a paving stone. Mildred, with fast reactions, kept Edith from falling.

Edith whispered conspiratorially: "Father said it was you who fixed the mechanical horse and that, based on that, it was probably you who fixed the clock, too."

Mildred looked around the yard. She could see Isaac working the new colt in the corral. She longed to go to the fence and watch him. She loved the way he broke and trained the horses, especially the new arrivals. But, Edith was gently pulling her toward the house, not as a way of avoiding the horse training session, but because that had been their established path. Mildred contemplated asking her friend to spend some time watching, but then remembered the withering plants and Edith's desire for tea.

"I did fix the horse, and the clock, and the rabbit, and just about everything Cole has ever attempted to create, but Cole is always to be given credit for the clock." She didn't look at Edith, not wanting to explain any further at the moment.

"Good afternoon, Miss Greene. Miss?"

"Willoughby, this is my friend, Miss Wickliffe," said Mildred, not slowing their already slow pace. She still hadn't decided to forgive Willoughby for his joke on her.

"Good afternoon, Miss Wickliffe."

Edith stopped and gave the man a nod.

"Not to bother you, Miss Greene, but I've been charged with finding Mr. Greene. Have you seen him recently?"

"Has your uncle returned?" asked Edith, excitedly.

"No, he means Cole. Willoughby is Cole's…" Mildred hesitated. She couldn't remember Roland Willoughby's official title.

"Valet. I'm young Mr. Greene's new valet."

"I haven't seen my brother all day. If he's not to be found, he's not to be found. He often disappears for hours and hours at a time," said Mildred. She turned abruptly, still tethered to Edith, and moved toward the house. As they entered, Marcus and another young servant were moving a rather large wooden crate through the foyer toward her father's study. She read the printing painted on the side of the crate; it was clearly addressed to her uncle and marked "Fragile Specimens."

They went into the study where Mildred pulled the knob to ring for the servants. A house girl quickly arrived and Mildred asked for tea. The girl nodded and departed. Such instructions had begun to feel natural.

"What do you think is in the box?" Edith asked.

"Let's see." She placed the basket of weeds on the small table and led Edith toward the crate. Marcus was looking at the box. "Get the crowbar and we'll open it."

"It's addressed to your uncle, Miss," advised Marcus.

"It's marked "Specimens" so we should open it at once. Uncle will have included instructions inside as he's done in the past."

Marcus left the room. Mildred began inspecting the shelves of books. She remembered that there were several that gave details of the English garden. She hoped the plants she had found would be illustrated there. As she explored the shelves, Edith wandered aimlessly around the room.

There were a great many wonderful items in the study. In addition to being one of the largest private libraries in England, her father had a penchant for collecting all manner of trinkets and souvenirs from his travels, as did her Uncle Parker. The former owner of Wickwillow Manor had been an avid animal hunter, so in addition to their possessions, there were many animal heads protruding from the walls, and several hides on the floor and draped over the sturdy leather-covered furniture. As Edith wandered, she touched many items. She didn't pick anything up, but did touch everything she could.

Mildred found the book she'd sought, just as Marcus came back into the room with several hand tools. Mr. Willoughby stood in the doorway, but didn't enter the room. Together, Marcus and Mildred worked at removing the long, front side of the crate, just as her uncle had shown her many, many years before. It took some effort, but eventually the front of the crate was ready to fall. Marcus dropped his hammer on the floor and caught the heavy wood. With some effort, he moved the panel and rested it on the side of the box. Mildred inspected the burlap wrapped items in the crate and, after some moments, discovered a letter attached to one of the sides. She pulled it out and quickly popped the wax seal and unfolded the sheet.

Dear Little Willow, for I know, Mildred, it will be you to open this crate. Inside are two sets of items. The three deep brown burlap-wrapped bundles should be delivered at once to the greenhouse. Please let Chesterland know of these, and he'll take care of them. There are individual instructions included inside the packages.

The bundles wrapped in paper are various things I've collected during the first half of my journey. You may, of course, open them and if anything strikes your fancy or that of your brother, feel free to display it as you desire.

Your loving father.

Mildred found the bundles and sent them with Marcus to the greenhouse. "Please, do tell Chesterland of their arrival."

"Yes, Miss," said the houseman and he departed under a great burden.

"Father!" Mildred whispered. "This letter is from my father not my uncle." Mildred dropped to her knees in the wood shavings that had fallen out of the crate. "This package is from my father." She looked hard at the letter, it held no date. She tore into the paper inside the crate.

"Do you think you should wait for your brother? I would love to discover this with you, but I do think that you and Cole should do it together."

Mildred looked hard at her friend trying to discover her reasoning. In the past, she had always opened such things and told Cole about them later. "He never seems very much interested."

"Maybe he doesn't show interest to hide the fact that his feelings are hurt," offered Edith.

"Perhaps."

"And, didn't you want to see about your plants. They'll be all wilted."

Mildred considered her friend's point. The thought of tea and a little snack caused her stomach to grumble. It made sense to have tea and look through the books first. "Fine, tea it is." The girls left the study and returned to the parlor to find the tea tray had arrived.

They sat close together on the sofa with the book opened on their combined lap. As they scanned the pages and pages of illustrations, they found two of the six plants Mildred had gathered were considered herbs of a healing nature. The others were weeds.

After the discovery, Mildred wanted to rush back out to the garden and do more work; she wanted to explore the contents of the crate. But she also wanted to be a good hostess. So, she arranged the plants back in the basket with those she wanted to keep on the top. She closed the book and placed it on the side table, knowing that she'd be spending time later reading through the pages of material to learn more about what she had discovered.

She liked the idea of healing and medicinal plants. She knew of a woman in the village who offered such herbs and treatments to those who came to visit her. The woman wasn't a doctor, but many in the village respected her, even the doctor, for her knowledge and great kindness. Mildred wondered if it would be acceptable for her to visit this woman just to talk, to learn more about the plants and herbs.

"Would you like some more tea?" Edith asked.

The girls hadn't moved even though the book was no longer between them. Their legs, sides, and arms still touched.

"No. I've had enough." Mildred was still lost in her thoughts, but as she felt Edith move away from her she came back fully into the room. "Oh, shall I pour for you?"

"No, no. I'm fine." Edith leaned forward to pour more tea into her cup, breaking their physical connection. "Where did you go just now?"

"I'm so sorry," Mildred said without further explanation at first. She watched her friend pour the tea and then lean back on the sofa. Their faces were very close. She thought about the servant who had accosted her over seeing her and Edith kiss. Almost as a reflex, she stood up, looked around the room, and as an excuse, picked up the book and basket of plants and moved them to a different table.

She wanted to tell Edith about what had happened, but decided not to. There was no reason to burden her with such a thing. She wanted to talk about the kiss and her changing emotions. She wanted to talk more about their brothers and what had happened between them, but didn't feel this was an appropriate conversation in a place where others might hear them. What she wanted, Mildred realized, was to be alone with Edith. To find some secret place where others would not discover them: A place where they could be together; a place where they could talk that was truly private. Yet, she also wanted to pull the packing out of the great box and see what her father, her father!, had sent. For a moment, she envied poor people. People without great means didn't have servants seeing and knowing their every move.

"What is going on with you, today?" Edith asked. She had a quirky smile on her face that caused Mildred to smile.

"My head is simply filled with all manner of issues today. I want…" she thought. "I want a great many things and I simply don't know how to make it all happen at once."

"Tell me what you want and we'll make it happen," said Edith, who sat forward on the couch for emphasis.

"You are so kind," she said to her friend. Yet, even with that kindness she still held back from saying more. There were several topics on that list that didn't seem appropriate even to say aloud.

"Well?"

Mildred censored herself. "I want to know more about these plants than the book says. There's a woman in town who might know."

"Well, that's easy enough. We could simply walk into the village and visit her," said Edith with a sensible air. And, because she was already leaning forward, she selected a small finger sandwich from the tea tray and playfully popped it into her mouth. "Why don't you put on a clean frock, and we'll go there now."

Mildred admired Edith's sensible tone and nature. She easily saw the world and worked out the details.

"Come, I'll help you pick out something and change." Edith stood, looking more matronly than young.

Together, they ascended the stairs and walked down the long hall to Mildred's door. Along the way, Edith let out gasps and ahs about the sculptures and paintings that lined their way. Mildred didn't offer any comment. No friend had ever been in her room. She didn't know the protocol of such a thing. Yet, Edith seemed so comfortable and confident. She decided to follow her friend's lead.

They entered Mildred's room and closed the door behind them. Mildred moved to her cupboard and opened the door, showing her dresses to Edith.

"Oh, this one in light blue will bring out the blue in your eyes."

Mildred smiled. "Can you help me with these buttons?" She gently elevated the coiled braids at her back, not wanting them to unravel.

Edith stepped close to her. As she undid the buttons, with her breath on Mildred's neck, her fingers gently brushing her back, chills of excitement ran all over her body. How could it be, one moment great interest, the next something more sisterly, and then back to this? How could one make any honest decisions with all these feelings going on?

"There," said Edith, having finished with the buttons.

Together, they removed Mildred's soiled smock and Mildred tossed it aside on a chair. She reached for the blue dress feeling Edith's hands on her through the layers of undergarments she wore. A gentle and easy touch, not sexual.

"I think it's time to have some new foundation garments made. These are rather worn. Your breasts have grown so full they strain the fabric." Her words weren't mocking or judgmental or sexual, but motherly.

Mildred was embarrassed. No one, except the maid who helped her dress, not even her brother, had ever seen her like this.

"Look, your breasts are already full," said Edith. "Mine are barely noticeable. Mother said she was a late bloomer, too."

Mildred felt the rush of blood into her face and her ears tingled. She both wanted this moment to be ended, yet strangely never wanted it to cease. This familiarity felt so off to her, but Edith, so matter of fact, this must be how she and her mother talked. Oh, to have a mother, to have had anyone, a sister or even a maid, who would be willing to talk so openly about these things, undergarments and growing breasts, and sexual feelings that made no sense to her. Without making eye contact with Edith, she said, "Based on your mother, I don't think you have anything to worry about." She felt it sounded inappropriate, but it was said. How could she want or hope to be intimate with another, with Edith, if everything that happened in a private setting was embarrassing to her?

She thought of married couples. Not only of those things they did together that produced children but of the intimate moments. Of a man helping his wife with a necklace. Of a wife helping her husband with his tie. How close they stood. How they touched each other's faces out of love and kindness. That's what the books she read were filled with, intimate moments between married couples and even others. But, this didn't feel like being married. This felt different. Mildred knew for certainty, she wasn't in romantic love with Edith. She loved her like a sister.

"What is this?" Edith held up the small, mechanical rabbit.

Mildred took the metal creature, little more than a series of cogs and pins in the rough shape of a bunny. She wound a spring and set the thing down on the table. It rhythmically walked for a few steps. "Cole gave it to me." She said. "It didn't work then, but I fixed it."

Edith's smile showed admiration and pride. She hugged Mildred with one arm. "Wind it up again."

Mildred showed Edith how to wind the rabbit and together they watched as it marched a few more steps for them both. They were invested in that movement and it felt good to Mildred.

Mildred turned to Edith, who remained standing close. "Will you help me?" She raised the dress over her head.

Edith easily slid into action, moving yet closer to Mildred and taking pieces of the dress in hand, helped her friend slide it over her head. When they'd finished that action, Mildred and Edith were very close, standing face to face.

"I want to kiss you again," whispered Edith. Her breaths had grown short. "I think I've fallen in love with you. I know it's wrong?"

Mildred looked into Edith's dark green eyes. "I don't know what to say. I have deep feelings for you, deep admiration. But, I don't understand my feelings, my thoughts, my..." A piece of a solution to a problem she'd been thinking about filled her mind. She thought she might know a way for all of their relationships to work. But, it was too new and fresh of a scheme. This solution wasn't like solving a mechanical riddle. Her mind didn't see the inner workings of all the pieces and parts. And, because this flash of thought had come so differently to her, she didn't yet fully trust it. But, she did know it was an idea worth thinking more about.

"What is it, Mildred?" Edith asked.

"If we're to make it into town and back by dinner, we should go," she said, not yet ready to share her thoughts with her friend. Mildred wondered if this is how married couples were, that they had thoughts and ideas but didn't share them with each other. Was it right and proper to have ideas of her own without sharing them? She didn't fully know the answer to that, but knew that she'd have to mull it over and watch for clues in the novels that she read.

Within a few moments, Mildred was buttoned into her blue dress. She chose a little straw hat with a flutter of colored ribbons at the back and pinned it to her head. Once dressed, the girls left the room and with a bounce in their steps they headed for the front door. None of the servants accosted them as they left and Mildred, once out of the house and walking along the river path with Edith's hand tucked into the curve of her arm, felt happy and safe. How very strange to feel safe out of doors, along a well-traveled road, but not to feel so in the intimacy of her own bedroom.

Fifty-Five

Desperation climbed for Parker Greene; being trapped on his home island gnawed at him. What if the Robin returned and left again and he was kept isolated here on this island? What if his plan began automatically when the proper conditions for escape existed, as it would, and he wasn't there to lead the charge, or even simply escape with the dwarfs? Greene tossed aside the plan before him. He stood, nearly knocking over his chair behind him, and paced.

"Sir? Is there something I can help you with?"

"Oh, hello. I thought I was alone." Greene turned toward the small woman standing in his office doorway. He'd never seen her before.

"I was nearby. They asked me to check on you."

"Who asked you?" Parker walked to the maid. "What is your name?"

"I'm Emma, sir." She curtsied deep. "I work for Miss Ebony. It was she and our other house servant, Jacob, who suggested I stop in to be sure the Lord had food to eat and a clean home to work in."

Greene's skin grew cold and clammy. He thought he might pass out.

"Sir, you've gone white. You should sit down." Emma rushed for a chair and pushed it across the office, catching Parker Greene as he fell. She fanned his face for a moment. "Lord, I'll be back in a flash." She rushed from the room, her heels clicking on the wood floors.

Parker blinked his eyes. Everything looked dreamlike. He watched a fly buzz near him. It didn't look like any fly he'd ever seen before, it was bigger, the size of a coconut, and all the colors of the rainbow. The horrible thought of this fly being one who plagued the men in the outdoor cage caused gooseflesh to rise on his arms. His skin shifted from clammy to hot. Perspiration quickly pooled and dripped into his eyes. Parker Greene was unable to move, unable to wipe away the sweat from his face.

Emma returned with a cool, wet towel. She sponged off his sweaty face. "Oh, I wish I had arrived a bit sooner. I might have gotten you to the chaise or your bed."

Parker was unable to speak. Try as he might, he could not force words from his slack mouth. His sense of being trapped on the island grew focused and intense. Not only could he not leave the island, his thoughts could not leave his mouth. He slipped in slow motion from the chair.

Emma's feet burst across the room; she was next to him now with a cushion. The small maid managed to get that cushion between him and the chair. As he dropped to the floor, his weight took the pillow with him, and it softened the blow to his head when that dropped off the chair and finally hit the floor.

"You'll be okay, Lord Greene. We've seen her do this to others. When we saw you with her this morning, we feared you'd…well, at least you didn't go home with her."

The door chimes sounded.

"Don't worry. I've locked all the doors and windows."

The giant fly, now the size of a melon, buzzed near his ear. If he could, Parker would have shuddered. Instead, he simply sweat more. His body trembled involuntarily.

"We can't have anything happen to you. You are our savior. All of us are available to you for support. We might be the only ones you can trust right now."

The door chimes continued. Knocking and then pounding was added to the chimes. Greene could hear his name being shouted. He knew the voice. It was…it was…he fell into sleep, an odd sleep. He was conscious of what happened around him, yet those activities were very distant from him in his mind. The greater focus of his mental imagery was on his plan of escape.

As he lay there, sweating and shaking, with his lover calling to him and a dwarf tending him, Parker Greene watched every detail of his plan unfold. The Balsa Robin would arrive, the dwarfs would work the generator and unload the cargo. The first night of the ship's return, the dwarfs would gather in the two spots.

Someone slapped his face, hard. He wanted to hit the slapper back, but still he couldn't move. Those around him talked, but now it was as if he was underwater. He could hear them, but the sound was muffled to the point of not understanding.

Strong arms came under and around him. Greene now floated through the air with the support of love. He was now in bed, naked, shaking. Covers were heaped upon him. Blankets, quilts, mountains of fabric, and still he shook and shuddered and sweat.

Fifty-Six

Cole entered the house through the kitchen. He picked up two apples from the basket next to the door and made his way up the servant's staircase to the second floor. He stopped at the top of the steps, listened. The house was quiet, except for the sound of the cook and a servant gossiping in the kitchen below him.

He walked slowly along the hall, keeping to the carpet so his feet wouldn't make any sound. It wasn't that he was avoiding being noticed, not really. He simply enjoyed the quiet of the big house. He liked feeling alone and invisible to any others who might be present.

Mildred's door was, of course, closed. It had only been a few days, but he had missed entering her room at night and sitting with her while she filled him in on her day. The absence of their private time together had begun to weigh on him. Cole stood for a moment at that door and then, with a purposeful movement opened it, entered the room, and closed the door behind him.

Her room was cool and well kept. Her bed was made. Her desk was neat. All the doors and drawers of the cupboards and cabinets were closed tight. Cole went to her desk. There weren't any stray notes or any beginnings of any letters, simply a neat, clean surface and that damn mechanical rabbit. He absently picked it up, wound the key, and set the thing down. It marched in front of the pen that was in its holder, the inkwell with its cap on. He wondered how she kept her inkwell and desk so clean. Even with a blotter, his own desk was heavily stained with ink and grease.

Cole looked out of her window, out at the great expanse of the grounds with their trees of green and grass of green and the gentle river of green reflecting a blue sky with fluffy clouds moving through. He sat in her chair and from that perspective could see over the garden walls. He admired her progress. It had only been a few weeks, but the center path of Mother's garden, as well as the areas near the wall nearest the house, were well defined. He could now see the dots of red, yellow, and pink: the roses she had unearthed from the thick masses of weeds, tall grasses, and debris.

He marveled at this view. He'd never sat in her desk chair before and he now realized that for her entire life, for the desk and chair had always held this place under the window, for her entire life she had been looking and watching as the garden become overgrown and reclaimed by the elements of time. How sad it must be for her to not remember Mother and then to watch as the thing most beloved by her went to seed.

Cole opened a drawer. He shuffled the paper there, clean stationary with her embossed initials: MG. He closed that drawer and opened another. There rested her notebooks. One was the garden notebook their uncle had given her before he left on this latest journey. Uncle Parker had asked him when he left this last time if he, Cole, wanted to come along. It was a good profession, plant hunting, his father had told him when he was small. And, it would be nice to spend time with his uncle, to be treated as a man by him and those around him. Cole was the first son. It was second and third sons who took to the sea, just as his father had when he was a boy and his uncle after him. Cole turned down the offer.

He liked his father, but didn't really know him well. He was gone most of the time, six or seven months at a time. He'd return with a flourish of excitement, gifts, and activity, stay home for a few weeks, maybe two months, and then would be off again to some other exotic destination. With him gone, his Uncle Parker picked up the role, maintained the pattern. Cole couldn't imagine being away from his home and his sister for that long. He asked his uncle if Mildred could come along, too, but his uncle's mood quickly changed. Life on the sea and in the air is no place for a little girl, he had chastised Cole.

Cole thumbed through the letters under the notebook. They were all from their uncle. He unfolded one. The rich paper had been thickened and crimpled from exposure to sea water. He sniffed the letter, smelling the ink, imagining he could smell the sea and the world that his uncle, and father, inhabited so easily. He imagined Lord Parker Greene, standing well over six feet tall, against a light blue sky that expanded as far as he could imagine. His father stood with him at the rail of the ship with his broad shoulders and long blond curls blowing in the wind created by the ships movement and great propellers. In the fantasy, they both looked happy, their view of the ocean waves below filled with expectation of possibilities that the next destination finally arrived at would provide and produce.

Cole tried to picture himself there in that scene between his father and his uncle, but, just as when his uncle had brought up the topic the first time and the second and third, Cole simply couldn't imagine himself there.

The boy had another fear that he hadn't shared with anyone. The thought and idea of being on a ship with all those men for months at a time was thrilling to him. Not because of the adventure of travel and seeing foreign lands, but because he found those flyers so attractive. Frequently, his father had sent stray sailors to take up positions in his home, just as he'd sent Willoughby and Marcus. Cole had seen the sailors, shoeless, climbing the ropes and ladders, working on the deck of their ships in tight trousers and wide open collar shirts. His heart pounded as he'd watched them work. He became sexually aroused at the sight of them. How could he spend months on end in that environment and not act? And, if he were to act, how could he disgrace his family in that way?

Cole tossed the letter back in the drawer, not attempting to place things exactly as he'd found them. He closed the drawer and opened the lowest one. Inside were two more notebooks. One he knew to be his sister's diary, which he ignored. The second he'd never seen before. It was a large black book whose pages were dog-eared and worn. This book he lifted to the top of the desk and opened. Inside, he discovered drawing after drawing, page after page of devices like he'd never seen before. There were pens that held their ink. There was a long driveshaft, like that of a wheat mill, with a faint drawing of their home above it. There were mechanical looking fans and cooking machines. One of the pictures detailed a mechanical page turner for a piano. On and on the pictures went. It was as if Mildred was creating a new world of some sort with a collection of devices, some fantastical, others practical.

This, he thought to himself, this is what I want to do. I want to invent and create fantastical things that will make life more enjoyable.

Just as he began to truly scrutinize the pictures, words, descriptions, and plans, the door to his sister's room opened.

"Oh, excuse me, sir," said one of the little housemaids.

They came and went so quickly he didn't recognize this one. She was very young, maybe thirteen or fourteen. She was very thin and still held the potential to be tall.

"What is it?" Cole snapped. He was embarrassed to be found going through his sister's desk, but yet had also embraced the idea that he was the master of this manor and therefore had the right to do as he pleased without question or judgment of others.

The girl stood motionless at the door.

"What is it?" Cole turned to look at her more fully.

She kept her head down, not making eye contact. "I've brought some fresh laundry of Miss Greene's to put away."

"Go about your business." He watched her open different drawers and cabinets, replacing pieces of his sister's wardrobe. Cole then turned back, took one more look at the book, and then dropped it into the drawer. He left the room before the maid had finished her duties.

Cole walked down the hallway. At the door of his own room he hesitated. The pause was first because he couldn't exactly remember why he had come upstairs. Then, remembering that he wanted to look for his field glasses, he reached for the handle to gain access to his room to discover that the door was ajar. He smiled thinking how funny it would be if he found Mildred rummaging through his own desk drawers. Although, they both knew there was no point in that, that she wouldn't find anything that would interest her. He flung open the door to find Willoughby there, placing an evening jacket on a hanger.

"Good afternoon, sir," said Willoughby.

Cole simply grunted in the direction of the servant. He didn't like that this man was now in and out of his room at all hours. Cole had suddenly lost any semblance of privacy, even in his own bedroom.

He looked around the space. It looked almost as neat as Mildred's bedroom. "What has happened here?" asked Cole. His tone, while quiet, held accusation.

"Just tidied up a bit, sir. Is there something I can help you with?"

"No," said Cole with some force. Then, reconsidered. "Where have you put my field glasses?"

"Here, sir," said Willoughby, opening a cupboard. The servant handed the glasses to his master.

Cole looked into Willoughby's eyes. They were an amazing shade of grey. Steel grey and piercing, yet also interesting. As he stared, Willoughby cast his eyes down and away. Cole continued to look and thought about the places those eyes must have seen. As he took the field glasses, Cole could smell him, a hint of shaving soap, and something else, a musky scent that reminded him of what? He knew he'd smelled something similar before, but couldn't remember where or what it was.

"Thank you," he said gruffly and turned to go. Cole hadn't yet figured out how to deal with this man who was now seemingly attached to him.

"You're welcome, sir. Will there be anything else?" Willoughby had a pleasant, almost playful look.

"No, no…" stammered Cole as he retreated. He walked down the hallway, back toward the front staircase, his heart pounded and he realized a film of sweat covered his body. The boy increased his pace and practically ran from the house.

Fifty-Seven

Parker Greene woke from a dream. He took his time opening his eyes, still enjoying the heavy, soft sensation, like he was adrift on a luscious feather bed, surrounded by—

"He's waking up!"

"Hmmm, no," Parker murmured.

Someone placed a cold towel against his forehead. He tried to reach for it, but his arms were pinned to the bed.

"No."

Now, a man's hand, rough and large, was softly slapping him. Not to hurt him, but to pull him forward into the world, into reality. He struggled to keep the dream going, but it was lost to him. No dream. No reality. He drifted in blackness, feeling the hand, thinking of the feather bed. Parker wondered if this is how God felt, how the great Creator experienced the world.

"Parker, come back to us."

That wonderful voice. Whose voice was that? He imagined warm breath against his ear as that voice emerged from swollen lips that tasted of him.

"Parker."

He struggled now to open his eyes. He realized something was wrong, very wrong.

"You can see he's coming back to us." This voice was a woman's. "Just let him come in his own time."

The man ignored her advice. "Parker!" More slapping, a little aggressive now.

"I…" He tried to speak, but nothing more came. Then, suddenly, as if filled with some new spirit, he opened his eyes. Before him, touching him, looking hard at him was Able Currant. Not his lover. Not his friend. The enemy. A pirate. "I…"

"You are back!" Able exclaimed and leaned down closer and closer and kissed Parker full on the mouth. A joyous kiss. "You've come back to us. We've all been so worried." Able indicated the room. Parker could feel people there, but couldn't raise his own head.

"Don't worry. Within a day or two you'll have a full recovery, sir."

"Who? You?"

"Oh, we are all here," said Dr. Collier.

"The last time…"

"Don't try and talk," said Collier. He sat now at the side of the bed and forced a tincture into Parker's mouth. "It shall be like old times. The kind women will bring you broth and help you eat it and I shall check in on you several times."

It was the man he remembered from his college days. The physician who taught biology and administered aspirin and casts to the collection of young boys. It was both a joy and a sadness to see the man again. To know that he, among the other pirates, must be left behind to die, or even killed in the scuffle. Parker had always liked the good, Dr. Collier. But, now, he was one more link in a chain that was binding the world.

Together, Able and Collier adjusted Parker up into a sitting position and one of the little women got up close to him and fed him broth one large spoonful after another. As her hand approached his face the ring she wore grew terrifyingly large before his eyes. When she saw him watching the ring, she smiled at him and then winked. Everyone knew what must be done, what must happen soon. He ate the soup as readily as he could in a desire to regain his strength as quickly as possible.

Fifty-Eight

Perry had made his way to the central path along the outside wall of the garden opposite from the honey bee hive. While he worked cutting grass and pulling weeds along the wide central path, Mildred had connected her portion of the path to the outside ring near the bees. She stood for a long time, watching the bees entering and leaving the hive. After her amazing experience being covered with bees a few days earlier, they had not accosted her. Occasionally, one or two of the creatures would hover near her, land on her sleeve, and then lift off again. It was, Mildred believed, their way of acknowledging her, of saying hello.

Mildred took out a handkerchief and wiped at her brow. It had taken the whole morning to connect that central path to the outer one. While there was still a great amount of work to do, she was proud of the effort she and Perry had put into the garden. One half of it was now open and navigable. Of course, now that this had been accomplished, it was easy to see the great amount of effort required to open up all the smaller paths that weaved in patterns amid the various flower beds and overgrown shrub hedges. But, even with the knowledge that there remained so much, she was proud of her efforts.

She took a brief break on the bend along the outside wall, nearest the bees, to work out some issues. She found their noise, their constant hum and buzz, to be soothing. There were three problems weighing on her. First, that she knew there had to be some way to both get the honey and not to kill the hive, but the matter stumped her. She'd talked to the stable master, who was the most knowledgeable person she had close to her when it came to the issue of the bees, but it appeared to her that they'd exhausted his knowledge. She was still waiting for Mr. Wickliffe's scientist friend to write back and inform them of some possible choices.

Second, problem: what to do to help poor Cole? There had to be a way to allow him to follow his heart and love who he wanted, without bringing disgrace to the family, or, more importantly, to bring shame to Horatio

Wickliffe's family. She didn't want the Wickliffe's to leave. Because of the next concern.

Third, what to do about her feelings for lovely Edith, and Edith's feelings for her? As Mildred considered Edith, her heart raced and she felt a flush rise on to her cheeks. She knew and understood Cole, although she hadn't told him. Of course, she sympathized with her brother. But, poor Edith was in love with her and somehow Mildred must help her shift those feelings into sisterly love, not romantic love.

That's when it occurred to her, the solution to the second problem. As she realized the resolution, their tower clock began chiming the hour of eleven. That was the newly agreed upon lunch time. She raced out of the garden and back to the house. She wanted to change from her dirty smock into a clean dress. There was so much to discuss with Cole.

She entered the house through the great front door. No one was in sight and she dashed up the staircase and ran right into Mr. Willoughby on the top landing. The two of them tumbled to the ground.

"Oh, Mr. Willoughby, I'm terribly sorry!" shrieked Mildred.

Roland Willoughby quickly righted himself, and once on his feet, offered his gloved hand to her. "Quite all right, Miss Mildred."

She took his hand and a chill shuddered through her body, but she allowed herself to be partially lifted to her feet again by this man.

"Shall I let Cook know that you'll be a bit tardy for luncheon." Now, he eyed her in obvious judgment of her state of disarray.

"Yes, thank you." Mildred turned toward her room, wishing to dash down the hallway, but knew that Mr. Willoughby was still watching her. She walked as quickly as she could, finally hearing his footsteps on the stairs.

She entered her room and felt that things were out of sorts, yet when she looked around the space, everything appeared to be where it was supposed to reside. In her mind she cursed the maids and housekeeper for always shuffling through her things.

Mildred quickly poured water from the pitcher into the basin, stripped off her smock and dress, and, standing in her undergarments, splashed water on her face and washed her hands. She dried them with the crisp towel and flung that off to the side table. She moved to her desk and dashed off a note of invitation for dinner to the Wickliffe family, and then with as few movements as possible, slipped a fresh dress over her head, added a few pins to her hair, and ran out of the room without even tying the laces at her neck.

A scullery maid was in the hallway, taking advantage of the afternoon meal time to clean out the grates and add new coal to them before the evening. The young girl, with her soot stained hands, face, and arms, took a step and pressed her back up against the wall. She cast her glance down at the dirty tools in her hands to avoid Mildred's face.

Mildred stopped, took a deep breath, and resumed her direction, walking as quickly as she could manage without running. "I go days without seeing a single servant, and now, today, when I'm in the greatest of haste, I run into all of them with every step," she muttered under her breath.

Another maid, her arms heaped with linens, appeared before her. "You must tie my dress."

"Yes, Miss." She set the bed sheets on a windowsill and tied a neat bow at Mildred's neck.

Mildred arrived in the dining room, perspiring again, but found herself alone. At least she hadn't kept her brother waiting. He'd been growing angry if he had to wait for her, yet never apologized if it was Mildred who had been waiting for him.

She looked hard at the room. The settings seemed neater and more regulated in their placement. The crystal and silver glistened in the afternoon sunlight. There was a vase of fresh cut flowers as a centerpiece. She liked the new touches and wondered what motivation the staff had received to bring things into such order.

Mildred took her seat at her place and, after taking several long, deep breaths and wiping her cheeks and forehead with her fresh handkerchief, she rang the bell. The girl arrived before Mildred had replaced the silver bell on the table. "Please have this delivered at once to Mr. Wickliffe and have the boy wait for a reply," she said.

"Yes, Miss," said the girl who backed away and out of the room.

Mildred poured herself a glass of water and in a single swallow, drained it off. She poured a second glass and took a sip before placing the glass back in front of her. She was glad to have a moment to catch her breath and to think. She contemplated her latest idea that had hit her in the garden and knew, without a doubt, that so long as the players agreed to the game, she had found the perfect solution.

Something on one of the rooms many glass panes caught her attention. It was a small honey bee moving in odd patterns over and over. She wondered about the secret language this bee was using to share its message. There was no way for her to know it, but she felt, as she watched the bee perform the pattern over and over in its movement, that the creature was attempting to share something with her. But, she knew, for the moment at least, there was no way for her to translate what she was seeing. Yet, she watched it move, delighted by the activity which kept her occupied until Cole finally arrived for lunch.

"Father has sent a letter," Cole announced as he entered the room.

"Another One! Where is it? Let me see the letter. What does he have to say?" Mildred watched her brother take his seat and ring the bell for service. When the girl appeared, Mildred gave the hand signal and the girl again disappeared behind the door. Not a breath passed before she and another serving girl brought in the platters and served lunch to their masters, or the children playing at being their masters.

Cole stabbed at the food offered him and flung it on to his plate.

"What has he written?" Mildred implored.

The tower clock droned on the noon chime with its twelve bongs. Mildred and Cole sat in silence as the bell tolled between them, a reminder to Mildred of her accomplishments. Her brother didn't make eye contact, but busied himself with some newly arrived mail on a silver salver beside his plate.

When the chiming stopped, Cole began again without missing those twelve beats. "He said that he'd changed his mind. That Mr. Willoughby was to become the new butler for the house. In charge of everything. His sister will be arriving whenever she's supposed to arrive and would still be your maid. And, your maid only. The girl's not to do anything else in the house but to take care of you." He filled his mouth with food.

"Cole, don't you think it strange? Father has been missing for years now. Suddenly a letter arrives from him with no mention of where he has been or what he's doing or if he's coming home." She looked hard at her brother. She tried to regulate her tone but it remained shrill. "Cole look at me." He did look up. "Something isn't right about this. These letters can't be from Father."

"Look, it's in his distinct hand."

Mildred snatched the letter from her brother. "Well, it does look like his handwriting, but there's no way. And, that crate from him? Oh. Never mind. Eat your lunch."

Cole had never stopped eating and was about ready for a second portion.

Mildred knew she should wait to share her plan. Her brother was in a foul mood, which she didn't understand. He hated having Mr. Willoughby as his caretaker and this way that was no longer an issue. They'd had butlers before and the house ran smoother than it had been running. Well, that is until recently. She wondered if the polished crystal and silver was the doing of Mr. Willoughby's taking action and providing guidance. Next, Mildred wondered how that letter had arrived. That, she decided to ask: "How did Father's letter come to you?"

Cole didn't speak at once. He swallowed the large portion of potato he was consuming and followed that with a swig of wine. "A ship arrived yesterday at the areo-port and a man on a mechanical horse, much grander than the Wickliffe's, brought the letter."

"Was there only the one? Nothing for me?" She pouted.

"It was special delivery," was the only thing Cole said.

Letters and parcels rarely came so close together. Normally, in the past, whatever father or their uncle sent would arrive together, all at once. But over the past series of days there had been something from their father almost every day. The thought caused her to remember the packing crate. Somehow, with all the recent activities, she'd completely forgotten it. She hadn't opened a single parcel from inside that crate.

She ate her lunch in small bites. Mostly, she moved the food around her plate as she thought about all that was happening. There was her brother, who was once again being a beast to her. There was Edith, who the more she thought about the more she cared for. There was the garden. There were the bees. There was the crate. There was the clock! It chimed the noon hour. Mildred took another bite with the knowledge that dinner was only six hours away and she had to plan her words carefully. She had calculated that she would tell Cole now, at lunch, about her plan, get his approval and praise, and then inform the others. But, she dared not broach the subject with him in this mood. But, if she didn't gain his approval it wouldn't work.

Mildred watched her brother's face. He was lost in his food, staring at it and shoving huge quantities into his mouth, and then chewing angrily. She wondered how he managed to stay so fit and trim considering the great quantities he consumed. She wondered, too, how he still had any teeth and didn't choke to death the way he chomped and swallowed like a dog finishing his bowl of food before any of the others in the pack attempted to encroach on the possession.

She looked back toward the window and there were now two bees, one following the other, as the first continued to make the pattern over and over along the center of the pane.

I'll wait, she thought to herself. Everything will simply work out perfectly throughout the day. I know this is a good plan; a perfect plan. I will wait and trust that it will unfold smoothly.

The serving girl arrived with pudding. Mildred played with it, just as she had her lunch, while watching her brother inhale his double portion before wiping his mouth on the cloth napkin and abruptly leaving the table. She listened to the sound of his boots as he traveled through the dining room, through the hall, and into the conservatory. She wished she had kept the letter, but she hadn't. She'd wished again that she'd talked to him about her plan, but knew, instinctively, that she'd selected the best course of action.

Mildred rang the bell and gave the hand signal for the table to be cleared. Just before she left the room, she said to neither girl in particular, "Let Cook know that we'll be six for dinner at six." She enjoyed the sound of those words as they left her mouth. She liked playing at Lady of Wickwillow Manor.

Fifty-Nine

Parker Greene had regained control of his faculties. He sat up in bed, eating a bowl of very good soup. "Bread! Is there no bread?"

"You are a horrible patient," said one of the housekeepers. She handed him a hard roll and her eyes sparkled and twinkled.

"Thank you."

"I think you'll be finishing your soup and getting yourself out of bed. No more lollygagging around for you." She plumped his pillows.

Parker took her arm. "Thank you for saving me."

"No, sir, it wasn't me. It was your doctor man."

He held her still. "Thank you."

She looked around to be certain no one would hear and then, in a lowered voice said: "You're welcome, I'm sure. We need you well."

As if her words were punctuation, the house began to hum, there was a vibration under their feet. The house maid rushed to the window. "The Robin!" She turned to Parker with a knowing, wry smile.

"So it begins," he said. "Fetch me my trousers, boots. We must be quick."

She raced around the room, helping Parker dress. While better, he wasn't yet solid on his feet. She braced him and then helped with buttons, ties, and belts. When she'd finished he looked rumpled and handsome, unshaven and masculine.

"Thank you," he offered again as the housemaid rushed from the room.

Once more, Parker Greene opened the top drawer of his dressing table. There, like on the ship, were his personal items. This time, there wasn't any choosing. He took the time to tuck letters, his pocket watch, the small pistol, and the bag of gold into their pockets and places. He knew he couldn't put on his side arm. A sword would draw too much attention to him, a man out for a stroll. He must hurry. If he didn't get into the elevator in the first fifteen minutes of the Robin's arrival, he might be trapped on his own island, and the plan would go off without him and he'd be left behind with the survivors. Parker doubled his pace until he was at the front entrance.

As he opened the great wood door, there, in jacket and cravat, stood Rifle Helms looking handsome and rugged. "Are you ready, my Lord?"

Rifle's smile so inviting, Parker forgot all protocol, leaned forward, and kissed the man right on the lips. They lingered together until an "Ahem," brought Parker back to the moment.

"I see," said Able Currant. "I misunderstood you then?"

"Oh, Able." It was an awkward moment. But, Parker had never grown to trust Able, despite having enjoyed the pleasure of his company many times.

"Oh, there's no misunderstanding. This man is with me," said Rifle Helms, stepping between Parker and Able.

"Are you challenging me to a duel?" Able laughed at the thought. His laugh was infectious, only this time, no one joined him and the song of that laughter fell silent.

"No," said Rifle who quickly thrust a dagger into his rival's gut. He held it there. "You won't be coming with us."

Able struggled for a moment, gripped Rifle's shoulders tightly, and just as it looked like he might take action, blood dribbled from Able's mouth and all life left his beautiful eyes.

"Why?" Parker asked as Rifle let Able fall into the flower beds.

"He's no friend of ours." Rifle looked around the street. No one appeared to be watching. He took out his handkerchief, wiped the knife blade clean, and tossed the cotton onto Able. "One less pirate for our battle," he hissed.

There was absolutely no turning back now. Not that Parker wanted to turn back. The two men headed toward the elevator and, along with a dozen dwarfs, descended into the tunnel, which was already filled with little men and women.

A small cheer went up as Parker Greene and Rifle Helms joined the crowd.

Nate pushed through the crowd in his waddle walk and tugged on Parker's sleeve. "All is ready from our end, sir. The plans, the people, the weapons. We have not relied or depended on any of the pirates. It is, as you asked, just our band and the two of you."

"Excellent, Nate. Now, you have to get me into the boiler rooms of the Robin. I have to get the lads there to join us, otherwise all will be lost."

"Then off," said Nate as he turned toward the tunnel. The crowd parted and Parker and Rifle followed the little man as he led the way.

Sixty

The tower clock chimed the sixth hour. Mildred descended the stairs in a white dress that moved well. When she entered the parlor all eyes turned to her and she thought she heard a gasp. She was glad she'd taken the extra time to pile her hair atop her head and to add the adornments of little white flowers. Mildred had thought the effect would be stunning, and based on the reaction of the Wickliffe family, she knew she'd been correct.

"Good evening," she said brightly to those assembled. Mildred made the rounds, shaking first Mr. Wickliffe's hand, and then Mrs. Wickliffe's. She nodded to Horatio who stood alone, apart from his family, and then moved gracefully to Edith. In her periwinkle blue dress, her eyes of blue sparkled. "Hello, Edith," said Mildred. Her hand trembled lightly as she reached for that of her friend's.

"You look amazing, Mildred!" exclaimed Edith who clutched to her. "Thank you so much for this dinner invitation." Then she drew her face close to Mildred's and whispered: "It has been unbearable at our home the past few days."

Mildred didn't comment, but turned to Mr. Wickliffe. "How is that horse of yours?"

"Working perfectly," said Mr. Wickliffe with a warm smile.

Mildred moved to the long upholstered banner and gave it a tug. One of the serving girls arrived with a tray of wine glasses around a large crystal decanter. "I thought we would have a little wine before dinner, if that is acceptable to everyone?" She looked around at her guests, wondering where Cole was. She had asked Willoughby that afternoon to be sure his charge, even though he was no longer Willoughby's charge, would be on time for dinner. Before the girl left the room, Mildred asked her quietly, "Where is my brother?"

"I don't know, Miss."

"Would you please find Willoughby and ask him?"

"Yes, Miss."

"I must apologize for my brother. He is, as usual, running a bit late. Why don't you pour us some wine, Mr. Wickliffe?"

"Of course, of course," said the man. She watched as he took up his task, offering glasses to Mildred first and then his wife and daughter. She saw Horatio wave off the offer of a drink.

Mildred moved easily to Horatio. "Would you prefer something else?"

"No thank you, Miss Greene." The boy didn't make eye contact with her.

Mildred desperately wanted to pull Horatio and Edith aside, in the hall, or out of doors so that they could all talk. But, such a thing wasn't acceptable, even in such a small group as this. She'd invited the whole family to dinner and, therefore, knew she must entertain all of them, not just the children.

For a long while, no one spoke. Mildred offered them seats and took up her favorite chair. She knew she was supposed to make conversation, since no one was speaking. It annoyed her that Horatio was keeping so separate from the rest of the little group, but she didn't know how to bring him into the fray from the fringe.

"This is interesting," said Mr. Wickliffe of a small wood carved statuette sitting on the side table. "I don't remember seeing it before." He picked up the small figure and turned it around and around in his hands, marveling at the intricate carving and detail of the tribal man.

"That was among the things Father sent in his last crate. I liked it so much, I decided to bring it out into the light."

"Your father? You've heard from him?"

"Well, Mr. Wickliffe, there have been two suspect letters. I believe the crate has simply been in transit for a very long time. What's that line? On a slow boat from China? Around the capes and all that."

"You finally went through the crate?" asked Edith. She looked a little disappointed, possibly because she'd hoped to have been present when the wonders in that box from the opposite side of the world had been revealed.

"I haven't gone through everything. As I was exploring the contents this afternoon, I kept being interrupted by one need or another of the house. So, I decided to wait to finish." She wanted to rush now with Edith into the library and allow her the fun of rummaging through the packing materials, but knew such a thing would be inappropriate.

Mildred gazed toward the door, hoping that the figure there who had caught her eye was her brother, but it was only Willoughby. The tall man entered the room and all eyes turned to him. His striking height and handsome looks arrested the room and what little conversation that had begun once again stopped as the man made his way to Mildred; he bent in half to get low enough to speak to her.

"I'm sorry, Miss Mildred, but I do not know where your brother has gone off to. I did convey your message and the importance of this evening's dinner to him, but he offered no words. He simply left the house again. That was several hours ago."

"Thank you, Willoughby." The man waited, remaining in his awkward position. Mildred ignored him and turned to her guests. "Friends, it appears my brother has lost track of time once again."

At the words, Horatio's eyes bore into her and then rapidly he looked away. She wondered about the man's pained expression. She wished she could provide comfort. She knew, deeply knew, that her plan would bring him ease and she longed to simply share it with him now. But, with everyone else present, it seemed to her most inappropriate.

"May I suggest we go in for dinner and allow my brother to join us when he arrives? I would hate for the dinner to be ruined because of his tardiness." Mildred didn't know if this was the correct thing to do or not, but she'd made a decision. As she stood from her seat, the others who had also sat stood to join her. Edith moved to her side and the girls led the way into the dining room. Mildred offered seating assignments, leaving the chair at the head of the table empty for her absent brother. Once everyone had taken their seats, she rang the bell for the start of service.

Just as the first course was being brought to the table, Cole strode into the room. He wasn't dressed for dinner, but still in soiled work clothes. "Couldn't hold dinner five minutes for me, Sister dear?" he barked.

Mr. Wickliffe stood to greet him, but Cole motioned for him to sit, which he did.

"If you'd like us to wait while you change, we'd be happy to do that." Mildred's tone was even, but a little dark. She had grown tired of her brother's unpredictable attitude. As her anger in the moment grew, she wondered why on earth she'd been so interested in crafting a plan that would make him happy and protect his name.

"I can eat in these," he said, tugging at his trousers for emphasis.

"Please, Cole. Won't you please…" Mildred didn't know what she wanted, beyond her sudden desire for this evening to be over and done. She wished now that she had only invited Edith. They could have dined together alone by candlelight in the conservatory, or…Mildred stopped herself from thinking, "my room."

"We'll be happy to wait for you," said Mr. Wickliffe. He'd adopted the tone of stern father. With that tone, his words were less an offer and more a command.

Cole responded. "I'll only be a few moments."

Willoughby joined him in the doorway as he left the room and the two men, with Willoughby a respectable few steps behind the master of house, walked away.

While this scene unfolded, the two serving girls stood silent and still near the door to the hall that led to the kitchen. With a mastered movement of her hand, Mildred sent them away.

The group sat silent for a moment. Edith looked expectantly first at Mildred and then at her mother. Neither woman offered her any solace. Horatio had taken up a butter knife and was absently playing with it, running his finger along the edge and back down to the handle. Mr. Wickliffe sat defiant while his wife looked to Mildred. It was obvious that she was trying to come up with something to say, but she didn't say anything. The woman who always appeared so kind and graceful, was now silent.

"How is your garden?" Edith asked.

Mildred looked with kindness toward her friend. "We've completed the circuit!" She touched Edith's hand and then, feeling uncomfortable, knowing that all the eyes in the room, save possibly Horatio's, were upon her; she removed her hand. "Not the full circuit, mind you, but we have fully uncovered half of the main paths around and up to the fountain." She was proud of the accomplishment.

"And, your bees?" asked Mrs. Wickliffe with a small, but noticeable shudder.

"The bees. I'd nearly forgotten," said Mr. Wickliffe. He reached into one of the inner pockets of his dinner jacket and produced a letter. "My scientist friend has written to me of a new invention by an American. It's a box designed for the keeping of bees. Amazing. There's a book about it and he's offered to send me a copy as soon as he can acquire one. Anyway, he saw the invention at an agricultural conference he attended in Paris recently and has offered some rough sketches and notes." Mr. Wickliffe gently waived the thick letter that he held.

Mildred wanted to get up and rush to his side of the table. She wanted to take the letter away from this room and sit with a lamp and read it alone. The possibilities, without even having seen the drawings or read the words, were already whirling through her mind. Instead of taking action she took a breath and said: "I look forward to reading of this discovery and I thank you so much for your kindness in contacting your friend."

On the heal of her words, Cole strode back into the room in evening dress. He cut a handsome figure with his combed hair and a face ruddy from being recently scrubbed clean. His mood and demeanor had changed along with his clothes and he now had the confident air of a man in charge.

"Please forgive my tardiness. It couldn't be helped," said Cole, taking his seat at the head of the table.

Mildred rang the bell for service just as the tower clock began striking seven. She watched her brother who took charge of the meal. He incited polite conversation about local politics, about the success of the fields, and about the fine weather. He prompted Mrs. Wickliffe and Miss Edith about new hats he'd seen in the milliner's window. As each course proceeded, he gave Mildred the signal to ring for service.

It was imperceptible, but while he spoke and listened, while he ate and drank, he offered glances again and again in Horatio's direction. Their guests could not have noticed the amount of attention and pleading he was sending to Horatio in those small glances. Mildred didn't even know if Horatio was picking up on the signs. And, once again, Mildred found herself more determined than ever to do all she could to aid her brother, and Horatio. To the others, Mildred knew she gave the impression of being fully engaged in the conversation at hand and in seeing the meal run smoothly, all the while, in her mind, she was thinking about her bees, thinking about her plan to save and aid her brother, thinking about her desires for there to be more than kissing between her and Edith. She thought, too, of Mr. Wickliffe's kindness as a piano teacher and of Mrs. Wickliffe's kind instructions in the ways of a lady of means. She thought of the rejuvenation of the garden that was taking shape under her own hands. She thought of the wonderful clock that was now beginning to chime the hour of eight with the full knowledge that it was her mind that had discovered the solution. She considered her drive shaft idea that would modernize the house. She again thought of her sisterly love for Edith and her desire that they be together as much as possible. Yet, feared still telling Edith of her feelings for fear of losing her friendship.

 Her life felt to her to be full and complete. She had so much to do and think about, more than she'd ever experienced before. And, she wondered how all of this had come to pass. Just a few short weeks ago she was a young woman with little more on her mind than Latin verbs and piano etudes. And, now, she was the Lady of this great house with problems, issues, and solutions to offer. While not the same as designing a powered house, Perhaps, the role of woman had something of interest to offer?

Sisty-One

Throngs of dwarfs ran in all directions. Some were unloading the Robin's spoils and booty from her latest venture, while others were restocking her with food, water, and arms in preparation of her next voyage. The great crane removed three mail schooners. In addition, two groups of dwarfs, one led by Rifle, the second by Parker Greene, assembled in their locations.

Greene and Nate entered the ship. There had been no fight, there had been no resistance. Nate blended easily, being among the little people. Parker stood several feet taller; there was no merging or hiding among the activity. The two quickly made their way to the lower decks, to the stokers. There was little time to convince them to join up with Greene and the dwarfs.

When they entered the boiler room, Lord Greene gasped at the sheer size of the boilers, each of the six at least twenty feet high by twenty feet wide. Great hoses were now filling them for their next journey. Shirtless young men, with goggles over their eyes, stoked fires. With each shovel of wood or coal, sparks shot out of the furnaces.

"Lord Greene?" He barely heard the voice.

Parker turned to the young stoker who called to him. Even covered in soot, he recognized the blond boy from his own ship, the Barkley. "Yes."

He pulled off his eyewear. The rubber and glass lenses bounced around his neck as he talked in an animated style. "Have you come to save us?"

"Are you all prepared to fight, to follow, and to fight some more?" Greene wanted to put an arm around the man's shoulders, but the furnace man was covered in soot and grime.

"We are prepared. We have a plan in place, a contingency really, for any opportunity."

"Good, lad. What is your name?"

"Albert Neyland."

Parker Greene continued: "Albert, is there anyone here you cannot trust?" Parker looked around the floor where dozens of young men, dressed in like fashion, worked on their own boilers.

"There is one." He pointed toward a young boy in the corner. Unlike the others here, he was clean, wearing a crisp white shirt. He held a book and walked from boiler to boiler taking notes. "He holds all the power here."

"That diminutive boy?"

"He is Flynn's son."

"Ah. Well, he must be the first one murdered. There's no turning back on that. As soon as the fighting begins, he must be taken out. Is there one among you who is up to such a task and can do it without remorse?"

"Choose anyone here, and they will gladly take on that burden." Albert smiled wryly at Parker Greene.

"Good. Well, you choose who it will be. Second, the doors to this chamber must be locked and secured from the inside. And, finally, the boilers must be ready for flight in a mere twenty minutes from…" Parker took out his pocket watch. He pushed a pin. "Now."

"Yes, my Lord. As you wish. I will see to all these details."

"Good man. You shall be rewarded."

"Regaining my freedom shall be reward enough for me, sir."

This formal exchange was British. They were now at war to uphold the morals of England and their dear Queen. The words weren't trite, but incendiary. Parker Greene, lost in the excitement, patted Albert on the back; his hand came away covered in coal dust, grime, and sweat. He turned and strode toward the door where Nate waited on lookout.

"All's clear, Lord Greene."

Parker liked that the men had taken to calling him "Lord" once again. They were all British. Subjects of their beloved Queen.

The plan of action was underway. He stepped through the door; there was a brief cry behind him, a grand "Hurrah!" from the crew, and then only the hum of the boilers, the scrape of the shovels. Once outside the boiler room, the door he'd traveled snapped shut; he heard the bolts cast.

"Next stop, cleaning up the upper decks. We must spare all we can."

"We're prepared to kill them, sir." Nate walked as fast as his legs could carry him. "I understand your morality, but we've been prisoners for decades. The captors must die." Up one flight of wooden stairs they came together with a group of dwarfs, each carrying some bizarre looking weapon. Some harnessed electricity; others were complicated collections of gears and cogs that when brandished delivered death in efficient ways. His favorite weapons among the new creations were those that gave the little men and women who brandished them the power of the pirates they fought. A bow with cogs and pulleys turned a full-sized bow into a child's, but allowed great power. Another gun-like defense, when shaken, gathered a charge, which could be administered to an enemy, but the two must be close together. And so, with a collection of toy-sized artillery, the growing band of small men and women moved forward with their task of clearing the Balsa Robin of any remaining pirates.

While Greene's plan was to allow the men to live, but to leave them on their island without workers or power, he respected the desire of the dwarfs. He brandished his sword, and along with his friends, cut down the unarmed pirates, those few onboard who were overseeing the packing and cleaning.

The mob of little men and women began spreading out, combing each nook and cranny, opening each door. Whenever the enemy was encountered, they were slaughtered. The halls and decks became slick with blood. No one looked back with any regret. After years of oppression and servitude, these small people were having the final word with their captors.

Parker Greene considered the mess, but continued forward with his rag-tag band.

Deck-by-deck the small band moved, footsteps moving together, almost as one, as each cabin and storage space were checked for pirates. One man, swinging in a hammock in a dark corner was cut in two by swords, his body left to drip and ooze as the mob moved on to the next set of stairs, the next cabins, systematically killing, leaving the bodies where they fell. Some tried to run from them, and those were taken down by the wonderful new weapons.

Finally, Nate, Lord Greene, and a band of twenty arrived at Captain Flynn's door. They stood silent for a moment and then burst through the door like an army. The dwarfs in page uniforms quickly joined the ranks. Upon entering the inner office, Flynn stood, outraged to see the band before him.

"Have you come with some complaint? What are you about, Greene? Representing the little people?" He laughed heartily.

Without warning, two of the pages, one to the left and the other to the right of their master, moved their hands in quick order, rubbing their pointed rings over Flynn's body. Red began to seep through his pants and shirt.

"What are you…"he gasped. "Bad form, Greene."

A lifetime passed in very slow motion and Flynn fell to the floor. He writhed for just a few seconds and was dead.

"How?" Parker asked toward Nate.

"Poison rings. Two or three pokes with intention and the contents inside are released into the victim. Quick, sudden death."

"Why haven't you ever used these weapons?" Greene couldn't believe they'd lived so long as captives with a mechanism such as this to deliver freedom.

"We needed a leader. Not just random killing."

With the ship cleared, Greene and his men began ordering the Robin prepared to sail. He hoped Rifle was meeting with a similar ease of success. They'd have to compare notes to discover who among those school chums had been killed, who simply left behind. It didn't feel like a satisfactory conclusion, yet the actions were happening and there was no changing the outcome now.

Sixty-Two

Dinner concluded, the men went into the library for brandy, and the women entered the drawing room for coffee.

Cole watched Horatio, who had never been in the room before; his friend walked around, sipped his brandy, and looked at the books and souvenirs that crowded all the walls. He avoided eye contact with both Cole and his father. On every surface was an object from some wonderful place in the world. "May I speak to you?"

"Of course," said Cole, still focused on the decanter.

"Father, would you mind if I spoke to Cole, alone?"

Mr. Wickliffe looked at the boys. "Of course. I'll see what the women are up to and maybe get Miss Mildred to play something for us." As he spoke, in a quiet voice, he left the room.

As the door closed behind Mr. Wickliffe, Cole and Horatio, still standing close to one another, moved into the arms of the other and kissed. It was a soft, easy kiss that lasted through eons and spoke volumes.

"Ahem," said Mildred politely.

Cole and Horatio broke off their embrace, yet neither, in that moment, felt or showed any signs of remorse. That kiss bonded them together. Without words or knowledge, they knew that they were a couple and would have to face the consequences of that decision. Yet, it was a decision, as unspoken as it was, that contained all the joy, love, and the weight of the world rolled into one.

"What?" Cole asked of his sister. He wasn't angry or upset, but resolved to the fate that her words, posture, and accusations might bring. It was a small sound, the "what" that he spoke.

Mildred closed the door behind her and moved to them. "Please, let's sit for a moment."

The boys did as instructed.

She removed the snifter from her brother's hand and took a small sip of the liquid in an attempt to steady herself. Cole watched her and wondered what she was up to. As he waited for her, the tower clock struck the hour of nine. He liked that there was now a demarcation of time in their lives. He liked that he had found the solution to the clock's…he remembered that it really wasn't him that had fixed the clock. Well, he had put the pieces in their correct places, but it had been his sister who had solved the problem. Cole wanted to cry and the look was so upsetting to Horatio that he took up Cole's hand into his own to comfort him. He wanted to explain to Horatio what had him so upset, but remained silent.

"I have found a solution of sorts to our trouble," she began.

"Our trouble?" asked Cole. "What do you know of all of this? What trouble is it of yours?" His anger began to rise. He hated that he was so often angry and out of sorts. Yet, there it was.

"Dear Brother, I know a great deal about what we're all going through, even though you and I haven't spoken directly about any of it. I wanted to talk to you at lunch today, but you were so horrible to me, I decided to wait until tonight."

Cole dropped his head down along with the barrier he'd been creating between them for a reason he himself didn't really understand.

"Now, I don't have much time. I have to get back to the drawing room before they wonder what has happened to me."

"Go on," said Horatio, still braced against Cole on the leather sofa.

"I know that you two are in love. It's obvious now if it wasn't before. And, I think it's wonderful, even if the rest of the world might not." She looked at them. Horatio was urging her forward with his eyes; Cole's focus was on Horatio; at the sign of negative reaction he would end this conversation with his nosy sister. "I have found great friendship toward Miss Wickliffe." That statement caused Cole's head to rise and then tilt slightly to the right like a dog hearing a sound in the distance.

Horatio's eyes sparkled while a smile broadened his handsome face. "I knew it. I knew something was up with her." He seemed pleased with himself at discovering the cause of his sister's recent spark in happiness and joy.

"While not love and romance such as yours, I care for her with the great affection of sisterhood. So, I've come up with a grand solution that just might keep us all together, keep you and your family from having to leave. Now, I don't yet have a good solution for the hunter, but we'll cross that bridge when it's built."

"Oh, get on with it," barked Cole.

Mildred sighed. "If I'm to tell you this solution and play my part in it, I must ask you, Cole, to start being a bit nicer to me. You've been horrible the past few weeks and it's getting the better of my nerves, for I certainly haven't done anything to you to warrant such dreadful treatment from you."

The room was eerily silent.

Finally, Cole spoke: "I'm sorry, please continue." His voice was soft and once again resolved to whatever fate might bring him.

"Now, I haven't yet had a chance to share this idea with Edith. But, here goes. I propose that…that for appearances only….that it look as if I am betrothed to Horatio, and you, Cole, are courting Edith. That will give us all the opportunity to spend as much time with each other in any combination that we desire." Mildred wanted more brandy, but refrained from disturbing her brother until he'd processed what she'd just said.

"Brilliant!" exclaimed Horatio. He looked to Cole for his response.

"I don't want to woo Miss Wickliffe." His tone was sullen, and he looked as if he'd burst into tears at any moment.

"You won't actually be courting her, Cole," chastised Mildred. "It will only be for appearances sake. If we are out in public or entertaining. In front of their parents and town people. If it appears that the four of us are romantically aligned as couples, as the expected male-female couples, no one will question you spending time with Horatio or me spending time with my future sister, Edith. We will, however, have to be discreet about your…romantic endeavors."

"It's brilliant, Cole, don't you see?" prodded Horatio.

The smile that formed on Cole's face was like the clouds parting and sun reappearing. "Oh…" was all he said.

"Do you think your sister will play along?" Mildred asked.

"I don't see why not. Cole is a handsome boy, and our parents keep pushing her to find someone nice to become engaged to. She's of that age, as are you, Miss Mildred."

Mildred's demeanor became playful. "If we're to be engaged, Mr. Wickliffe, I suggest you start calling me Mildred." She laughed.

"Mildred," he said and then turned to Cole, placing a hand on his friend's knee. "This will work, and we can be together forever. Don't you see? If we marry each other's sisters and live together in the same house, only the servants will know."

"The servants? That's why this won't work," said Cole, falling back into his dejection.

"That's another bridge to cross later," chastised Mildred. "Cole, why can't you just go with this, work with this for a few moments." Mildred stood up. "I really do have to go back to the parlor. Please, join us in there in a few minutes. I'm going to play the piano."

"What about the difference in our class distinction," Cole offered.

Mildred dropped her voice to a barely audible whisper, "Cole, we are new money. Father has bought his title and all of these trappings." Mildred raised her arm and took in the room. "No one will speak any more ill of us than they already do."

Horatio stood up and reached out for Mildred's raised hand. He caught her a little off guard which caused an uncomfortable laugh to escape her lips. Electricity shot through her at his touch. Other than a few kind handshakes and pats, he'd never touched her. She liked the feel of his hand now grasping hers to hold her in place. Horatio smiled at her warmly. "Thank you, Mildred." He boldly kissed her cheek, which caused her to flush.

"You're welcome." She held his eyes for a long moment. "Now, bring him along." She tried to release her hand from her captor, but he held her a beat longer before allowing her fingers to slip out of his own. Mildred glided out of the room as quietly as she had entered, leaving the boys behind to discuss their new fate.

Sixty-Three

The pages cleared Flynn's body away, as if he were a pig carcass after a feast: two in front, two behind and one underneath. Two more pages easily cleaned up the blood from the floor before turning to Lord Greene.

"We await orders, Lord."

"Gather those who know how to fly the Robin. Bring them to me."

The small men laughed.

Parker Greene looked from one mirth-filled face to another. "What have I missed?"

A Nubian dwarf, with shining black-as-night skin, stepped forward. "sir," he stifled another pleasant laugh. "Everyone of us knows how to fly, rig, and captain our beloved Robin. Granted, most of us," here he indicated to those assembled, "can't climb the rigging. But, we can instruct anyone over four feet exactly what needs to be done. We have been preparing for this day for a very, very, very long time." He smiled bright white teeth and stepped back into formation.

"Excellent. What is your name?" Greene stepped aside as several small men unrolled a grand map of the world on the desk before him.

"I am Samuel."

"Samuel," Greene stepped up and held out his hand. "You shall be my second. You shall get us to," Greene scanned the map. "Here. You shall get us to this spot in England as quickly as possible. We all serve at your honor."

"It shall be my honor to serve you, Lord Greene." Samuel took the offered hand and pumped it joyfully. Before he'd even released it, the man had begun barking orders and the others were on their way.

"We must await…"

"We are here and we must be off. The power will shut down in less than seven minutes." Rifle Helms stood before Greene, covered in a coat of blood.

"What on earth has happened?" Greene stepped back, not toward

Rifle.

"They put up a fight. We fought back. Only lost two men. Everyone is onboard. Even Miss Ebony and those men."

"She got them? All of them?" Lord Greene sat down. A page placed a glass of whiskey in his hand and he drank it off. He thought back to those men with flies walking on their faces. Near death. And, Miss Ebony, who had attempted to kill him, saving them. Such a strange turn of events.

"All but one. He bade them leave without him. He was nearly dead." Rifle pointed to the bottle. "May I?"

"Of course."

Before the blood-soaked fighter could reach the decanter, two pages arrived. One poured whiskey, the other began undressing Helms. It only took a few moments. Rifle stood naked while several men and women washed him down, blood draining into a basin he stood in. Others toweled him dry. And, still others, redressed him in perfectly fitted clothes. It was such a wonder to behold, Greene remained dumbfounded throughout the process.

"There, fresh as a daisy," Rifle finally said.

"Close enough." Greene walked to the great windows. The buildings around him were smoke and flames. He glanced over to his home island, it too belched smoke.

Samuel stopped pacing for a long moment. "Sir, we must depart. If we don't launch before the power shuts down, there will be no hope of getting the Robin into the air."

"There should be one more."

"Who?"

"Nate. He left when we arrived here. He said not to leave until he returned." Parker Greene paced before the windows. He checked the time on his watch. "How much longer?"

"Two minutes."

The energy of the great ship could be felt. It was steamed. It was ready.

"Give word to open the doors." Greene wanted an assurance, but there wasn't any.

"Once we begin, the sequence can't be stopped." Samuel stared at Greene.

"Begin." Greene strode out of the captain's quarters and began making his way to the lowest door. Much of the blood had already been cleaned up.

The bodies were neatly stacked. They would be delivered to the sea once the Balsa Robin were in the mid-Atlantic. He shuddered at the numbers of dead, but continued moving downward, toward the main hatch. He scrutinized every red-headed dwarf he passed, hoping it would be Nate. None of them were.

Lord Greene passed a cabin where each little person was stopping at and depositing a heap of mail or plans that they'd been carrying on their person. They chose to save that material instead of large amounts of personal items. He admired their loyalty to the Queen.

It felt like the great air ship was pulling at its tethers. It was raring to go, to begin another journey, as if it had a life and will of its own.

Parker Greene arrived at the last hatch. This was the last one that would be closed. A few stragglers were now racing toward the gangway. None of them were Nate.

"We must close it, sir." A small man and woman reached for the ropes. "It will be ripped away if we don't."

"Hold it until the last possible second," he instructed, again eyeing the time on his watch. Merely thirty seconds. Without thought he began counting. "Twenty-nine…twenty-eight…twenty-seven…"

"We must pull it up now," said the woman to the man. "We can't stay aloft for days, let alone weeks, with this hole gaping in the hull. And, if we need to land in the water, we'll see our death."

"Nineteen…eighteen…"

No one else was in sight. They closed up the hatch tight. A few more beats and the ship rose from its birth. It was a rocky, bumpy rise, but they were over water now. Ascending into a blue sky.

Lord Greene considered that if Nate had made the ship at that last moment, that this would now be the perfect ending for the story. Instead, the mastermind of so much of the plan was nowhere to be seen. Greene hoped, for his own sake, that the little man wouldn't be murdered for his actions today.

As the ship pulled away from the islands, gaining height and distance with each belch of smoke and steam, everyone near an opening or open deck could see the islands in smoke and flame. While the reassuring hum stopped abruptly.

Sixty-four

Mildred entered the parlor and the eyes of the Wickliffe's all focused on her at the same time. She smiled, feeling a light blush rise to her face. It had been a long day and Mildred suddenly felt fatigued. She licked her lips, tasting a hint of the brandy upon them. She desired more, but knew that was impossible. "Shall I play for you?" she asked, approaching the pianoforte.

Mr. Wickliffe joined her at the instrument and said: "That would be lovely."

Mildred watched as the vicar looked through a small stack of music. "This, I think. You can perform, and I can see if you've been practicing. Two birds, as the saying goes."

Mildred smiled at her teacher. She so wanted to talk to him, to declare her sins, to gain his acceptance and love as an in-law, a substitute father. In that moment she realized how much she missed her father. And, she also realized that for her romantic plan to truly work that she'd have to lie to her uncle in each letter she wrote from now on. At the thought, her stomach twirled. She was grateful for the bench beneath her as she sat with a thump.

"Are you all right, Miss Mildred?" asked Mr. Wickliffe.

"I think the heat has gotten the best of me for the moment."

The vicar turned to the maid who was bringing a fresh pot of coffee into the room. "Please bring us some port." The maid, without a word, curtsied and left the room. "A little wine will steady you," said Mr. Wickliffe.

"Thank you." She looked at the music he had placed on the stand. She hadn't practiced it enough. She knew she'd have trouble in the allegro passage. Mildred wanted to confess. She knew he'd be able to tell that she hadn't appropriately prepared the piece. She wanted the wine to arrive. She wanted the boys to come into the room and create a diversion. She wanted to look toward Edith and see her sweet face. But, all she could manage was to look at the keyboard, afraid to touch it with her trembling fingers.

The solution and the boys arrived at the same moment.

"Mr. Wickliffe," began Mildred. "Can you show me a better fingering for the middle of the allegro section?"

The question pleased him. He quickly turned to the place she spoke of. "Everyone has trouble with that. Let's not put you on the spot at the moment, but instead, you'll play something else for us and we'll work on the fingering during our lesson tomorrow. I'm so pleased that you discovered the problem."

Mildred breathed a little easier as the vicar replaced the difficult, unpracticed piece with a Brahms Intermezzo she was more familiar with.

Time blurred for her as the maid arrived with the port. Everyone took a seat on the plush furniture, their attention turned toward Mildred at the pianoforte. She played the lush, romantic music, all the while eyeing out of the corner of her eye the glass of wine that had been placed for her at the edge of the piano.

She desperately wanted to be alone with Edith, to tell her of the plan she'd concocted. She wanted to be alone with her thoughts. She wanted to…she simply wanted to be alone. But, as the hostess, it was her responsibility to entertain her guests. The music flowed as her hands, without her having to think about them, glided over the worn ivory keys. This place, this spot, sitting on this bench, playing this instrument, was so familiar to her. It required no thought to make this music. She'd played this piece hundreds of times. Her mind flashed to the workings of the clock, then to the interworking of the mechanical horse. She envisioned once again her driveshaft idea that would provide power to all manner of new devices throughout the great house. Mildred followed her thoughts as they wandered through the cellars and tunnels below the house. She could see where some new tunnels would have to be dug to provide the lines and direct reach of the massive shaft that would churn constantly. She could almost feel the hum of the great machine whose steam and torque would turn the shaft every moment of every day. With that thought, she realized the house would require a much larger furnace and boiler. That's when everything went black.

Mildred enjoyed that blackness for a moment. She could hear the buzzing of bees around her as she searched the blackness for them. She saw nothing, but the sound grew more intense. A streak of light flashed past her line of sight. In her mind, she turned to follow the light, which flashed once again as it passed her. Her world spun.

"Hello, dear," she heard clearly amidst the buzzing, but she didn't recognize the voice.

She attempted to speak, but nothing came out of her mouth. She instead thought the word, "Hello?"

"That's it. That's how it works." Laughter filled her head. It was a soft, kind, gentle sound that gave her great comfort.

"Who are you?" she thought. But, before an answer was offered, the buzzing of the bees increased in volume and intensity, so loud she couldn't hear the words, although she instinctively knew they were there. The buzzing grew even louder and then stopped, leaving absolute blackness and silence in her head.

"Mildred? Mildred?"

She could hear her name but couldn't make the words of acknowledgement leave her mouth.

"Mildred?"

That was her brother. He sounded bewildered to her, yet she couldn't comfort him.

"Father, do something!"

She hated that Edith sounded so panicked and upset. Mildred wanted to reassure her friend but couldn't move. She knew something wasn't right. She could feel that she was lying on something very hard and a little cool. But, Mildred had no ability in that moment to identify it. She could feel her hands being patted and her face being dampened with a cool, wet cloth, yet, she couldn't move, couldn't speak. Once again, she heard the heartening laughter in her mind, a slight hum of her bees.

Mildred tried to envision the great shaft, the workings of the connectors, the flow of power that would drive fans and lights that would work by some mystical force of spinning wheels. Yet, suddenly, she couldn't see any of it. Everything that was or had been familiar in the dark reaches of her mind was now beyond access to her. That, more than not being able to speak or move, was unsettling to her. She could fathom going through any hardship or challenge the universe might present, but not losing her capacity to envision how things worked. That would be madness.

"She's coming around."

The voice was Mrs. Wickliffe's. The woman's face was blurred, but as her eyes fluttered open, that's who she saw and felt the kind woman's hands cradling her head. Next to her mother, Edith, with a look of fear and worry such as Mildred had never witnessed before, knelt fanning Mildred with a piece of sheet music.

"You gave us all such a fright," said Cole. In that moment, he was his "old self." The caring concerned brother she had known all her life.

"Most amazing thing I've ever seen. One moment you were playing and then, BOOM!, you fell backward off the stool and hit the floor."

With Horatio's words, Mildred raised her hand to the back of her head and felt the throbbing bump. She tried to sit up, but the room spun horribly, so she rested again against Mrs. Wickliffe.

"Stay still a bit longer," the vicar said. He handed his wife a glass of water, which she dutifully held to Mildred's lips.

Mildred drank some. With each breath she could feel herself returning more fully to her body. When she tried to sit up again, she was successful. She wanted to speak about the sensations she'd experienced, about the bees buzzing in her mind, about the voice she'd heard. Mildred looked around her at all the faces so intensely focused on her and she remained silent. They all looked so hurt and pained. While she knew they were worried and supportive, she also knew that this was not something she could speak of to them. She realized in that moment that she couldn't even share this experience with her closest friend, Edith. In all her life, Mildred never felt as alone as she did right then. She longed for her father's return. He had seen so much of the world. He'd told Mildred of tribal peoples in South America who spoke the words of others that they heard in their heads. He'd told her of American Shaman who channeled gods and healers. Certainly, her father would understand. But, he was lost to her, gone, as during most of her life.

The boys and Mr. Wickliffe assisted her to stand and helped her to the sofa. As she sat, Edith plopped down next to her and gently held and stroked Mildred's hand.

It was all too much for her. She wanted them to go, but knew it would be unkind to ask them. She drank some more water, now able to hold the glass on her own. She wanted a sip of wine or brandy to further steady her nerves, but there wasn't one within reach. She eyed her glass of wine, still sitting on the pianoforte. She willed that someone would bring it to her, but no one did.

For the next quarter hour, everyone in the room fawned over her. But, as the mantle clock struck the tenth hour, they finally released her from their attention. She was feeling better, she'd said. She didn't require the attention of a physician, she'd assured them. Really, they must go, she'd be fine. Mildred stood and led the vicar's family to the door.

She and Cole waved good-bye to the Wickliffe's as they drove up the tree-canopied lane. As their carriage disappeared, Mildred was certain she'd seen fairies or sprites accompanying them, but assumed that must simply be some residual effect of the throbbing bump on the back of her head.

Sixty-five

Parker Greene joined in the boisterous cheer that rang through the Balsa Robin. The great ship lunged quickly toward the clouds, rocked a bit, but finally came calmly to a cruising altitude of several hundred feet. All the men and women in the captain's grand quarters fell silent. Several people cried. Parker Greene and Rifle Helms were more than a head above these people.

There was no need for an explanation of the mood. Horrific acts had been committed that day, in that very room. And, worse actions had played out over the years and years that most of these wee humans had been held captive.

Around the room hugging began. Thanks to the great Lord Parker Greene. He would be a legend now.

"No! You must never speak my name in conjunction with these actions. I am working undercover, under the cloak of secrecy. It cannot be me whose name you use." Parker Greene looked around the room and easily, by instinct pushed Rifle Helms before himself. "Mr. Helms shall receive the credit, the praise."

"No, truly Parker, you have done this."

"No, you and they have been working on your escape plan for years. If you'd known the stokers would go along—"

"No, it's more than them."

"Stop! We understand, Lord Greene. Rifle Helms shall receive full credit. And, when we meet again, which I trust we will, you and I and they will always know the truth." Samuel touched the side of his nose and gave a wink. "That shall be our symbol of good will and knowing. But, we will never speak your name. We have only given you a lift, saved you, as has Rifle Helms."

"That's it. He's saved me, too." Parker Greene took Rifle's hand and squeezed it for a long time. "So, Captain, I appoint you Captain of this mighty vessel." He turned to Samuel. "I have been waiting weeks for a proper tour of the Balsa Robin, Mr. Butler. Shall you guide me?"

"It would be a distinct honor, Lord Greene. Won't you come this way." He raised an arm and indicated the cabin door.

"Captain Helms, you'll see us safely back to England?"

"I will, my Lord. Where shall we roost?"

Parker Greene studied all the expectant faces in the room. "Well, I suspect they are from all over the nation. So, we shall land comfortably in the great field near the river in Wickwillowshire. It is in the middle of the country. There is room for those who might wish to stay on and build a life. For those who want to return to their villages and homes, we are in the near center of England and they may take train transport easily."

"Solved. Very good, sir." Captain Helms began to study the charts rolled out by the pages. "Men, you may dress as you wish. I require no costumes of you."

Samuel led Parker Greene out of the cabin for his tour of the great Balsa Robin.

Sixty-Six

Mildred and Edith worked at cleaning out the fountain. Perry had to spend the morning grooming the horses because old Isaac was under the weather, despite the fine sunny day.

"Edith, I have to talk to you about everything."

"I told you, I'm fine with the four of us playing at this game."

"No, us, I have to talk to you about us." Mildred stopped raking the muck growing at the fountain's floor.

Edith didn't say a word, her eyes bore longingly into Mildred's. We're to play the charade like the boys, right? We're to pretend…"

"I don't love you like that," Mildred blurted out. "I—"

"You what? I thought." Edith sank to the ground. She wiped a dirty hand at her tears, bringing mud onto her cheeks."

Mildred rushed to her side. "I do love you, but like a sister, only like a sister."

"Like a what?" Edith regained her strength. She reached into the fountain, took a handful of muck and threw it at Mildred. It landed on her neck.

"What is this?"

Edith hit her with another glob. "We kissed. We touched." Her voice grew louder, more shrill.

"I was confused." Another handful of mud and leaves hit her in the face. "Listen," said Mildred, wiping at herself, "I've never known the love of a woman and I was confused by you, by us." More stuff hit her. "That's enough!" Mildred reaped her own handfuls of slimy leaves and threw them at Edith, hitting her square in the face.

Edith choked and sobbed. Mildred rushed to her, helping to clean the leaves from her face. At one moment, the girl was about to strike, but then Mildred laughed. Edith laughed, too.

"Edith, I do love you like a sister."

A long pause was followed by Edith pulling Mildred into an embrace.

"It will have to do," said Edith.

She heard the ship before she saw it. A great humming, like when she was covered with bees, both jolted and comforted her. Mildred turned her eyes skyward. Searching the cloudless blue for the dot. The dark dot grew larger. It was the biggest airship she'd ever seen in her life. Perhaps ten or even twenty times the size of a mail schooner. Those are the ships that usually came through Wickwillowshire.

The thing grew larger and closer. It was descending. It passed over the garden, over the manor house, barns, and stable. Toward the great field and the river.

Forgetting her state, Mildred clutched Edith's sticky hand and the girls ran toward the ship as it continued to descend.

"What? What is it?" Cole shouted toward his sister. He looked in the direction she was headed and saw the massive ship with its great propellers, gliding easily to the ground and a solid landing in the river. It verily created a dam that caused the water to flood out over the banks and into the field around the ship. He wiped his hands and began running with Edith and Mildred.

"Wait for me," Horatio called, having finally put down the book he was reading and looking around at the activity. He got up and ran after the others.

The name was easy to read from their vantage. "Balsa Robin." It had only been a rumor, a tale. But no, here it was, the big ship, in their very yard.

"Ahoy!" shouted Parker Greene. The gangplank lowered, he made his way quickly to his wards. "Whoa! What a mess you are." He refrained from hugging them.

"Uncle! Uncle! You've returned in great style," said Mildred. "This is Edith Wickliffe, my great friend."

"Ah, yes, Miss Wickliffe, how is your dear father?"

"Fine, sir." Edith curtsied. "And, this is my brother, Horatio."

"Fine name." Parker, after checking the boy's hands, offered his own hand forward and the two men shook.

Men and women began disembarking from the ship. Samuel and Rifle barked instructions and orders.

"Uncle!" Mildred held a hand over her mouth. "There are so many… little people." She stifled a laugh.

"Yes, yes, I'll explain it over lunch. Come, it must be nearly time for luncheon." As Parker Greene spoke the tower clock chimed eleven times. "You've done it. You've fixed the clock!" He looked toward Mildred who pointed at Cole. "My boy, you've done it." He shook his nephew's greasy hands.

Cole didn't speak, just smiled and cast his eyes down toward his feet.

"Rifle, ladies, Samuel, Cole, come. It's time for luncheon. We shall dine in an hour." He turned toward the charges. "That will give us all time to clean up and dress properly. Come come. Into the house."

Sixty-Seven

Mildred knew the routine. Their lives would be chaos for a few weeks while Uncle Parker was home. She took her time undressing, bathing, and putting on clean clothes

A few days. All these new people, or most of them, would be gone, dispersed into the body of England. Uncle would visit London, but have no playbills or ticket stubs or stories to share upon his return.

Mr. Gilbert would dine with Uncle Parker. The two drinking one or even two decanters of brandy while stories of the latest escapades were shared. Mildred used to try and listen in, but not any longer. The smoke. The hushed tones. The eyes of the servants upon her crouched in the hall outside the library. Just to hear war stories elaborated.

For now, she would only answer questions as they were asked. All else would be placed on hold. That's how it worked, for these few weeks, maybe six, that their uncle would be in the household.

Then, in the dark of night, because that's usually how it happened, a messenger arrived and Uncle Parker kissed her forehead and say good-bye. She'd not had a moment alone with him this time; she hadn't shown him the letter from her father about Willoughby; she hadn't talked about the crate of things sent home by her father. How could that be if her father truly was dead?

Mildred wound the rabbit and watched it march across her desk. What would become of all those dwarfs?

About the Author

Gay-Contemporary author, Gregory A. Kompes (MFA, MS Ed.) has written a bunch of books. He lives in Las Vegas, Nevada, with his husband. Learn more at www.Kompes.com

Sixty-Seven

Mildred knew the routine. Their lives would be chaos for a few weeks while Uncle Parker was home. She took her time undressing, bathing, and putting on clean clothes

A few days. All these new people, or most of them, would be gone, dispersed into the body of England. Uncle would visit London, but have no playbills or ticket stubs or stories to share upon his return.

Mr. Gilbert would dine with Uncle Parker. The two drinking one or even two decanters of brandy while stories of the latest escapades were shared. Mildred used to try and listen in, but not any longer. The smoke. The hushed tones. The eyes of the servants upon her crouched in the hall outside the library. Just to hear war stories elaborated.

For now, she would only answer questions as they were asked. All else would be placed on hold. That's how it worked, for these few weeks, maybe six, that their uncle would be in the household.

Then, in the dark of night, because that's usually how it happened, a messenger arrived and Uncle Parker kissed her forehead and say good-bye. She'd not had a moment alone with him this time; she hadn't shown him the letter from her father about Willoughby; she hadn't talked about the crate of things sent home by her father. How could that be if her father truly was dead?

Mildred wound the rabbit and watched it march across her desk. What would become of all those dwarfs?

Printed in Great Britain
by Amazon